The

VIRGINIA CARYS

An Essay in Genealogy

PRIVATELY PRINTED

THE DE VINNE PRESS

NEW YORK

1919

TO

TWO CARY WOMEN

MY MOTHER
AND
MY WIFE

CONTENTS

ILLUSTRATIONS

NOTE. *The eighteenth century portraits here reproduced are heirlooms and are given the names attributed to them by tradition; evidence for critical identification of either subjects or painters is not available to the present editor.*

[IX]

[x]

[XI]

INTRODUCTION

IN the summer of 1843, Rumor took wing from Ovid's House of Fame and flew about Virginia, spreading a report that there was a fortune in England waiting to be claimed by the common law heirs of the Virginia immigrant Miles Cary. No one knew who was responsible for the story, but it profoundly affected the peace of mind of a wide-spread family connection; not Carys only, but the nearer kin of their several branches—Randolphs, Pages, Nicholases, Seldens, Peachys, Hays, Leighs, Skipwiths and Egglestons. Lawyers and family Bibles were diligently consulted, heirlooms were furbished forth and a vast deal of traditional misinformation was distributed and recorded in the form of pedigrees. The excitement was fed by highly colored specifications in great variety, disregarding geography as much as probability. An age-old leasehold in London had fallen in, the property it had covered having an actual value of from six to eighteen millions of dollars, with no one in England to claim the reversion; Lord

Brougham had moved a parliamentary commission to investigate such hoary eleemosynary trusts as had outlived their usefulness, and a report had come in that, among others, a property known as "Cary's Rents" should revert to the heirs of the founder; this was described as lying, forsooth, on the Thames opposite Windsor, but already swallowed by the growth of London: the Lord Chancellor, clearing his docket, had exhumed an estate which had remained in chancery until the direct representatives of the original litigants had become extinct; a new interpretation of a Tudor marriage settlement had overturned long established property rights. It was even averred positively that the British Government had asked the State Department at Washington to produce the Cary heir. In due time, when replies to frantic inquiries in England came in, there was found to be no foundation whatever for the story: it was a purely American invention; no one had heard of it in England. The bubble was pricked.

Although sensible people then put away the visions of Alnaschar in which the soberest of them had indulged for a time, the agitation persisted for the ensuing ten years, reappearing at intervals as more "Cary heirs" were heard from in the West and Southwest. As late as 1852 a "Colonel Mulberry Sellers" from Georgia, then shepherding the sheep of Fortune in New York, advertised in the Richmond newspapers that he had new and mysterious information on the subject. When interviewed he offered to sell his proofs, or, if the inquirer preferred and could produce legal evidence of his descent from Miles Cary, he was ready to buy out the claim: a modest sum, say $100,000, was proposed as the consideration either way.[1]

The suggestion of the need of proof had brought home to some among the Carys a disagreeable realization that they had no such evidence of their breeding as could stand the test of the law. While they might no longer have any belief in the existence of the visionary fortune, they did still cherish vaguely a traditional confidence that among them was the heir to the Hunsdon peerage which had been in abeyance for a century. There was, in fact, no more foundation for this dream than for that of

---

[1] This was one of the earliest instances of a traffic which afterwards became an industry, the exploiting in America of imaginary claims to English estates. The most conspicuous case, in which some Virginians were involved, was that of the Jennings claim to the property of Earl Howe: this had some merit, but when it was finally quashed by the English Court of Chancery in 1878 and several merely fraudulent promoters of syndicates of American "heirs" of other names were jailed in the United States, the industry languished and died. The epidemic is historically interesting as one of the last symptoms of colonialism: the toll which, with curious manifestations, the present generation takes from its ancestors is membership in a patriotic society. The serious study of genealogy has profited by both.

the fortune, but it was not pleasant to have to forego it.[1]

This lack of documentary evidence of origin, while conspicuous in the Cary family in the middle of the nineteenth century, was not peculiar to them: other Virginia families shared a like destitution. The explanation is not far to seek. After the Revolution and Mr. Jefferson's level-

[1] The descendants of Miles Cary, sprung from Cary of Bristol, are the same relation to the Hunsdons that they are to the Falklands, namely, all three are derived from cadets of the same Devon stock: but the cadet who founded Hunsdon and Falkland left home generations after the ancestor of the Virginia Carys was established in trade at Bristol. Not even when the lion and the unicorn were fighting for the crown could a serious claim of inheritance be made out on such facts: but it was not until 1868 that the Hunsdon ghost was finally laid in Virginia. In 1866 Colonel Joseph L. Chester drew the attention of Captain W. M. Cary to the Heralds' College pedigree of 1699, which established the origin of the immigrant Miles Cary among the Bristol merchants; and two years later Mr. Robert Dymond, of Exeter, told him of the record (*Harleian MS.*, 6694) of the Hunsdon peerage case in 1707, from which it appeared that the Virginia Carys were then, by name, considered by the House of Lords only to be eliminated from the Hunsdon pedigree. On the authority of Richard Randolph, "the antiquary," Hugh Blair Grigsby had meanwhile given the myth a literary currency in his *Virginia Convention of 1776* (1855), p. 91. Speaking of Colonel Archibald Cary, he said: "He was a descendant of Henry Lord Hunsdon and was himself at the time of his death the heir apparent to the barony." Grigsby repeated the statement, again without qualification, in 1858, in his *Virginia Convention of 1788*, ii, 302, and it was thence taken over as recently as 1883 into John Esten Cooke's romantic *Virginia*, p. 229; doubtless to it also may be related Fiske's (*Old Virginia*, ii, 25) inclusion of the Carys in his farrago list of cavalier families in the colony. Colonel Archibald Cary was not even the head of the family in Virginia in the feudal sense. As it happened, he had living about him in Chesterfield a numerous tribe of distant kinsmen who had precedence of him among the descendants of the Virginia immigrant, and there were those then still extant in Warwick who had precedence over them.

ing legislation there was no longer any reason to keep up the proofs of gentility, but, on the contrary, a strong popular pressure to forget them, which was felt by all who took part in politics.[1] No more in their own social intercourse than in public was it necessary for the representatives of the group of families which had governed Virginia in the eighteenth century to prove who they were. They shared a common foible of unabated confidence, supported by mutual admission, that they were all conduits of the oldest and bluest blood of England.

They had, too, evidences of the past which amply satisfied their own demands. In every family there was some Aunt Patty or Aunt Polly to rehearse to the children glittering tales of the brave days of old when their Virginia forebears had been "King's Councillors" and "High Sheriffs," sprung from cavaliers whose

---

[1] Bagby's *Bacons and Greens* is a just picture of the immediate effect of democracy on the domestic manners of the Old Virginia Gentleman. One of the most interesting evidences of the process in the making is the story of the familiarity of some of Colonel Thomas Mann Randolph's neighbors at Tuckahoe in 1779, told by the Saratoga convention prisoner Lieutenant Anburey: "When they were gone some one observed what great liberties they took; he [Colonel Randolph] replied it was unavoidable, the spirit of independency was converted into equality and every one who bore arms esteemed himself upon a footing with his neighbour; and concluded with saying, 'No doubt each of these men conceives himself in every respect my equal.'" (*Travels through the Interior Parts of America* (1791), ii, 330.) In the same connection, we may note the prohibition by Colonel Wilson-Miles Cary, in his will of 1810, against such a funeral as he had been proud to give his father in 1772, because even a dignified pomp had become "unrepublican."

loyal sacrifices of blood and treasure on behalf of ungrateful but fascinating Stuarts had driven them out of their far-descended English manor-houses. These stories were seconded by the effigies on the dining-room walls of scowling stout gentlemen in periwigs flanked by full-bosomed ladies whose similitude of figure, pose and costume in every household proved either the accepted belief that they were all close of kin or else that the itinerant "artist" who had painted them lacked imagination. There was store of inherited table plate from which long use had rubbed all but the suggestion of the arms with which it had been engraved; there were heraldic book-plates in the heavy broken-backed folios of Echards's *Ecclesiastical History* and Chamberlen's *Queen Anne*, which were the despair of the dust-pursuing housekeeper; somewhere in the tidewater region there stood in an open field near the crumbled foundations of a long gone house an array of ruined ancestral tombs originally built altarwise of brick to support ironstone slabs, carved in England with arms and achievements of the past, reminding one in their plight of Shelley's *Ozymandias*.

But the fact remained that when one came to look for them there seemed to be few written evidences of any kind. Virginia had never taken much care of immigration records, and with a few exceptions, Virginia families even less of their private papers. Casual fires in isolated country houses are always destructive of stored muniments. Such fires had combined, with the ravages of war and removals from Tidewater to Piedmont, to wipe out much of the raw material there might once have been available to the genealogist.[1]

In the midst of the first discussion of the "Cary Fortune" my grandfather Archibald Cary returned to Virginia from Port Gibson, Mississippi, where he had been for some years established in the practice of the law; he came to take a long vacation among his own people while recuperating from yellow fever contracted in Cuba. Having leisure and being impressed with the observations on the lack of family evidence made by the eminent lawyers who had been consulted, Governor Littleton Waller Tazewell and the Hon. Benjamin Watkins Leigh, he then began a systematic collection of genealogical facts about the Carys and their kin. All these he recorded in a beautiful script,

[1] Ante bellum Virginians were not antiquarians but were satisfied with the traditional accounts of their origins. Had it been otherwise we might now know much more of Virginia families than we do, for before 1861 most of the county records so fertile in genealogical material were still extant, reaching back to the beginnings of the colony. They were then generally neglected except in the emergency of a law-suit. How little comparatively is now provable is strikingly illustrated by the necessary omissions from Dr. Stanard's illuminating *Some Emigrants to Virginia*.

putting to shame our modern slovenly MS., in a great blank book in which he had previously kept notes of law lectures at Transylvania University; of the breeding of horses; recipes for the characteristic potations of the Southwest, whose exotic names still have a cooling and stimulating import; scraps from the Code Napoleon and from the code duello; and his own secret essays in lyrical verse. Once started, this genealogical work· became a hobby; as the difficulties developed, the appetite grew. With Archibald Cary it was unfortunately satisfied by ingenious but futile conjecture under the influence of the distorted current tradition,[1] for he made no such effort, as did his distant kinsman Guilford Dudley Eggleston a little later, to go back of the printed word to the MS. sources of history.[2]

[1] "For what is the character of a family to an hypothesis?" insisted the philosophical Walter Shandy, Esq. As we have noted, the Virginia Carys believed, in Archibald Cary's day, that they were the representatives of the Hunsdons. Starting back from the tombstone of the immigrant Miles Cary, his attempt was to identify the John Cary there named with one or the other of his contemporaries, the cavaliers of the same name, who appear in the pedigrees of Cary of Devon, viz.: John Cary of Long Melford, co. Suffolk, or John Cary of Ditchley, co. Oxford. Such traditional myths are still current in Virginia, but what will undoubtedly be the last serious exposition of them in print was Mr. Moncure Conway's *Barons of the Potomac and the Rappahannock* (1893). As literature, this is a charming book, but as history it withered under the destructive criticism of one who had studied the MS. sources and bridled his imagination with fact. (See *Va. Mag.*, i, 213, 326.)

[2] In 1851 Mr. Eggleston journeyed from Indiana to Virginia to make a systematic search for evidence of his Cary descent. To

In a few years Archibald Cary found in his· young nephew Wilson Miles Cary of Baltimore an ardent disciple of his hobby, and before he died in 1854 turned over to him his MS. *Cary Book*. With this start, Captain Cary took upon himself, after the war between the States, a vow to compile and edit a complete record of his family. During the remainder of a long life he collected material to that end with unflagging zeal.[1] He brought to the work not only energy

his MS. notes (herein cited as *Eggleston Notes*) we owe the preservation of the immigrant's will *in extenso* and much of the genealogical material on which the following pages are founded. The Warwick *Will Books* which Mr. Eggleston consulted were subsequently removed to Richmond for custody during the war between the States and there destroyed, with the records of the Colonial General Court, and of other tidewater counties, in the conflagration which followed the evacuation of Richmond in April, 1865.

[1] In 1872 Captain Cary sent out a prospectus of the Cary pedigree chart which he then contemplated publishing, in which he described his work in the compilation of it as follows:

"By simple persistence, in many instances I have been finally rewarded with information I sought for years from indolent, unwilling or over-occupied possessors. I have corresponded with antiquarians of England and America in elucidation of my Genealogy: and to authenticate it have myself ransacked the extant records of Virginia, which are, alas! scanty indeed, owing to the wholesale destruction of the late war. I have visited in person the County Court Houses of Warwick, York, Elizabeth City, James City, Henrico, Chesterfield and Fluvanna, in search of what was left; have haunted graveyards and unearthed tombstones, procured documents from home and abroad, from public and private archives, pedigrees and testaments from Heralds' College and Doctors' Commons, records from family Bibles; taken statements from the lips of octogenarians, and have well-nigh exhausted all sources of information, including the old letters and family papers of our connection. Much of this labor has been entailed by the conflagration of our residence at Carysbrook in 1826, when ·unfortunately trunks

but modern genealogical methods into which he was initiated, in 1866, by that long foremost American genealogical authority, Colonel J. L. Chester. The plan grew, but never took literary form. There was frequent postponement in the hope that newly discovered proof might illuminate the dark places in the pedigree; for Captain Cary was by nature and training a scholar of the standard Mr. Fitzgilbert Waters set for himself in the same studies: "With might-have-beens, however glittering, I have nothing to do."[1]

Captain Cary's historical bent was, moreover, acquisitive of fact, but not synthetic. His voluminous amplifications of his uncle's MS. *Cary Book* and the mass of his own notes, collected from public records in Virginia and in England in a series of minute, much worn pocket-books, were never systematically arranged or indexed, and require no little industry to master their contents; but their fine legible penmanship, their recurrent evidences of scholarly self-restraint

of the accumulated papers of generations perished in the flames, and with them a full genealogy of the family."

The genealogy last mentioned was undoubtedly a transcript and continuation of the Heralds' College pedigree of the Bristol Carys made in 1699. The last Cary of Bristol had such an extension and mentioned it in her will (1795, P.C.C. *Newcastle*, 584). Captain Cary ultimately had the satisfaction of making a copy from it, then in the hands of Mr. D. C. Cary-Elwes, to replace the one lost in the Carysbrook fire.

[1] Hosmer, *Memoir of H. F. Waters.* New England Hist. and Gen. Reg., 1914, lxviii, 3.

and historical honesty, the implacable use of the logical process of elimination, and, most of all, the prodigious amount of hard work they represent, cannot fail to stir with respect whoever follows in Captain Cary's footsteps. It is well to record this appreciation of the *W. M. Cary Notes,* for, as Lord Morley said when he had finished his pursuit of Diderot through the mountains of volumes of the *Encyclopédie,* "I have a presentiment that their pages will seldom again be disturbed by me or by others."

Captain Cary died in my house in Fauquier in the summer of 1914, leaving his life work incomplete. Because of my sympathetic interest in his studies, he gave me my grandfather's *Cary Book* and his own notes relating to Carys, both in England and Virginia,[1] with the request that if ever I had opportunity I would preserve them from destruction by putting them together in print. In the summer of 1918 I had an interval of unwonted leisure when, with the same excuse that Rabelais gave for writing his book,[2] I took up the pious task of completing what my grandfather and my cousin had both essayed and had

---

[1] Capt. Cary's surviving MS. genealogical collections are now distributed; those relating to Maryland families are in the library of the Maryland Historical Society, those relating to Virginia families, other than the Carys, in the library of the Virginia Historical Society (catalogued as *The Cary Papers.* See *Va. Mag.* xxvi, 305), and those relating to the Carys at Belvoir House.

[2] Rabelais, *Prologue du tiers livre.*

not finished. This book is a part of the result.[1] It is a very different thing than either of its progenitors planned, and their memories must, therefore, be absolved from any responsibility for its deficiencies, though to them I gladly yield whatever credit there may be in preserving an honorable tradition. The peace of mind generated by these studies during a difficult period has been my reward.[2] The results are printed for the information of a now widely scattered family connection, in the hope that the record may tend to renew the old bond of blood.

[1] I have also compiled, and plan to print, an historical and genealogical study of the various branches of Cary of Devon and Bristol, in England.

[2] I have a pleasant precedent. In his Life of Dr. Robert Sanderson, the author of the prayer "For all Sorts and Conditions of Men," who became Bishop of Lincoln after the Restoration, Izaak Walton tells how one day during the Commonwealth, after that good man had been ejected from his Oxford professorship, "I met him accidentally in London, in sad coloured clothes, and God knows far from being costly. The place of our meeting was near to Little Britain, where he had been to buy a book, which he then had in his hand. We had no inclination to part presently, and therefore turned to stand in a corner under a penthouse, for it began to rain, and immediately the wind arose and the rain increased so much that both became so inconvenient as to force us into a cleanly house where we had bread, cheese, ale and a fire, for our money. This wind and rain were so obliging to me as to force our stay there for at least an hour, to my great content and advantage: for in that time he made to me many useful observations with much clearness and conscientious freedom." Dr. Sanderson rehearsed the occupations of his temporary retirement and concluded, says Walton, that "the study of old records, genealogies and heraldry were a recreation and so pleasing that he would say they gave rest to his mind. Of the last of which I have seen two remarkable volumes and the reader needs neither to doubt their truth nor exactness."

[XXIV]

The printed literature of the Cary family is fugitive. For the picturesque Devon traditions we have the pleasant pages of old Prince, Westcote and Pole. Two able modern antiquarian scholars have systematically sifted the family archives in England on the purely genealogical side, and published their notes in J. G. Nichols's *Herald and Genealogist* 1866–1873; to both of them, Mr. Robert Dymond of Exeter and the Rev. C. J. Robinson, all Carys owe a debt of gratitude for the preservation of records which, but for them, must surely have been lost. There are records of the family in England in all the standard peerages, the substance of which, with notes of some American Carys (but very little about the Virginia family), is uncritically reproduced in Albert Welles's *American Family Antiquity* (5 vols., New York, 1880). The numerous descendants of John Cary, of Bridgewater, Massachusetts, an early member of the Plymouth colony, who have spread through the Middle West and include the literary ladies Alice and Phœbe Cary, have found their diligent historians (S. F. Cary, *Cary Memorials,* Cincinnati, 1871; Henry Grosvenor Cary, *The Cary Family in America,* Boston, 1907); while they have a similar origin, they have not proved their relation, if any, to the Bristol family.

There exist in MS. numerous pedigrees of Cary of Virginia, most of which relate back to an advertisement entitled *The Cary Tradition,* dated June 14, 1852, which was published in the Richmond *Whig* newspaper in July of that year by Anderson Demandville Abraham, of Buckingham Court House, as a reincitement to the discussion of the fabulous Cary fortune. Mr. Abraham had perhaps access to Mr. Guilford Dudley Eggleston's notes of his researches in the Warwick records in 1851, but undoubtedly supplemented them by some original investigation of his own. While his production is still of value when used critically, it is the source of most of the erroneous genealogical notions which prevail among the Cary connection. Not the least, the Rev. Philip Slaughter was misled by it.

Pending the publication of Captain W. M. Cary's long promised book, there have appeared several incidental discussions of the Virginia Carys. The best of them are, for the Peartree Hall family, Goode's *Virginia Cousins* (1887), though that book is not free from mistakes of fact and typography; and, for the Richneck family, an appendix in the third (1878) edition of Dr. Slaughter's *Randolph Fairfax*. There are notices in Bishop Meade's *Old Churches,* etc.; in Page's *Genealogy of the Page Family in Virginia* (1893); and in Mr. Charles P. Keith's valuable *Ancestry of Benjamin Harrison* (1893). More recently, Louise Pecquet du Bellet has published four large volumes of detailed pedigrees of *Some Prominent Virginia Families* (Lynchburg, 1907), as a record of the ramifications of the Jaquelin, Ambler and Moncure families, in which seventy-three pages of Volume II are devoted to the Carys. More branches of the family were here explored than had ever before been undertaken in print, but the compilation, while a monument of industry and enthusiasm, should be used with caution as genealogy. Its value lies in its preservation of traditions even when they prove to be erroneous.

In the following notes there is cited for each family, if not for each individual, some evidence of the character the lawyers call primary; but by reason of the destruction of most of the records of Warwick County, where the earlier Virginian generations principally dwelt, as well as many family papers, it has, unfortunately, been sometimes necessary to piece out with secondary proof and, indeed, some argument. The effort has been to collect and array such evidence as still remains.

The principal sources are: (1) the wills, of which a calendar is given in an *Appendix;* (2) for Bristol, the Heralds' College pedigrees and parish registers; (3) for Virginia, gleanings from surviving public records: for the MS.

sources I have relied almost entirely on the *W. M. Cary Notes* and the earlier *Eggleston Notes*, covering the *Will, Deed* and *Court Order Books,* tax returns, etc., of the various Virginia counties in which Carys lived or did business, some of which are still at the court-houses, some in the Virginia State Library, and scraps of others in the library of the Virginia Historical Society; the older parish registers which were deposited by Bishop Meade at the Theological Seminary near Alexandria, Virginia; the record of early patents in the *Virginia Land Register,* at the Land Office in Richmond; and the *Virginia Quit Rent Rolls,* 1704, of which a copy has recently been acquired by the Virginia Historical Society: for what is in print I cite Hening, *Statutes at Large,* 13 vols., 1823; Palmer and Flournoy, *Calendar of Virginia State Papers,* 11 vols., 1875–1893; the British Record Office *Calendar of State Papers, America and West Indies,* which, so far as yet published, includes the Virginia colonial papers sent to England down to 1708; Kennedy and McIlwaine, *Journals of the House of Burgesses, 1619–1776,* 13 vols., Virginia State Library, 1905–1916; and *Legislative Journals of the Council,* 3 vols., 1918; Stanard, *Colonial Virginia Register,* 1902; Swem and Williams, *Register of the General Assembly of Virginia,* 1776–1918; *History of the College of William*

[XXVIII]

and Mary, 1874, containing a catalogue of alumni; (4) family Bibles and MS. pedigree charts preserved in various branches of the family; (5) statements by contemporaries as to recent generations; and (6) those invaluable repositories of material for Virginia history and genealogy, the *William and Mary Quarterly* and *Virginia Magazine*.

I have pleasure in acknowledging my obligation to the various representatives of the Cary connection who have, in generous response to my requests, taken the pains to collect material which I have used; and particularly to those foremost genealogical authorities on Virginia families, my friends Dr. L. G. Tyler and Dr. W. G. Stanard, who have not only cheerfully and patiently satisfied all the demands for advice made upon them by an exigent amateur, but have done me the honor to read and criticize my proof sheets.

F. H.

Belvoir,
   Fauquier County, Virginia.
May, 1919.

THE
VIRGINIA
CARYS

CHAPTER ONE

THE ORIGINS

The Surname In the language of the Celtic peoples who covered the British Isles in the time of Julius Cæsar, a fortified place was called *caer*. This passed into a place name and by extension was given to streams on which the forts were built. These names have persisted in Devon, Cornwall, Wales, Scotland and Ireland, where the Celts last held dominion of the land. When the inhabitants of these countries emerged from the family anonymity of the middle ages some of them assumed the names of the lands on which they dwelt. In this way we find family names derived from *caer,* in English and Irish variants Cary, Carey, Carew; in Scotland Ker and Carr. They were of widely scattered origins, and doubtless of different races as well, Celts, Saxons and Normans, so that all Carys are not necessarily of kin, even the remotest, least of all in America, where representatives from all their places of origin have met and mingled.

In spelling, the Devon name has undergone

change. In Domesday it was *Kari,* and so continued down to the end of the thirteenth century: we find it in the form *Kary* in a marriage settlement as late as 1357. It appears as *Cary* in the Rolls of Parliament, *temp.* Richard II, and as early as 1313 in the Bristol *Tolzey Book;* but in the next century is indifferently *Care, Carie, Caree* and *Carree.* By the sixteenth century it has become quite uniformly *Carye,* and seemed destined to crystallize in that form; but towards the beginning of the seventeenth there is a distinct separation of practice, which has persisted ever since. On the one hand the Devon and Bristol families, and the Falklands as well, then drop the final *e* and revert to *Cary.* The Hunsdons, on the other hand, then begin to transpose the final letters and spell *Carey,* which, with some inconsistency of practice, they maintained to the end of their history. This latter standard was apparently set by Sir George Carey, second Lord Hunsdon. His father represents the transition: thus in his marriage license 1545 and when he first went to Parliament 1554 he spelled *Carye,* but at last it appears *Carey* on his tomb in Westminster Abbey.[1] No other recognizable branch

[1] In his *Curiosities of Literature,* ii, 237, Isaac D'Israeli has collected illustrative examples of the mutations of orthography of proper names at the time of Queen Elizabeth, beginning with the conspicuous instances of Shakespeare and Sir Walter Raleigh. Any one who has ever examined even casually a collection of sixteenth and seventeenth century wills could extend the list through many private families. D'Israeli judiciously observes: "The truth

[4]

of the Devon stock has at any time deliberately followed the Hunsdon precedent; but they have all had it imposed on them more or less. Perhaps some of the numerous Carey families of to-day, who may be descended from the Devon stock, simply represent a loss of tradition upon which the "right" lines have come to stickle.

As the Hunsdons were the first Carys to take a conspicuous place in the world, their spelling of the name has entered largely into the literary tradition. Thus the editors of Clarendon, whose trumpet gave the name its widest fame, had their historical and political memory fixed on the Hunsdons of the preceding generations when they spelled the name of the second Lord Falkland, *Carey,* although Falkland and Clarendon himself spelled it *Cary.*[1] Sir Walter Scott (*Woodstock,* ch. 31) made the same mistake with respect to another of the Falkland family. Finally, the crowning inconsistency is that the modern British ordnance map spells the name

seems to be, then, that personal names were written by the ear, since the persons themselves did not attend to the accurate writing of their own names, which they changed sometimes capriciously and sometimes with anxious nicety." The second Lord Hunsdon was in this last category.

[1] The early editions of Clarendon's *Rebellion* and *Life* were founded on transcripts of the original MS. and were freely edited. Later editions restored Clarendon's full text, but Mr. Nichol Smith says (*Characters of the Seventeenth Century,* The Clarendon Press, 1918): "No edition has yet reproduced his spelling." This Mr. Nichol Smith has himself done in his extracts from the MS. still preserved at Oxford, whence we learn that Clarendon took no liberties with the name of his dear friend, though he did with many of his contemporaries.

[5]

Carey in respect of the manor from which the Devon family derived their patronymic.

The Christian Until quite recently the Carys
Names have been consistent, throughout
their long history and in all their environments, in England as well as in America, in the use of Christian names. They have reproduced again and again the wholesome English John, William, Thomas, Richard, Robert and George, in about that order of frequency. For the sake of an old tradition it is to be hoped that these names may be continued.

Miles, which has multiplied in Virginia, was not originally a Cary name, but was derived, with maternal blood, from the Hobsons in Bristol. Likewise Wilson, which has been handed on from father to son for seven generations among the Richneck Carys, was first given to a grandson of the Virginia immigrant, in honor of his maternal grandfather. Harwood, which has persisted among the Prince Edward Carys, like Archibald in other lines, was first given in compliment to a friend.[1]

Cary of About the end of the twelfth century,
Devon *temp.* Richard I, the first Cary of
Devon appears in possession of the

[1] The later Richneck Carys are, however, descended from Dr. Archibald Blair, although Colonel Archibald Cary, of Ampthill, who was the first Cary to bear his name, was not.

manor of Cary (called in Domesday Book *Kari*). This is a bit of bottom land on the western border of Devon, not far from the Cornish town of Launceston, and may be identified on the modern British ordnance map. It lies on a stream known, time out of mind, as Carywater, flowing south down a combe which reaches up into the western hills of Dartmoor. This progenitor of a persistent and widespread race is called, on the authority of the traditional pedigrees which crystallized in the *Visitation of Devon of* 1620, Adam de Cary. Arguing from the known and quite uniform characteristics of his descendants, he was perhaps the man of business of some Norman baron; certainly he was not a warrior. To him succeeded at the manor of Cary a line of Williams and Johns, all "de Cary" (it was not until the end of the fourteenth century that they dropped the particle), who married prudently into Norman families and after two centuries had by that means established themselves in possession of a large collection of the best manors in Devon. Following a centrifugal instinct, they found their principal seats far from their place of origin, on the southern and northern coasts of the shire, at the Domesday manors of Cockington on Tor Bay and Clovelly on the Bristol Channel. They were generally magistrates, lawyers and parliament men.

Despite two attainders and various other vicissitudes of fortune, they have managed to hold on to their place in the world for more than seven hundred years, and are still represented in the possession of Devon soil by the squires of Tor Abbey and Follaton. One of the notable names in their history is Sir John Cary, the unfortunate Chief Baron of the Exchequer, *temp.* Richard II; he died in banishment in Ireland with other great judges of England who, in a political crisis, had advised the king in accordance with his desires rather than in accordance with the law and their oaths. Another is Sir George Cary, always styled "of Cockington" to distinguish him from contemporaries of the same name, a busy and responsible local magistrate at the time of the Armada, and afterwards Lord Deputy of Ireland, *temp.* James I.

Cary in the Peerage A penniless cadet of this family was forced to leave Devon after the temporary ruin of his name in the Wars of the Roses: each of his two sons founded in Hertfordshire a race of successful courtiers.

One of them, becoming a gentleman of the Privy Chamber of Henry VIII, at the instance of his king complaisantly married Mary Boleyn. Her son bearing the Cary name became a great figure at Elizabeth's court as Lord Hunsdon, whose descendants were earls of Monmouth and Dover under the Stuarts: this line became extinct before the middle of the eighteenth century.

The other son of the disinherited cadet made an equally fortunate, though more dignified, marriage, and, through it and court favor, shared in the spoils of the monasteries. His family was raised to the peerage as Viscounts Falkland, *temp*. James I, and produced that sweet and gentle soul who became the most famous of all Carys, the cult of the modern High Church and Tory party in England: this line and title are still honorably represented.

Cary of Bristol As early as the fourteenth century there were Carys in Bristol holding high municipal office and engaged in the cloth trade; undoubtedly they gave .their name to the textile fabric known as *cary* which is mentioned in *Piers Ploughman*. While the record is lacking, it seems likely that they were ancestors of those later Carys of Bristol who were, at the end of the seventeenth century, formally acknowledged as kinsmen by the head of the Devon family. What is known of them genealogically, before they became finally extinct in Bristol at the end of the eighteenth century, is set forth in the next chapter.

[9]

The Emigrants Prior to the civil wars, *temp.* Charles I, these Bristol merchants had been almost as prosperous as they became again after the Restoration. The interference of that war with their foreign trade nearly laid them flat on their backs. A number of the younger and more enterprising among them then emigrated, one to New England, certainly two, and perhaps more, to Virginia, and one to the sugar islands in the West Indies. Our Miles Cary was one of those who so sought his fortune in Virginia, but the only one of them who is definitely identified as having established his race on that soil. The New England emigrant also left descendants who still flourish in Massachusetts.

Miles Cary went out as a young merchant with the tradition of a mercantile family, and suffered a sea change into a planter and public officer after he was established in the new world. On the other hand, the descendants of his New England uncle continued to maintain in their new environment, and in a most interesting way, the Bristol seafaring and mercantile tradition.

THE CARY HOUSE
ON BRISTOL BACK
WHICH STOOD UNTIL 1817

CHAPTER TWO

THE BRISTOL FOREBEARS

In 1699, thirty-two years after Miles Cary, our
Virginia immigrant, was dead and buried, three
of his kinsmen of the Bristol family, who had
achieved fame and fortune as English merchants engaged in overseas trade, united in an
application to the Heralds' College for confirmation to them and their descendants of the
right to bear the arms of Cary of Devon, which
they certified they and their ancestors in Bristol
had borne "time out of mind," in accordance
with "the constant tradition," that they were
descended from a cadet of the Devon family.[1]
With the consent of the contemporary head of
the Devon family, the application was granted

[1] Although many of the Bristol Carys were buried in the crypt of
St. Nicholas Church, including the two Mayors, they do not seem
to have erected there any family monument showing an achievement of arms; certainly none has survived. It may be noted then
in passing that Miles Cary's 1667 tombstone in Virginia (see *post,*
p. 36) is the only recorded and surviving evidence of such use of
arms by the Bristol family prior to 1699. In accordance with
the Virginia fashion Miles Cary's descendants displayed the arms
consistently, throughout the eighteenth century, on tombs, signet
rings, table plate, coach panels, book plates, etc. At the end of
the nineteenth century the practice was resumed.

[11]

by the Earl Marshal.[1] (See *Appendix II.*) In support of this application there was filed a certificate of the Chamberlain of Bristol from the *Great Red Book* of Bristol, then known as the *Tolzey Book,* as to Carys who had held municipal office in Bristol, viz.: Lawrence de Cary, Senister 1313; John de Cary, bailiff 1350 and 1353; William Cary, sheriff 1532 and Mayor 1546; William Cary, sheriff 1599 and Mayor 1611; and Christopher Cary, sheriff 1612. There was submitted also (1699) a pedigree beginning with the William Cary who was

---

[1] As these Carys were hard-headed men of business, still deep "in trade," one naturally asks why they incurred the obviously large cost of this proceeding. The answer is that they deemed that their prosperity was sufficiently assured to justify them in preparing for the reversal at home, as Miles Cary had already done in the new civilization of Virginia, of the change of social status which their ancestors had made under economic pressure when they established themselves in Bristol: a reversal which duly took effect in the case of the descendants of the only one of the Heralds' College petitioners whose race has persisted. It was a characteristic English phenomenon.

William Harrison (*The Description of England,* first published in the 1577 edition of Holinshed's *Chronicles*) has some pleasant and judicious observations upon the society of Elizabethan England, which are here *apropos.* After noting that merchants "often change estate with gentlemen, as gentlemen doo with them, by a mutual conversion of the one into the other," he proceeds to define the status of a gentleman under the English law: "Moreover as the King dooth dubbe Knights, and createth the barons and higher degrees, so gentlemen whose ancestors are not knowen to come in with William duke of Normandie doo take their beginning in England after this maner in our times. Who soever studieth the lawes of the realme, who so abideth in the universitie giving his mind to his booke, or professeth physicke and the liberall sciences, or beside his service in the roome of a capteine in the warres, or good counsell given at home, whereby his Common-wealth is benefited, can live without manuell labour and thereto is able and

Mayor in 1611, which was subsequently supplemented by fuller pedigrees of 1700 and 1701, all still on file in the Heralds' College.[1]

By means of the surviving wills and parish registers, it has been possible to carry the Heralds' College pedigrees back two generations to the William Cary who was Mayor 1546; but with him the evidence fails. There are no earlier surviving parish registers on which to construct a detailed pedigree, neither have there appeared, although diligent search has been

will beare the port, charge and countenance of a gentleman, he shall for monie have a cote and armes bestowed upon him by heralds (who in the charter of the same doo of custome pretend antiquitie and service and many gaie things) and thereunto being made so, good cheape, be called master, which is the title that men give to esquiers and gentlemen, and reputed for a gentleman ever after; which is so much the lesse to be disalowed of, for that the prince dooth loose nothing by it, the gentleman being so much subiect to taxes and publike paiments as is the yeoman or husbandman, which he likewise dooth beare the gladlier for the saving of his reputation. Being called also to the warres whatsoever it cost him, he will both arraie & arme himselfe accordinglie, and shew the more manly courage, and all the tokens of the person which he representeth. No man hath hurt by it but himself who peradventure will go in wider buskins than his legs will beare, or, as our proverbe saith, now and then bear a bigger saile than his boat is able to susteine."

Somewhat later the learned John Selden (*Table Talk,* ed. Arber, 52) confirms this: "What a gentleman is 'tis hard with us to define; in other countries he is Known by his Privileges: in Westminster Hall he is one that is reputed one: in the Court of Honour he that hath Armes."

[1] In his (incomplete) collection of Cary wills from Bristol, Mr. Fitzgilbert Waters (*Genealogical Gleanings in England,* ii, 1052 ff.) has reproduced portions of the pedigrees of 1700 and 1701 from *Stowe MS.,* 670, fols. 229 and 230.

made in Bristol and elsewhere, any wills, monu-
mental inscriptions, gild rolls, real estate muniments, etc., upon which might be *proved* the
connection which in 1699 the Bristol Carys evidently claimed by tradition between William
Cary, Mayor in 1546, and the earlier Lawrence
and John de Cary. Doubtless such evidences,
if any, as once existed were destroyed, either
during the life of the first Mayor of the family,
when the churches were pillaged, *temp*. Henry
VIII and Edward VI, or later in the disorgan-
ization of Bristol during the civil wars, *temp*.
Charles I. The persistent modern attempts to
establish identifications with specific members
of the Devon family have, therefore, been genealogically futile. Thus *e.g.* the assertion, by one
who has not proved his own connection with the
Bristol family (*The Cary Family in England,*
Boston, 1906), that William Cary, the Mayor
of 1546, was the William Cary who was the last
of the Ladford line, not only proceeds directly
in the face of Prince's statement (*Worthies of
Devon*) that the Ladford line was extinct in
his time, say 1697, but is contradicted also by
Colonel Vivian's demonstration (*Visitations of
Devon,* Exeter, 1895) that the last William Cary
of Ladford left a daughter and heiress, who
married and carried Ladford into the Helyar
family.

ST NICHOLAS' CHURCH, BRISTOL.

We begin our record, then, with

I. WILLIAM CARY (1492?–1572), "the Elder, dwelling upon ye Backe in St. Nicholas Parish in ye citty of Bristoll."

He was sheriff of Bristol 1532, and Mayor 1546, *temp.* Henry VIII. He had five children by two wives, but outlived all his sons and was buried in the crowd (*i.e.* crypt) of St. Nicholas Church, March 28, 1572, *temp.* Elizabeth, leaving a will dated April 2, 1571, and proved June 10, 1572 (P.C.C. *Daper,* 19). Having evidently retired from business when he made his will, he does not give his trade, but he was undoubtedly a "draper" like his son Richard, "the younger," who lived, and so carried on his business, in his father's house.

He m.,

1st: (name unknown) and by her had:

I Richard, 1515?, "the elder," see p. 16,

II Agnes, m. *1st,* 1544, Humphrey Cooper, and *2nd, ante* 1569, Thomas Dickinson, of Bristol,

III Susan, m. *ante* 1571, John Lacy, of Bristol,

IV William, "of London, citizen and clothworker,"

[He m. Elizabeth and had a son William and a daughter Anne. The son is mentioned in the will of his uncle Richard, "the younger," but not in that of his father nor in that of his grandfather, who leaves a legacy to Anne. William Cary[2] was executor for both his brothers, and died leaving a will dated March 2, and proved March 13, 1572, O.S. (P.C.C. *Petre,* 9.) In this he mentions 20 marks his father gave him by will, which, as Mr. Fitzgilbert Waters has acutely pointed out, is the precise equivalent (at 13*s.* 4*d.* the mark) of the £13 6*s.* 8*d.* bequeathed him in the will of William Cary[1], made the previous year, thus proving the identity.]

[15]

2nd: ? Agnes (d. 1559), and by her had:

v Richard, "the younger, draper, dwelling upon the Back in St. Nicholas Parish of the City of Bristol."

[He was buried at St. Nicholas, Bristol, August 11, 1569, and left a will, dated August 8, "an⁰ 11⁰ Eliz. Regᵃᵉ" (1569), and proved September 17, 1569 (P.C.C. *Sheffelde*, 20), in which he mentions his wife Elizabeth, his father, his brothers Richard and William, his brothers-in-law John Lacy and Thomas Dickinson and the children of his brothers—but no children of his own. He had had a daughter Bridget, baptized at St. Nicholas, February 28, 1560, O.S., who may have died before her father's will, or may be the Bridget Cary who married Roger Taylor at St. Nicholas, May 12, 1583.]

SOURCES:

(1) The Bristol wills (see *Appendix I*); (2) St. Nicholas parish register (the surviving book begins only at the end of this generation).

II. RICHARD CARY (*William¹*), 1515?–1570, "the elder, of the City of Bristol, Merchant."

He was buried June 17, 1570, two years before his father, in St. Nicholas Church, leaving a will, dated June 11, 1570, and proved November 3, 1570. (P.C.C. *Lyon*, 31.)

He m.,

1st: Anne (d. *ante* 1561), and by her had:

I Richard, 1542–1591, *o.s.p.*,

[Baptized at St. Nicholas, August 18, 1542, he is mentioned in the wills of his father and grandfather, and was buried in St. Nicholas, June 14, 1591. There is no evidence for any marriage or children.]

II Lettice, 1543–*post* 1570, m. Mellen,

III Mary, 1544, d. *infans*,

[16]

IV   Mary, 1546–*post* 1570,

V   Elizabeth, 1548, d. *infans,*

VI   Frances, 1549–*post* 1570,

VII   William, 1550, see p. 18,

VIII   Elizabeth, 1551–*post* 1570,

IX   Agnes, 1555?–*post* 1570,

X   Martha, 1558–1561, d. *infans.*

2nd: ? 1561, Joan, sister of Robert Holton, Chamberlain of Bristol, and by her had:

XI   Martha, 1562–*post* 1570,

XII   Anne, 1564?,

XIII   *Filia,* 1565, d. *infans,*

XIV   *Filia,* 1567, d. *infans,*

XV   Christopher, 1568?–1626, "of St. Stephens parish in the City of Bristol, Merchant,"

[He was Sheriff of Bristol 1612 (Bristol *Tolzey Book*). He m. Lettice Young, and by her had two sons who survived infancy, Christopher and William; and five daughters. He died, leaving a will dated October 30, 1615, and proved May 31, 1626 (P.C.C. *Hele*, 60). His eldest son, Christopher, "of the Citty of Bristol, Merchant," left a will dated September 10 and proved October 28, 1672 (P.C.C. *Eure*, 118), mentioning sons Richard and John, as to whom, see query, *post*, p. 147. The second son, William, "citizen and haberdasher of Coleman Street, London," left a will dated January 28, and proved February 13, 1664, O.S. (P.C.C. *Hyde*, 12), mentioning sons, as to one of whom, William Cary, "silkman," see query, *post*, p. 144. The marriages of all the daughters of Christopher[2] are identified by the will (1625, P.C.C. *Clarke*, 67) of Francis Bannister, the husband of one of them.]

XVI   *Filia,* 1569, d. *infans.*

SOURCES:

(1) The Bristol wills, see *Appendix I;* (2) St. Nicholas parish register.

III. WILLIAM CARY (*Richard², William¹*), 1550–1633, "the elder, of the City of Bristol, draper."

As shown by the Bristol *Tolzey Book,* he was Sheriff of Bristol 1599 and Mayor 1611, and thereafter Alderman. The St. Nicholas parish register shows his baptism October 3, 1550, his first marriage January 14, 1572, O.S., and his burial March 1, 1632, O.S., with the baptism of most of his children. The annals of Bristol (Alderman Haythorne's MS. in *Chronological Outline of the History of Bristol,* 1824) record of him: "This Mayor was afterwards Keeper of the Back Hall [*i.e.,* the Merchant Venturers' headquarters, on Bristol Back, otherwise known as Spicers' Hall], in which time his wife, an ancient woman, died; and four score years old or more he married his servant, by whom he had a son, having then sons living that were nearly three score years old." He left a will dated March 1, 1632, O.S. (the same day he was buried), and proved June 15, 1633. The record is in *Great Orphan Books* (Council House, Bristol), iii, 311.

He m.,

1st: 1573, Elizabeth (or Alice) Goodale (d. 1623), and by her had:

I   William, 1577–1638, *o.s.p.m.,*

[Baptized at St. Nicholas, January 3, 1576, O.S.; he married two wives, and was buried in St. Thomas Church, October 2, 1638. Although the St. Thomas parish register shows the baptism of several children, including two sons, the Heralds' College pedigree of 1699 testifies that he died without surviving male issue.]

II   Richard, 1579–1644, draper, of Bristol,

[Baptized at St. Nicholas, August 1, 1579, he m. 1606, Mary, dau. of Nicholas Shershaw, of Abergavenny, Monmouth, and had eight sons and nine daughters. According to his grandson's pedigree of 1700, he was buried at St. Nicholas, 1644; the parish register does not contain the record. Of the sons, only one, Shershaw (1615–1681), merchant, of Bristol, who died at Lisbon (P.C.C. *Admon. Act Book,* 1681), left issue. His three sons were John (1647–1730), the Bristol sugar merchant and publicist (see *Dict. Nat. Biog.,* iii, 1153, and P.C.C. *Admon. Act Book,* 1730); Richard (1649–1726), London merchant and director of the Bank of England (see his will, P.C.C. *Fairant,* 32), from whom are descended the family of Cary-Elwes, of Throcking, now of Great Billing, co. Northants (see Burke, *Landed Gentry*), and Thomas (1650–1711), Canon of Bristol and Rector of All Saints' Church (see his will, P.C.C. *Barnes,* 45). John and Richard of this family were two of the Carys of Bristol to whom the arms of Cary of Devon were specifically confirmed in 1699. (See *Appendix II.*) For John's sons, Richard and Warren in Virginia, see *post,* p. 154. The descendants of the clergyman Thomas carried on the family through three generations in the church until 1795, when the name became extinct in Bristol (see P.C.C. *Arran,* 48, and *Newcastle,* 584).]

III   John, 1583, see p. 20,

IV   Walter, 1588–1633, draper, of Bristol,

[Baptized at St. Nicholas, June 18, 1588, he m. Grace Browne, of St. Swithin's in Gloucester, who is styled in the Heralds' College pedigree of 1700 "an extraordinary enthusiast." Walter Cary left a will dated September 28, and proved February 18, 1633, O.S. (P.C.C. *Seager,* 77), mentioning children; but, according to the Heralds' College pedigree of 1700, none survived.]

V   Robert, 1589–1628, draper, of Bristol,

[Baptized at St. Nicholas, November 3, 1589, he married Anne, dau. of William Thomas, of Abergavenny, and had four daughters and two sons, of whom two daughters and the sons are mentioned in his will, dated August 11 and proved October 7, 1628 (P.C.C. *Barrington,* 90). According to the Heralds' College pedigree of 1700, this family became extinct during the civil wars.]

VI   Anne, 1590, *o.s.p., ante* 1632,

VII   Susan, 1592, *o.s.p., ante* 1632,

VIII   Margery, m. Hugh Yeo, of Bristol,

[A daughter of this marriage, Mary Yeo, married Shershaw Cary, son of Richard[5], *supra,* as his second wife. There was subsequently a family of Yeos in Elizabeth City County, Virginia, who were perhaps of this kindred.]

IX   Thomas, 1596–1648,

[Baptized at St. Nicholas, April 11, 1596, he m. Joan Milner and had a son Walter, baptized at St. Thomas, January 12, 1646, O.S., being himself buried at St. Thomas, February 12, 1648. Nothing more is known of the son Walter, who probably died *infans.*]

[19]

X   James, 1600–1681, of Charlestown, Massachusetts,

[Baptized at St. Nicholas, April 14, 1600, he emigrated to the Massachusetts colony in 1639, the pioneer American emigrant of his family. His record at Charlestown is complete to and including his tombstone recording his death "November 2, 1681, aged 81 years." (See Savage, *Genealogical Dictionary . . . of New England*, 1860.) From him descended a line of sea captains, merchants and clergymen, who have maintained the Bristol tradition in New England.]

2nd: 1624, Mary, dau. of Gregory Llewellyn, of Keynsham, and by her had:

XI   Anne, 1624, *d. infans,*

XII   Henry, 1625–*post* 1700, of Marlborough, Wilts.

[Baptized at St. Nicholas, November 20, 1625, he was, according to the Heralds' College pedigree of 1700, living 1700 at Marlborough. Thus he and his father together spanned 150 years, from Edward VI to Queen Anne. The pedigree also certified that he had married and had issue. In the book of *Skinners' Apprenticeships* there is an entry that in 1675 "John Cary, son of Henry Cary of Marlborough, Wilts, haberdasher of hats," was apprenticed to the Skinners' Company in London. If this family has persisted, its identity has been lost to the record.]

SOURCES:

(1) Bristol wills, see *Appendix I;* (2) Parish registers of St. Nicholas and St. Thomas, Bristol; (3) Heralds' College pedigrees of 1699 and 1700.

IV.   JOHN CARY (*William³, Richard², William¹*), 1583–1661, draper, of Bristol.

Baptized at St. Nicholas, April 10, 1583, and buried with his second wife in the Church of All Saints, February 13, 1661, he is described as "draper" in Henry Hobson's funeral certificate of 1637 and the will, of 1660, of his granddaughter, Alice Cary. There is no record of any will by him. It is evident that, with others of his family, he suffered severely in estate during the civil wars, when Bristol was alternately in possession of roundheads, cavaliers, and roundheads again, both parties preying on the resident merchants. The Heralds' College pedigrees of 1699 and 1701 give all the other information we have for him.

He m.,

? *1st:* 1609, Elizabeth Hereford,

[The evidence for this marriage is the Heralds' College pedigree of 1701, filed by John Cary, 1644–1701, sometime of Surry County, Virginia (see *post,* p. 155), and later of London, and a director of the "English Company trading to the East Indies," to support his application as a representative of the Bristol Carys for confirmation of the arms of Cary of Devon. This pedigree begins: "John Cary of the City of Bristol in com. Somerset and Elizabeth Hereford married 29th May 1609." No reference is made to John Cary's descent, or to William Cary, who was Mayor of Bristol 1611, with whom the pedigrees of 1699 and 1700 begin. The pedigree of 1701 was then apparently intended to be read with the pedigree of 1700, filed by John and Richard Cary, sons of Shershaw, in amplification of their original pedigree of 1699. There is no other possible John Cary, of Bristol, shown on the pedigrees of 1699 and 1700 than the John Cary who was the father of the Virginia immigrant by Alice Hobson; but as there is no reference on the pedigrees of 1699 and 1700, or elsewhere than on the pedigree of 1701, to any other marriage of John Cary than that to Alice Hobson, the identification of the John Cary who married Elizabeth Hereford with the John Cary who married Alice Hobson is not conclusive. It is persuasive, however. On the date of Elizabeth Hereford's marriage, the John Cary who afterwards married Alice Hobson would be 26 years of age. We have no proof of the date of Alice Hobson's marriage; the surviving parish register of All Saints', Bristol, in which we might expect to find it recorded, does not begin until 1621, and so the first evidence of that marriage is the baptism of the third son, Richard. Receding from this date, 1621, and allowing as many years as may be necessary for the births of Henry and Matthew, the sons of Alice Hobson who preceded Richard, as shown by Henry Hobson's will and the pedigree of 1699, we still have an ample margin for John Cary to have had his first experience in matrimony with Elizabeth Hereford and to have been the father, after 1609, of her five children enumerated in the pedigree of 1701. In any event John Cary could not have married Alice Hobson before 1617, when he would be 34, a late age for a first marriage in that family and at that time, but a probable age for a second marriage in a family which had con-

[21]

sistently practised second marriages. Finally, there is no inconsistency in the names of the children of Elizabeth Hereford (John,
Thomas, Philip, Prudence and Elizabeth) and those of Alice Hobson (Henry, Matthew, Richard, Miles, Alice, Honor and Mary).]

and by her had:

I   John, 1610?–1656?, of Hackney,

[The Heralds' College pedigree of 1701 says that he married,
left issue and "died about the year 1656." He has not been further
identified. A John Cary died at Hackney 1667 (see P.C.C. *Admon.
Act Book,* August 3, 1667), on whose estate his widow Dorothy
administered. Whoever was the John Cary, of Hackney, of the
pedigree of 1701, or the John Cary, of Hackney, of 1667, neither
may be identified with the interesting family of Nicholas Cary
(1650–1697), goldsmith, of Hackney, and later of Upcerne in
Dorset.]

II   Thomas, 1613–?, m. Susanna, dau. of
Philip Limberry, of Dartmouth, co.
Devon,

[The Heralds' College pedigree of 1701 shows that the claimant
John Cary, of London, was the son of this Thomas Cary, but gives
no further facts as to Thomas except that he was baptized December 27, 1613,—where not stated. No confirmation of this fact has
been found in any Bristol parish register.]

III   Philip,

[The Heralds' College pedigree of 1701 records him simply as
"3rd son of John Cary and Elizabeth Hereford." No further
record of him has been identified. It is possible that he may have
been the Philip Cary, of St. Martin's in the Fields, London, who
died 1765 (P.C.C. *Admon. Act Book,* 1675).]

IV   Prudence, "eldest daughter,"
V   Elizabeth, "2nd daughter."

2nd: 1617? Alice, dau. of Henry Hobson,
Innholder and sometime Mayor of Bristol,

[See Henry Hobson's will and funeral certificate in *Appendix I.*]

and by her had:

[22]

VI Henry, 1618?–*post* 1634,

[No record of him has been identified except the name in the Heralds' College pedigrees and the reference in Henry Hobson's will of 1634 as then living.]

VII Matthew, 1620?–1648, of Stepney, mariner,

[He is named in his grandfather Hobson's will of 1634 and himself left a will, dated October 22, 1647, and proved August 12, 1648 (P.C.C. *Essex*, 115), describing himself as "mariner," naming his daughter Alice, his brother Richard, and his wife Isabel, the latter then living "upon Wapping Wall in the parish of East Stepney." The daughter Alice completes the identification by her will of 1660 (P.C.C. *Nabbs*, 206, see *post, Appendix*, p. 163).]

VIII Richard, 1621–*post* 1660,

[He was baptized at All Saints', Bristol, July 29, 1621, is mentioned in his grandfather Hobson's will of 1634, in that of his brother Matthew, and in that of his niece, Alice Cary, of Stepney, as living 1660.]

IX Miles, 1623, the Virginia immigrant, see p. 34,

X Alice, 1625?, m. *1st,* Thomas Hayman and *2nd,* William Payne,

XI Honor, 1627?–1644,

XII Mary, 1630.

[The record of the daughters is the mention of Alice and her marriages in the Heralds' College pedigree of 1699; all three are named, in the order given in the will of their grandfather Hobson, as living 1634; the baptism of Mary, November 8, 1630, and the burial of Honor, November 6, 1644, are registered at All Saints', Bristol.]

SOURCES:

(1) The Bristol wills, see *Appendix I;* (2) the parish registers of St. Nicholas and All Saints', Bristol; (3) the Heralds' College pedigree of 1699.

CHAPTER THREE

CHARACTERISTICS IN VIRGINIA

The immigrant Miles Cary flourished in Virginia in the second consulship of Sir William Berkeley. After a busy career in trade and politics in which he attained prosperity and a seat in the Council, he was "killed by ye Dutch" during their foray upon Hampton Roads in June, 1667. He left four sons, who, we gather from the surviving records, began life respectively as a merchant, a builder, a surveyor, and a miller; all were considerable landowners and all took part in public life, the third with the largest measure of success. Each of these sons founded a family; by intermarriage their descendants allied themselves with other "Peninsula" families of their own kind and similar origin, and so established a wide connection of Virginia cousins.[1] We have noted that the Eng-

[1] In a warm and characteristic appreciation of the Peninsula between James and York Rivers, Governor Henry A. Wise says (*Seven Decades of the Union*, 1872, p. 29): "It is a land of genial climate, of generous soil, of majestic rivers, of fruitful fertility of fields, and of forests of richest frondage; above all distinguished for its men and women. It was settled by a race, or rather stock, of families the like of which will rarely be seen again—so manly,

AUTOGRAPHS OF THREE OF THE IMMIGRANT'S SONS

No autograph of the immigrant himself or of his eldest son has come to light. The only surviving official document on which the immigrant's signature appears is of 1667, a remonstrance to the King in Council signed by Sir William Berkeley and all the Virginia Council including Miles Cary, representing that Lord Baltimore had failed to ratify the engagement of his commissioners for a cessation of planting tobacco. The record of this, now in the British Public Record Office (Cal. State Papers, Am. & W. I., 1661–1668. No. 1509, p. 475), turns out to be only a copy of the original certified by Secretary Ludwell.

lish Carys have maintained throughout their history relatively the same place in the world with which they started, that by their marriages in the early generations in Devon they acquired with their lands a local self-conscious clan sense: but they did not become great nobles or compelling popular leaders. Such, precisely, is the family history in Virginia also. During the eighteenth century they were leading public men in their several communities, magistrates and legislators. Their official vocations were practically hereditary. Most of them were in the commission of the peace and took their turns as High Sheriff; actively serving in the militia as well, they were, after the Virginia fashion, always designated by military titles. In one

so refined, so intelligent, so spirited, proud, self-reliant, independent, strong, so fresh and so free. The family names of this Peninsula known to honour and to fame are countless: the Armisteads, Bollings, Byrds, Blairs, Burwells, Amblers, Carters, Cloptons, Christians, Carys, Dandridges, Digges, Fontaines, Gregorys, Harrisons, Coles, Inneses, Mallorys, Nicholsons and Nicholases, Randolphs, Pages, Nelsons, Kennons, Griffins, Barrons, Sclaters, Sheilds, Dudleys, Tuckers, Tylers, Tabbs, Tazewells, Wallers, Peachys, Saunders, Wythes, Lightfoots, Semples, Bassetts, and others no less known, from whom have sprung names of note in every Southern and Western State, as well as in other parts of Virginia." An illustration of the justice of terming the Peninsula immigrants a "stock". is found in the following record of one among these families, in which recur twenty-three of the forty names in Governor Wise's list; if we had followed up the distaff lines we could doubtless have included them all. For the names of other families who had their first Virginia homes in Warwick cf. Bishop Meade, i, 240.

As the bluest tincture of Cary blood in Devon was a dilution of Plantagenet, so in Virginia, measured by Virginia standards, we may reckon the Randolph infusion of Pocahontas!

branch they produced six successive clerks of the old County Court, most of whom served also in the important function of permanent clerks of legislative committees;[1] another branch produced four successive Naval Officers in the revenue service, a lucrative and much sought office in eighteenth century Virginia; among their several burgesses at·least three (the immigrant, Miles[2] of Richneck and Archibald of Ampthill) were of first-rate importance in the General Assembly, and they claim one member of the Council and one of the Judges of the first Supreme Court of Virginia. One of them was an original trustee named in the royal charter of

---

[1] *The Old Virginia Clerks.* In the *Virginia Law Journal* (1880), iv, 381, is a just tribute to a class of men peculiarly racy of the old-time Virginia civilization:

"The body of men which once filled the offices of clerks of courts in Virginia have left as decided impressions upon the history and traditions of the State as any other class that have lived in it. They exerted possibly more influence than any other men in the communities and times in which they lived, and their influence was always for good. They were the general advisers of the people; their advice was generally followed, and in nine cases out of ten it was good, whether viewed from a financial, moral or legal standpoint. The race of these valuable members of society, which gave it a tone peculiar to Virginia, has almost become extinct, but those who remember them still love to dwell on the characters of such men, who were universally regarded as having been the most exemplary that any people were ever blessed with."

In the course of some interesting observations upon the historical changes in the status of occupations, in which he cites the reversal of the social position of merchants and physicians in the seventeenth and nineteenth centuries, the Rev. H. E. Hayden (*Virginia Genealogies,* 1890, Preface, xviii) says: "The offices of High Sheriff and of County Clerk are slowly losing their ancient honour. Until reconstruction days these two offices were filled by the best blood and brains of the colony and State . . . descendants of such men

William and Mary College of 1691, who later served also as Rector; following him there was an uninterrupted identification of the name with that ancient and honorable institution for six successive generations, including eighteen students whose names appear on the incomplete surviving records, and three Visitors. Two of them were educated in England, one at Trinity College, Cambridge. Throughout the colonial period they were steadfast adherents of the Established Church, usually serving in their respective vestries, though two of them affiliated for a time with the Quakers.

For a century past, as democracy has spread, they have taken but little part in public life.[1]

. . . will feel ashamed in the atmosphere of sheriffs and clerks, who can do little more than read and write, to speak of their gentle ancestors as having held such positions."

The office of County Court Clerk came to be almost hereditary in some families in Virginia during the eighteenth and the first half of the nineteenth century. We have seen how a succession of · Carys held it during the colonial period. In his valuable *Memorials of Old Virginia Clerks* (1888), Mr. Frederick Johnston, sometime clerk of Roanoke, shows from the surviving records accessible to him (which in few cases went far back into the eighteenth century) that the following families were clerks of court for several generations, viz.: James Steptoe of Bedford and his descendants of other names, the Millers of Goochland, the Wallers of Spotsylvania, the Chews of Fredericksburg, the Pollards of Hanover, King William and King and Queen, the Youngs of Isle of Wight, and the Christians of Charles City. If this was true of the nineteenth century, the list could doubtless be considerably extended in the eighteenth when there was a general recognition of an hereditary claim to office. The record of the Carys, of whom Mr. Johnston had no trace, is evidence for this assumption.

[1] Some of the Carys, stirred by the idealism of Mr. Jefferson's doctrines, early declared themselves Democrats, but there was that in their breeding which made it as difficult for them, as for their descendants, to act on the principles they avowed.

[27]

They have, however, steadfastly maintained their ideals. In the American Revolution they stood, without exception, on the patriot side, and made substantial sacrifices in doing so. While as soldiers they have never been foremost, yet in the Revolution, in the War of 1812, in the Mexican War of 1846–48 and in that against Spain in 1898, several of each generation bore arms for the Commonwealth. In the epic war between the States conspicuously they did their part; then practically all of them (actually eighteen are identified) were in the field and made poignant sacrifice. In the war against Germany just ended, their youngsters have once more been under arms, one of whom dauntlessly gave his young life in a fine attempt to aid a comrade.

Descendants of each of the immigrant's sons are still to be found in Virginia after two hundred and fifty years: of all but the second in the male line, and by intermarriage, his blood is now represented by the family of the third. While this is an interesting fact, demonstrating not only persistence but a characteristic conservatism, the family has not been altogether sitfast. Each of its branches has contributed emigrants to the westward growth of the United States. Soon after the Revolution most of the representatives of what is now the senior line moved to the new lands of the western frontier, and reseated themselves in Kentucky and Tennessee; many of their descendants, spreading further west, crossed the Mississippi and have since lost touch with their Virginia kin. Again, in the renewed economic migration which bled the Old Dominion during the second quarter of the nineteenth century, a number of them established themselves in the Southwest and in Maryland. Still again, in another crisis, after the war between the States, some of them sought new opportunity in the far South, in the West and in New York. Wherever they have been, at home in Virginia or adjusting themselves to strange environments, they have held up their heads with dignity and self-respect, and have continued to reproduce inherited characteristics. They have clung to an intense local pride in their origin, and, without being the less good Americans, have continued to cherish the memories and institutions of colonial Virginia, and to speak its racy tongue[1]; even those who have joined in the national Western migration have remained *tuckahoes*.[2] Their women have maintained their old tradition of charm and character; their men have generally acquired a liberal education, sometimes under

[1] See that scholarly study, *Word-Book of Virginia Folk Speech*, 1899, by a loyal son of Warwick, Dr. B. W. Green.

[2] One wonders whether the present generation has ever read a book which delighted our grandfathers,—Joseph G. Baldwin's *The Flush Times of Alabama and Mississippi* (1853), picturing the Southwest about 1835. If not, it is cordially recommended, particularly the chapter on the transplanted Virginian in that environment, a characterization at once amusing, sympathetic and true.

[29]

difficulties, and with spotless honor have done their work, chiefly in the professions. They have been usually successful; but despite their later tincture of Scots blood, again and again they have turned the course of their careers at critical moments by a certain high sensitiveness which was not what the world called practical.[1]

Not the least interesting characteristic of this family is the periodical revolution which may be observed in their domestic habits. Roughly stated, for the first two hundred years of their history they were feudal landlords in rural Devon; then, in Bristol, for two centuries more, part of the highly centralized and circumscribed urban and gild life of a medieval municipality; then in colonial and "ante-bellum" Virginia for another like period, once more patriarchal landlords, so attached to the soil, indeed, as to resist

---

[1] This was, of course, the outstanding characteristic of the second Falkland. That gentle soul and fine intelligence lacked a fibre coarse enough to play the useful part in English history for which he had conspicuous opportunity. In smaller theatres of activity throughout the history of the family we note similar traits in other Carys at moments of crisis, in England as well as in America. It was true of the Chief Baron, *temp.* Richard II; of Sir William Cary, the liegeman of the Red Rose, and of the later Jacobites. In making this observation we have not overlooked the Hunsdons. In their earlier generations they exhibited an immense physical vigor and energy, and with it a coarseness of speech and deed, and an eye single for the main chance, which distinguishes them from any other Carys of whom there is a recognizable record. The explanation is that the Hunsdons were not Carys at all: if they were not, as seems historically most likely, entitled to a Tudor bar sinister, then they certainly derived their physical and mental equipment from their maternal blood, and were Boleyns to the end.

all attempts of government to herd them in towns; now, in a fourth cycle, with the changes in American civilization, they are, with few exceptions, again "citizens."

The distinction of this family is its persistence and even, honorable tenor: if they have not risen high, neither have they lapsed low. These are qualities which, if not romantic, make a strong appeal to the imagination of most men of gentle breeding, not the least in a world engaged in making "the world safe for democracy," for they spell Home.[1]

In all respects the Carys are a typical Virginia family.

[1] Even in the midst of revolution men crave permanence in something: our age *finds* it in religion, but, undaunted by experience, still seeks it in the ideal of Home. A thoroughly modern poet has, finely, combined the two cravings in the phrase:

"God, who is our home."

CHAPTER FOUR

WINDMILL POINT AND
PEARTREE HALL

The first home of the Warwick Carys in Virginia was the high bluff which divides Warwick River and Potash Creek at their confluence, facing Mulberry Island (or, as it is locally called, "Mulbri'land").   Here in 1643, on a plantation known as Windmill Point,[1] a Bristol

[1] *The Windmill Point property:* The first settlements on Warwick (then known as Blunt's Point) River, below Martins Hundred, were made after the Indian massacre of 1622. From the patents it appears that John Baynham (spelled also Bainham and Burnham) had an "ancient patent" dated December 1, 1624, for 300 acres "adjoining the lands of Captain Samuel Matthews and William Claiborne, gentleman." (*Va. Mag.,* i, 91.) This was Windmill Point and there John Baynham was living in 1625. (Brown, *First Republic,* 622. A Richard Baynham "of London, goldsmith," was a shareholder in the London Company in 1623 and one of the Warwick faction, Brown, *Genesis,* ii, 904, 982, and an Alexander Baynham was burgess for Westmoreland in 1654.) This John Baynham's daughter, Mary, married Richard Tisdale, who succeeded to the property, and from him Captain Thomas Taylor purchased it, taking out on October 23, 1643 (*Va. Land Register,* i), two patents, one calling for 350 acres, including Windmill Point proper, and the other for 250 acres known as Magpy Swamp. In the first of these patents Windmill Point is described as "butting upon Warwick River, bounded on the S. side with Potash Quarter Creeke and on the N. side with Samuell Stephens his land." The Stephens place (patented 1636 "adjoining the land of John Bainham," *Va. Mag.,* v, 455) was "Bolthrope," which passed through the hands of the governors Harvey and Berkeley

merchantman, Captain Thomas Taylor, found a snug harbor, safe from the privateers of the Parliament (cf. Neill, *Virginia Carolorum*, 178), and here he was succeeded by his son-in-law Col. Miles Cary; here in turn succeeded the eldest son of our immigrant. This Major Thomas Cary, "the merchant," is, on the surviving records, a somewhat shadowy person after his earliest youth, but he became the fertile progenitor of more of his race than any of his brothers and is still numerously represented. From him descended during the eighteenth century the neighboring households at Windmill Point and Peartree Hall,[1] with the

(*Va. Mag.*, i, 83), was afterwards long the home of the Coles (*Hening*, ii, 321), and eventually the property of Judge Richard Cary[5]. In his will the immigrant Miles Cary describes Windmill Point as "the tract of land which I now reside upon," refers to Thomas Taylor's patent, and says that a resurvey shows it to include 688 acres, exclusive of the Magpy Swamp. We trace the title through eight Carys to 1837, when the senior line became extinct and Windmill Point passed to the Lucas descendants of the youngest daughter of Captain Thomas Cary[6], one of whom Mr. G. D. Eggleston found in possession in 1851. In 1919 the site of the original house is marked by a grassy cavity. A modern house stands nearby, the residence of J. B. Nettles, who is now the owner of the small surrounding farm. The property is sometimes referred to as "Cary's Quarter." This Windmill Point must be distinguished from Sir George Yeardley's Windmill Point (originally Tobacco Point) on the south side of James River in Prince George, where, it is supposed, the first windmill in the United States was erected.

[1] *Peartree Hall*. It appears from the will of his son Miles[4] that Miles, Jr.,[3] dwelt on Potash Creek, a description which is persuasive that he established the house which in the next generation and thenceforth was known as Peartree Hall. That house stood on the bluff over Potash Creek, about a mile above Windmill Point. It was destroyed by fire about the beginning of the nineteenth cen-

branches of the latter which were maintained for several generations in Chesterfield, in Southampton and at Elmwood[1] on Back River in Elizabeth City, whose descendants have since spread far and wide.

THE SENIOR LINE AT WINDMILL POINT, EXTINCT 1837

I. Colonel MILES CARY (*John⁴, of Bristol, William³, Richard², William¹*), 1623–1667, of Windmill Point, Warwick County, Virginia.

Baptized at All Saints' Church, Bristol, January 30, 1622, O.S. Emigrated to Virginia about 1645, where the first record of him is on the bench of the Warwick County Court 1652. Major 1654, Lieutenant-Colonel 1657, Colonel and County Lieutenant 1660. Collector of the Tobacco Duties for James River, Escheator General for the Colony, Burgess 1660–1665, being member of the "Publique Committee" of the Assembly (*Hening*, ii, 31); advanced to the Council 1665. He maintained a water-mill and a mercantile business, both of which are mentioned in his will. Died, probably

———

tury, when the land was sold, Richard Cary⁶ being the last Cary of Peartree Hall. The bricks from the older house were used in the construction of the dwelling now standing on the property, which for two generations past has been occupied by a branch of the Tabb family, who represent also the Cary tradition. See B. W. Green in *W. & M. Quar.*, xv, 52. Miss Frances Tabb is the present gracious chatelaine.

¹ ELMWOOD, which harbored three generations of the Back River Carys, and later belonged to the Jones family, now of Hampton, lies in the midst of a land which reminds one of Holland, low rich fields between diked hedgerows in which the elm predominates. It adjoins the U. S. aviation station known as Langley Field and is now (1919) included in the prosperous farms of the Hampton Normal and Agricultural Institute. The original house, a modest but comfortable abode, still stands in the shelter of an ancient grove to testify to the tradition of the abundant hospitality there practised.

[34]

from wounds, during the Dutch raid on Hampton Roads in June, 1667. He had acquired his father-in-law's lands at Windmill Point and Magpie Swamp, and others, aggregating more than 2600 acres in Warwick, including the plantations afterwards known as The Forest, Richneck, and Skiffs Creek (Mulberry Island).

He m. (in Virginia not later than 1646) Anne, dau. of Captain Thomas Taylor,

[The surviving evidence for the marriage is the reference in Miles Cary's will to "my father-in-law, Thomas Taylor, deceased." In his patents of 1657 Miles Cary recites that he had acquired Thomas Taylor's property by devise and he returns Anne Taylor by her maiden name as a headright. She is described in the 1682 patent of Miles[2] as "his mother Mrs. Anne Cary" and so was living fifteen years after her husband's death. She was undoubtedly buried, as was also, probably, her father, in the graveyard at Windmill Point. No evidence has yet appeared to identify this Taylor family definitely. Thomas Taylor was one of the original patentees in Elizabeth City in 1626 (*Hotten*, 273), and in 1643 took up 600 acres in Warwick. In 1646 he sat as Burgess for Warwick and as late as 1652 was in the commission of the peace. In the patent of 1643 he is styled "mariner." He was probably a Bristol sea captain long engaged in the Virginia trade who retired from the sea in Warwick. His relation to Miles Cary suggests that he may have been of the family of John Taylor, alderman of Bristol, who is mentioned in relation to the Bristol Carys in the 1652 will of the Bristol clergyman, Robert Perry (P.C.C. *Bowyer*, 243. See *Va. Mag.*, xi, 364). We have seen that there had already been a Taylor-Cary marriage in Bristol.]

and by her had:

   I   Thomas, 1647?, of Windmill Point, see p. 37,

   II   Anne, 1649?, unmarried?,

   III   Henry, 1650?, of The Forest, see p. 86,

   IV   Bridgett, 1652?, m. Captain William Bassett, of New Kent,

[For the Bassett family, see Keith, *Ancestry of Benjamin Harrison*.]

V   Elizabeth, 1653?, m. Emanuel Wills, of
       Warwick,

[For descendants of this marriage, see *W. & M. Quar.*, xxiv, 200.]

VI   Miles, 1655?, of Richneck, see p. 100,
VII   William, 1657?, of Skiffs Creek, see p. 129.

SOURCES:

(1) Bristol wills in *Appendix I;* (2) Parish register of All Saints' Church, Bristol; (3) Pedigree of Cary of Bristol, filed in the Heralds' College, 1699; particularly the following item (which is not repeated in the pedigree of 1701) among the children of John Cary and Alice Hobson, viz., "Miles Cary, settled in Virginia and had issue Thomas Cary who married Anne, daughter of Francis Milner"; (4) Hening, *Laws of Virginia*, 1660–1667, *passim;* (5) Testimony as to Miles Cary and his family in Hunsdon peerage case 1707, *Harl. MS.* 6694, in the British Museum; (6) Miles Cary's will in *Appendix I;* (7) Miles Cary's tombstone at Windmill Point, *infra;* (8) Gleanings from public records.

TOMBSTONE OF MILES CARY, THE IMMIGRANT
AT WINDMILL POINT, WARWICK COUNTY,
VIRGINIA.

ARMS OF CARY OF DEVON

[Ar. on a bend sa. three roses
of the field. *Crest:* a Swan ppr.]

HERE LYETH THE BODY OF MILES CARY, ESQ[R]
ONLY SON OF JOHN CARY & ALICE, HIS WIFE,
DAUGHTER OF HENRY HOBSON OF THE CITY OF BRISTOLL,
ALDERMAN:
HE WAS BORN IN Y[E] SAID CITY
AND DEPARTED THIS LIFE THE 10TH DAY OF JUNE 1667
ABOUT THE 47TH YEAR OF HIS AGE,
LEAVING FOUR SONS AND THREE DAUGHTERS, VIZ:
THOMAS, ANNE, HENRY, BRIDGETT, ELIZABETH,
MILES & WILLIAM

NOTE. *The monument was a brick altar tomb surmounted by a heavy iron stone slab, evidently carved in England. It is now in*

[36]

CARY GRAVEYARDS

1. The fragments of the tombstone of the immigrant Miles Cary *in situ* at Windmill Point, Warwick County, Va., April 10, 1919
2. The legible fragments from No. 1 placed against the tree which stands beside the site of the grave
3. The fragments of the tombstone of Mary Milner and Miles Cary[2] *in situ* at Richneck, Warwick County, Va., April 10, 1919
4. Peartree Hall graveyard, April 10, 1919

complete ruin. The inscription was preserved by at least three copies, independently made, which agree, viz.: in 1844 by Mr. William Robertson, Clerk of Warwick; in 1851 by Mr. Guilford Dudley Eggleston and Mr. William B. ("Hell-cat Billy") Jones, then Clerk of Warwick; and in 1868 by Captain Wilson Miles Cary.

It will be noted that, as so often is the case in respect of traditional records, the inscription contains two errors of fact: (1) Miles Cary was not the only son of John Cary of Bristol, though at the time of his death he may have been the only surviving son; (2) Miles Cary was at the time of his death in his forty-fifth year, as appears from the following contemporary entry in the parish register of All Saints' Church, Bristol:

"The 30 January, 1622, [o.s.] was Baptized Miles, the sonne of John Cary."

The grave is on the high bluff over the mouth of Potash Creek, looking down Warwick River, in the midst of an ancient grove. In 1868 it was described as "at the foot of a giant walnut and in the deep shade of a bower formed by the festoons of a mighty grapevine which embraces the entire grove in its snake-like folds." This description held good on April 10, 1919, both the walnut and the grape-vine being extant. The brick tomb has entirely disappeared, while the slab which bore the inscription is shattered into many pieces, some of which have been carried away; but enough remains after two hundred and fifty years clearly to identify the inscription with the aid of the copies made a half century ago.

II. Major THOMAS CARY (*Miles[1]*), 1647?–1708, of Windmill Point.

He was employed 1666, before he was of age (as appears by his father's will), in the construction of the fort at Old Point Comfort. (MS. notes by Conway Robinson from General Court Order Book, 1666, in *W. M. Cary Notes*. See also *Va. Mag.*, xvii, 246.) Captain, Major and J. P. for Warwick. He ranked third in the Warwick Militia at Berkeley's array for defence against the Indians in 1676, prior to Bacon's rebellion. (*Hening*, ii, 330.) He inherited Windmill Point and Magpie Swamp under his father's will, and perhaps carried on the immigrant's mercantile business in Warwick, in the tradition of which we find his son and grandson engaged.

By reason of the facts that no Virginia evidence has appeared for any activity, after 1676, by the immigrant's eldest son, and that his sons affiliated with the Quakers, it was at one time conjectured by the genealogists that Major Thomas Cary[2] of Warwick might be identified with Colonel Thomas Cary, the North Carolina "rebel" of 1711. (*Spotswood Papers*, 81.) Apart from the stubborn fact of the Warwick will of .1708, the *W. M. Cary Notes* prove beyond peradventure that Colonel Thomas Cary of North Carolina was a son of Walter Cary of Cheping Wycomb, co. Bucks, and a stepson of John Archdale, the Quaker proprietary of North Carolina.

He m., not later than 1669, Anne, dau. of Captain Francis Milner, of Nansemond,

[The evidence for the marriage is the statement of it in the Heralds' College pedigree of 1699, in which Thomas, alone of the immigrant's sons, is named. By reason of the destruction of the Nansemond records, not much is known of the Milner family. It is possible that they were from Bristol; it may be noted that there had already been a Cary-Milner marriage in Bristol; that the pedigree of 1699 goes out of its way to record Milner as a name apparently known in Bristol, while the earliest settlement of Southside Virginia, including Isle of Wight and Nansemond, where the Milners were established, was largely recruited from Bristol. The Milners used, however (*e.g.* on Mary Milner's tomb at Richneck), the arms which are attributed by Burke to Milner, co. Lincoln. Francis Milner was Sheriff of Nansemond in 1699 (*Va. Mag.*, iv, 168), J. P. as late as 1702 (*Va. Mag.*, i, 369, and *Colonial Records of N. C.*, i, 645 and 675), and in 1704 appears on the *Quit Rent Rolls* for Nansemond under the title of Captain. He was a brother of Lieutenant-Colonel Thomas Milner, whose daughter married Miles Cary[2] (*W. & M. Quar.*, xiv, 139).]

and by her had:

I   Thomas, 1670, of Windmill Point, see p. 42,

II   Miles, Jr., 1671, of Potash Creek, see p. 49,

[The evidence for, and the deduction of, this identification is as follows:

At the beginning of the eighteenth century there were six contemporaries bearing the name Miles Cary in Virginia. In the order of age, they were:

1. Miles Cary[2], of Richneck, the third son named on the immigrant's tombstone, who died in 1709;

2. Miles Cary², called in the public records "Mr. Miles Cary, Jr.," prior to 1702, and thereafter "Captain Miles Cary" until the death of his uncle in 1709, when he becomes "Miles Cary, the elder," who was clerk of legislative committees as early as 1693 and during most of his life Clerk of Warwick;

3. Miles Cary³, named in the will of Henry Cary² as his second son. He was probably not born earlier than 1680, being the youngest of the five children by his father's marriage in 1671 with Judith Lockey. That he died young and unmarried is a reasonable deduction from the complete silence as to him of all other records than his father's will.

4. Miles Cary³, the second son of William Cary², described in his father's will in 1711 as then under age;

5. Miles Cary⁴, second son of No. 2 *supra*, and in time also Clerk of Warwick; and

6. Miles Cary³, the second son of Miles Cary², of Richneck, and Mary Wilson, who was not born until 1708.

During the agitation in Virginia from 1843 to 1852 over the fabulous "great Cary fortune in England" there were several attempts made to state the pedigrees of the various branches of the Cary family in Virginia. It was then that the *Eggleston Notes* were drawn from the Warwick records, and as those notes showed no Miles Cary among the sons of Major Thomas Cary², the genealogists seem to have agreed that "Mr. Miles Cary, Jr.," must be one or the other of the Miles named in the wills of Henry² or William². Since then these two theories have been so persistently advanced in the genealogical columns of newspapers that they have almost become sanctified. (See *e.g.*, Goode, *Virginia Cousins*, p. 283, advocating the Henry Cary origin, and Pecquet du Bellet, ii, 66, advocating the William Cary origin.) Meanwhile, however, the immediate family tradition contradicted both these theories. In 1843 John Cary⁷ of Lynchburg testified generally in a letter now *penes me* that his grandfather Colonel John Cary⁶ of Back River always maintained that the Peartree Hall household was of the senior line of the family in Virginia. Again in 1868 Miss Susan Cary⁶ (1789–1873) of the Back River family, a clear-thinking repository of tradition, asserted stoutly and specifically that whatever the wills showed, the constant tradition of the family was that her ancestor, Miles Cary, Jr., was a son of the eldest son of the immigrant. Evidence is now available to support and establish this tradition.

As nothing more is known of the *Milner* shown in the *Eggleston Notes* to have been named in the will, we might readily begin the argument with the assumption that Mr. Eggleston misread *Milner* for *Miles* in the difficult MS. of the Warwick records; but Mr. Eggleston did not have access to the Heralds' College pedigree of 1699 (which was unknown in Virginia until Colonel J. L. Chester brought it to the attention of Captain W. M. Cary, of Baltimore, in 1866), and so, having no knowledge that the wife of Thomas Cary[2] was a Milner, would have no mental predilection to read that name in this connection. We conclude on this evidence that there was a son *Milner* and must find proof elsewhere than in his will that Thomas Cary[2] had a son *Miles* and that that son is identical with the first Clerk of Warwick of the name.

We begin then with the fact that there was only one Thomas Cary of the third generation in Virginia and he was unmistakably the eldest son named in the will of Thomas[2]. He married Elizabeth Hinde in 1695. The Quaker missionary Story says definitely, in his *Journal*, that the Thomas and Miles Cary he met in Warwick in 1698 and 1705 were brothers, and that Miles was Secretary (*i.e.,* Clerk) of the County. By one of those happy accidents, which give zest to the patient study of genealogy, there has recently come to light in a most unexpected place a paper which goes far to establish the tradition now under consideration, checking with Story's statement also. Among the old records of Albemarle County, North Carolina, at Edenton, are several affidavits filed July 18, 1713, in a suit concerning a slave named Stephen, who had been sold some years before by Anne Akehurst to "Miles Cary, Jr." (*N. C. Hist. & Gen. Reg.*, 1901, ii, 151.) The witnesses are "Miles Cary, the elder," aged 42, whose signature is the unmistakable autograph of our first Clerk of Warwick, Thomas Cary of Warwick County, Virginia, "aged 43," and Elizabeth Cary "aged 34," who says that she went to dwell in the house of Daniel Akehurst in 1695. This Akehurst was a Quaker. He lived in Warwick but had been the Proprietor Archdale's deputy in the North Carolina Council, subsequently Secretary for the Proprietors and died in 1699. (Weeks, *Southern Quakers*, 65.) It was at his house that Story first met the Carys in 1698, and so it is persuasive that Thomas Cary[3] might have met his wife in the same house. The York records show (*W. M. Cary Notes*) that in 1701 "Mr. Miles Cary, Jr.," was attending to business for "Ann Akehurst, executrix of Daniel Akehurst, dec'd." All of this suggests that the witnesses for "Miles Cary, the elder," in 1713 were his brother and sister-in-law. Moreover, the Miles Cary who was Clerk of Warwick was the only one of the third generation who had a son named Thomas except the Thomas[3] who, Story says, was his brother. It seems likely that each of these sons was named after a common grandfather.

The negative evidence against any other identification is:

(*a*) The Clerk of Warwick was not the son of Henry Cary[2], because the latter's will dated January 27, 1716, naming his son Miles as beneficiary was proved by the oath of a Miles Cary who was one of the subscribing witnesses. As the law then stood (*Black-*

stone, ii, 377; *Harwood* v. *Grice,* 1735 Barradall's *Va. Reports,* 43)
a legatee was not a competent witness to a devise of lands, so that
the witness must have been another than the beneficiary. The original
will has survived and shows the signature of the subscribing witness to be identical with that of the Clerk, which may be seen on
several surviving official documents.

(*b*) He was no more the son of William[2], than of Miles[2], and for
the same reason because the Clerk was in active official life when
those other Miles Carys were infants.]

III   James, 1673?,

[This James is one of the unsolved problems of the Cary pedigree. There is no extant proof for him in relation to the Warwick family, except the *Eggleston Notes* of his father's will. As
we have definite dates for the births of his older brothers, he could
not have been born before 1673, and so would have been too young
even at a time of early marriages to have been, as has been conjectured (Richmond *Times-Dispatch,* April 16, 1911), the James
Cary of Abingdon parish, Gloucester, who had a son baptized in
1689 (see *post,* p. 149). He may have been the James Cary who patented lands in King William in 1720 (*Va. Land Records,* xi, 106),
but he seems too early to have been the James Cary who patented
lands on the Nottoway River in 1736 to 1740, and of whom there
are traces as late as 1759. For this last named James see *post,*
p. 43.]

IV   Milner,

[There is no record of him except in the *Eggleston Notes* of his
father's will. He must have died young.]

V   Elizabeth, ?m. . . . Jones of Gloucester,

[The only evidence for the marriage is a tradition in the Jones
family which takes color from specifications that this Elizabeth
Cary was mother to the Judith Jones of Gloucester who m. William Cary[3] of Prince George (see *post,* p. 138), and that one of the
children of Frances (Jones) Anderson, a sister of Judith (Jones)
Cary, was named Thomas Cary. See statement of L. B. Anderson,
1872, in *W. M. Cary Notes.*]

VI   ? Dorothy, m. *1st,* 1694?, John Pleasants, of Henrico, and *2nd,* 1720, Robert Jordan of Nansemond.

[41]

[The only evidence for this Dorothy is the tradition in the Pleasants family that the wife of John Pleasants, son of the Pleasants immigrant, was Dorothy Cary (*Va. Mag.*, xvi, 219, and *W. & M. Quar.*, xxiv, 266). This is the only place she can be fitted into the pedigree. The Quaker affiliation of this generation of the Carys, the marriages of Miles Cary[3], of Potash Creek, and Joseph Pleasants, brother to John, with daughters of Richard Cocke, and the references to the wife and children of John Pleasants in his mother's will of 1708 (*Va. Mag.*, xviii, 450), are all consistent with the tradition.

The second husband was the first of several generations of Quaker preachers of repute of his family. For these Jordans see *The Harrisons of Skimino* (1910), 23. Under their influence Dorothy Cary's son Thomas Pleasants also became a Quaker preacher, and married a daughter of Robert Jordan by his first wife (*W. & M. Quar.*, xxvii, 121).]

SOURCES:

(1) The *Eggleston Notes* for the will of Thomas Cary[2], recorded 1708 in Warwick *Will Book*, I, 23, naming children Thomas, James, Milner and Elizabeth. (2) Gleanings from public records, as cited.

III. THOMAS CARY (*Thomas[2]*, *Miles[1]*), 1670–*post* 1713, of Windmill Point.

He affiliated with the Quakers in 1698 and 1705 but in 1712–13 was High Sheriff of Warwick, indicating that he did not remain "convinced."

He m. 1695, Elizabeth Hinde, of Elizabeth City, and by her had:

I   Thomas, 1696?, of Windmill Point, see p. 43,

[As no record evidence has appeared for the names of the children of Thomas Cary[3] and Elizabeth Hinde, it is a deduction that this Thomas[4] (who cannot otherwise be placed) was son of Thomas[3], the evidence being that we find the descendants of this Thomas[4] in possession of the entailed lands at Windmill Point, while he himself sells Magpie Swamp to his cousin Miles Cary[4], of Peartree Hall, as the latter testifies in his will.]

II   ? James, of Nottoway River.

[42]

[In 1736 one James Cary patented lands on the Nottoway River, then in Nansemond, describing himself as "of Isle of Wight," and in 1738 and 1740 adds to these lands (*Va. Land Records,* xvii, 143, xviii, 50 and xix, 752). In 1753 the Vestry of the upper parish of Nansemond established a chapel of ease on the lands of James Cary "over Nottoway." (See parish register.) In 1759 James Cary is paid for maintaining a ferry. As Thomas Cary[2] and Thomas Cary[4], of Warwick, both had sons named James, it is possible, in the lack of record evidence to the contrary, that Thomas Cary[3] also had a son named James who might be identified with the James of Nottoway River, as he was apparently a contemporary of the fourth generation of the Warwick family.

In 1750 James Cary, Jr., was appointed Clerk of the Vestry of upper Nansemond and a year later is recorded to have removed from the parish. (See parish register.) We find the clew to his removal from Nansemond in Lunenburg *Deed Book,* iii, 385, which shows James Cary, Jr., acquiring, in 1753, lands on the Roanoke River in that part of Lunenburg now included in Mecklenburg. This James Cary, Jr., was too early to be identified with the James Cary[5], an authenticated member of the Warwick family (see *infra*), and may be assumed to be the son of James Cary, of Nottoway River, especially as there are further evidences of the name on the Southside, and in relation to North Carolina, where the Whitakers were established on the Roanoke River near the Virginia line (see *infra*). Thus there was a James Cary, Jr., member of the North Carolina Assembly in 1760. (*N. C. Colonial Records,* vi, 367.) Again, one James Cary patented lands in Halifax in 1761 (*Va. Land Records,* xxxiv, 867), and there is a James Cary listed in the U. S. (Va.) Census of 1785 as then living in Halifax. There are also traces, after 1759, of a Benjamin, an Edward and an Elphinstone Cary in Nansemond and Southampton, all mentioned in relation to lands of James Cary.]

SOURCES:

(1) *N. C. Hist. & Gen. Reg.,* ii, 151, for affidavit of Thomas Cary[3] that he was "aged 43" in 1713; (2) Kendall's *Life of Thomas Story* for the Quakers; (3) Elizabeth City records for the marriage license of Thomas Cary[3] (*W. & M. Quar.,* ii, 210) and the fact that he was Sheriff; (4) the *Eggleston Notes* do not show the record of any will of Thomas Cary[3].

IV. THOMAS CARY (*Thomas[3], Thomas[2], Miles[1]*), 1696?–1764, of Windmill Point.

There is no evidence for his wife, but his will named his children, except James, viz.:

I   Thomas, 1720?, of Windmill Point, see p. 44,

II Elizabeth, 1725–1800, m. Richard Whitaker, 1720–1794, of Halifax County, N. C.,

III Martha (d. 1762), m. Gough Whitaker, of Halifax County, N. C.,

[Both these Whitaker brothers removed about 1760 with their Cary wives, from Warwick to Halifax County, N. C., where the Cary name has persisted among their descendants. See traditions in Pecquet du Bellet, ii, 127. For some notes on the Whitaker family in Virginia, see Richmond *Standard*, 1880, iii, 9. Dr. J. S. Ames, of Johns Hopkins University, who has made exhaustive genealogical collections of the Whitakers, records over 15,000 descendants of these two marriages.]

IV James, 1728?–1788, of Isle of Wight, m. Mildred, *o.s.p.*

[He acquired lands in Newport parish in 1768 (Isle of Wight *Deed Book*, xii, 251), and by will, 1788 (Isle of Wight *Will Book*, x, 140), left such lands to his wife Mildred for life with remainder "to my brother Thomas Cary's son William of the County of Warwick." In 1796 (Isle of Wight *Deed Book*, xviii, 84) William Cary[6] and Sarah his wife conveyed these lands.

SOURCES:

(1) The *Eggleston Notes* for the will of Thomas Cary[4], in which he styled himself "the elder," recorded 1764 in Warwick *Will Book*, O, p. 488; (2) Dr. J. S. Ames' Whitaker Collections, MS.; (3) Gleanings from public records, as cited.

V. Captain THOMAS CARY (*Thomas[4], Thomas[3], Thomas[2], Miles[1]*), 1720?–1792, of Windmill Point.

As "Thomas Cary, Jr.," he appears in the court records prior to his father's death. He commanded the Warwick militia in the Revolutionary army (*Va. Mag.*, vii, 151, 254, 256). J. P. in 1785 and High Sheriff for Warwick in 1786. In the *Virginia Census* of 1782 his household is listed for 7 whites and 18 blacks.

He m.

1st: Martha, dau. of ?William Whitaker, of Warwick,

[The evidence for the Whitakers in Warwick is not complete; but, the family tradition being that Captain Thomas Cary's first wife was a Whitaker, the *W. M. Cary Notes* conjecture on such records as survive that this Martha Whitaker was first cousin to the Richard and Gough Whitaker (*supra*) who married her husband's sisters: that they were sons of John, and she daughter of William, Whitaker.]

and by her had:

I William, 1745?, of Windmill Point, see p. 45.

2nd: Frances, dau. of Robert Goodwyn, Sr.,

[For the Goodwyns of Surry and Sussex, see *W. & M. Quar.*, xxvi, 126. Frances (Goodwyn) Cary m. 2nd, 1795, John Bendall, who administered on Captain Thomas Cary's estate, which accounts for the fact that Windmill Point was, later, sometimes called *Bendalls*.]

and by her had:

II ? Robert, 1752?, of Charles City, see p. 46,
III Miles, 1755?, of Charles City, see p. 47,
IV Anne, m. Edmund Curtis, of York,
V Martha, m. Thomas Lucas, of Warwick.

SOURCES:

(1) Statement of "Kit" Curtis, of Warwick, 1868, in *W. M. Cary Notes;* (2) The *Eggleston Notes* for the will of Thomas Cary[5], dated 1790, recorded 1792 (Warwick *Will Book*, F, p. 774), naming his children, except Robert who is added from Charles City records; (3) Gleanings from Charles City and York records in *W. M. Cary Notes.*

VI. WILLIAM CARY (*Thomas[5], Thomas[4], Thomas[3], Thomas[2], Miles[1]*), 1745–1808, of Windmill Point.

He was J. P. for Warwick and (apparently) the William Cary, Jr. (so designated in distinction from his contemporary kinsman, William Cary⁴, of Yorktown), who was Naval Officer at Yorktown in 1782. See *Cal. Va. State Papers,* iii, 262.

He m.

1st: Polly, dau. of Judge Richard Cary, of Peartree Hall, and by her had:

I William, *o.s.p., ante* 1807,

2nd: 1789, Sarah (living 1821), dau. of Josiah Massenburg, "the elder,"

[Joseph Massenburg was a member of the Revolutionary Committee of Safety for Warwick. See *W. & M. Quar.,* v, 250, and for others of the family, *Va. Mag.,* xix, 397.]

and by her had:

II Thomas Whitaker, 1790, of Windmill Point, see p. 48.

SOURCES:

(1) The *Eggleston Notes* for the will of William Cary⁶, proved in Warwick 1808 (*Will Book,* 1793–1808, p. 388), recording the deduction from it that he left "one child, William." This conclusion is contradicted by the statement of William Cary⁶ himself in the bill in *Cary* v. *Wynne* 1807, that his son William was then dead (see *W. & M. Quar.,* xx, 67). That the surviving son was Thomas Whitaker appears from the statement of Mr. "Kit" Curtis (b. 1800) made in 1868, and other family traditions collected in the *W. M. Cary Notes.* (2) Elizabeth City *Deed and Will Book,* 1787–1800, p. 191, for deed dated 1795 referring to the second marriage.

VI. ? ROBERT CARY (*Thomas⁵, Thomas⁴, Thomas³, Thomas², Miles¹*), 1752?–1800, of Charles City.

He first appears on the records in 1792, as the purchaser of 150 acres in Charles City.

He m. ? Elizabeth, dau. of David Roper, of Charles City, and by her had:

I   David, 1775–1824, of Charles City, who had children Robert and Elizabeth,

II Frances,

III "all my surviving children except David and Frances."

SOURCES:

Gleanings from Charles City records in *W. M. Cary Notes.* The chief evidence is the will of Robert Cary[6], proved 1800 (Charles City *Will Book,* 1787–1808, pp. 508, 578), which names his father-in-law and the children and grandchildren as above. No further record of this family has appeared. It is not accounted for in any of the general family traditions, and is here included tentatively only.

VI. MILES CARY (*Thomas[5], Thomas[4], Thomas[3], Thomas[2], Miles[1]*), 1755?–*post* 1806, of Charles City.

He appears as a party to real estate transactions in Charles City from 1792 to 1799 and as late as 1806 in York court.

He m. Rachel, dau. of ? Anthony Lamb, of Charles City,

[For the Lamb family, see *W. & M. Quar.,* vii, 51 at p. 53.]

and by her had:

I   John, *o.s.p.,*

II William Miles, *o.s.p.,*

III Frances, m. John Morse,

IV Elizabeth, 1803–1835, m. Christopher Curtis, of Warwick,

[It was this Christopher Curtis, the second of his family to marry a Cary, who in 1868 conducted Captain Wilson-Miles Cary to the haunts and tombs of his ancestors and gave him the surviving local family tradition. His great-nephew S. S. Curtis, Sheriff of Warwick, performed the same hospitable office for other like pilgrims in 1919. For the Curtis immigrant, see *Va. Mag.*, v. 344.]

v Amelia, unmarried ?,

vi Alice, unmarried ?.

SOURCES:

(1) Statement of "Kit" Curtis 1868 in *W. M. Cary Notes;* (2) Gleanings from Charles City and York records in *W. M. Cary Notes.*

VII. THOMAS WHITAKER CARY (*William⁶, Thomas⁵, Thomas⁴, Thomas³, Thomas², Miles¹*), 1790–1819, of Windmill Point.

He was Clerk of Warwick and represented Warwick in the House of Delegates 1815–1817.

He m. Eliza, dau. of Captain Joseph Middleton, and by her had:

i William, 1816–1837, *o.s.p.*

[He was the eighth and last Cary of Windmill Point. His father died while he was an infant, leaving him a considerable property in negroes. His mother married again and removed to Norfolk, where he grew up. Studied medicine in Philadelphia and with Dr. Francis Mallory in Norfolk, and died as he came of age, reputed a youth of promise.]

SOURCES:

(1) Will of T. W. Cary, dated September 30, 1817, and proved August 12, 1819, in *Williamsburg Wills;* (2) Chancery record at Williamsburg, *Cary v. Dunn,* 1821; (3) Statement of "Kit" Curtis, 1868, in *W. M. Cary Notes;* (4) Swem and Williams' *Register,* and gleanings from other public records in *W. M. Cary Notes;* (5) Statements, 1871, in *W. M. Cary Notes* by Charles K. Mallory of Hampton and Charles S. Allmand of Norfolk as to their boyhood friend William Cary[8].

AUTOGRAPHS OF THE PEARTREE HALL CARYS

The numerals indicate generations

III. Captain MILES CARY, JR. (*Thomas[2]*, *Miles[1]*), 1671–1724, of Potash Creek, Warwick County.

In 1691 he began his career (and so determined the vocation of several generations of his descendants) as a clerk in the office of the Secretary of State at Jamestown, of which his uncle Miles, of Richneck, was then in charge as clerk of the General Court. By the same influence he was appointed 1693 (McIlwaine, *Journal of the House of Burgesses*, 1659–1693, 450, 451) Clerk of the legislative committees of Privileges and Elections and of Public Claims. A few years later he was chosen Clerk of Warwick. He held all of these posts until 1718, when he retired by reason of ill health. In 1702 he was Captain in the Warwick Militia, his uncle Miles[2] of Richneck then being Colonel (*Cal. State Papers, Am. & W. I.*, 1702, No. 237, p. 158). It seems probable from entries in the York court records that he carried on the mercantile business which the immigrant had established; this surmise is supported by the clearly established fact that his son and official successor Miles[4] was engaged in such a trade. "Captain Miles Cary" appears on the *Quit Rent Roll* for 1704 as paying quit-rents for 600 acres in Warwick; as both his father and elder brother were then living and neither appears on the roll it is possible that this Miles[3] was lessee of the Windmill Point lands; certainly he was at that time the most active representative of the eldest line. Though there is no stone to mark his grave, it seems quite certain that he was the first of his family to be buried in the Peartree Hall graveyard. That is as serene and restful a place to await the Day of Judgment as could be selected. In a secluded nook, "far from the madding crowd," flanked by a stately forest and pleasant cultivated fields, six generations of Carys lie in the shadow of ancient mulberries, beneath a blanket of riotous jonquils, which in spring clothe the entire area as with a golden oriental rug. This last home of his ancestors has been fenced, and is piously maintained by T. Archibald Cary[8], of Richmond.

He m. 1695, Elizabeth, dau. of Richard Cocke, of Bremo, in Henrico,

[For the Cocke family, see *Va. Mag.*, iii, 282 ff.]

and by her had:

I   Richard, 1696?–1721,

[He served an apprenticeship in the office of the Clerk of York County, and in 1718 succeeded his father as Clerk of Warwick, etc. He died unmarried after a brief career.]

II   Thomas, 1698?, of York and Chesterfield, see p. 62,

III   Miles, 1701?, of Peartree Hall, see p. 51,

IV   Nathaniel, 1703?–*ante* 1761, of Chesterfield, *o.s.p.*,

[The will of his sister-in-law Dorothy Philipson Cary, 1761, shows that he had married, lived in Chesterfield and died without issue.]

V   Anne, 1707?,

VI   Elizabeth, 1709?,

VII   Bridget, 1710?,

VIII   Dorothy, 1712?,

IX   Martha, 1714?.

[No proof has yet appeared for the marriages of the daughters, nor is there any convincing tradition. Abraham (*Cary Tradition* in Richmond *Whig*, July, 1852) stated that Dorothy married George Dudley. This appears to be the origin of the unproved statement in Pecquet du Bellet, ii, 67, that Dorothy Cary of the Warwick family was the mother of the Dorothy Dudley who in 1755 married John Cary, Jr., of Kingston Parish, Gloucester (see *post*, p. 151, and for the little which is *known* of the Dudleys of Gloucester and Middlesex, *Va. Mag.*, xxiii, 148). Again, Goode (*Virginia Cousins*, 283 and 50) states that "one of the daughters [of Miles Cary[3], of Potash Creek] probably" married a Collier; but Goode had already confused the daughters of Miles Cary[3], of Potash Creek, with those of his son Miles Cary[4], of Peartree Hall, and the Collier he selects was, he says, a Revolutionary soldier, and so contemporary also with the fifth generation.]

The order of the children. The *Eggleston Notes* on the record of the will of Miles Cary[3] state that he left children "Anne, Elizabeth, Bridgett, Dorothy, Martha, Miles, Thomas and Nathaniel." As the will was not quoted, this is merely a deduction, but it has been accepted as the order of seniority of the children. The evidence leads to another conclusion. In his will dated November 18, 1706, Richard Cocke, of Bremo, leaves legacies to each of his grandchildren then in existence, Cockes, Carys and Pleasants, boys and girls, naming them. The children of his daughter Elizabeth Cary he enumerates as follows: "Richard Cary, £20; Thomas Cary, £10; Miles Cary, £10; Nathaniel Cary, £10." It would seem to follow that that was the order of their birth (Richard was undoubtedly the eldest, receiving a double portion), and that none of the daughters of Miles Cary[3] was born prior to 1706. We have accordingly followed that order in our enumeration. The question is now of interest, as upon it depends the seniority of the extant Chesterfield and Peartree Hall lines.

SOURCES:

(1) *N. C. Hist. & Gen. Reg.*, ii, 151, for affidavit of Miles Cary[3] that he was "aged 42" in 1713; (2) McIlwaine, *Journals of the House of Burgesses*, 1693-1724, for his service of legislative committees; (3) *W. M. Cary Notes* for documents signed by him as Clerk of Warwick. See also *Va. Mag.*, i, 232; (4) Henrico records for his marriage license, August 22, 1695, and Register, St. John's Church, Church Hill, Richmond, for his marriage, August 25, 1695; (5) *Eggleston Notes* for record of his will proved 1724 in Warwick *Will Book*, I, 313; (6) Will of Richard Cocke, of Bremo, dated November 18, 1706, from Henrico records; (7) *W. M. Cary Notes* for documents signed by Richard Cary[4] as Clerk of Warwick after 1718; (8) *Journals of the House of Burgesses*, 1718-1722, for this Richard Cary's legislative service, and the date of his death.

IV.   Major MILES CARY (*Miles, Jr.[3], Thomas[2], Miles[1]*), 1701–1766, of Peartree Hall.

In 1722 he succeeded his father and elder brother as Clerk of Warwick and Clerk of the legislative Committees of Privileges and Elections and of Public Claims, and continued to act in both capacities until 1748, when he passed over the legislative duty to his eldest son; remaining in the County Court until two years before his death, a total service of forty-two years. After his father's death and his own marriage he dwelt at Peartree Hall, but at the end of his life was living in retirement, with his second wife, at a more remote property which he describes in his will as "Persimon Ponds"; a locality which may still be identified on the eastern border of Warwick, near Bethel. His mercantile business, carried on with Hinde Russell under the style "Miles Cary & Co.," was active and prosperous, as appears from many entries in the surviving York records. The cartouche on the title-page is a reproduction of his book-plate, after a design by Chippendale about 1751.

[51]

He m.,

1st: 1726?, Hannah, 1706?–1750?, dau. of Major William Armistead, of Elizabeth City,

[For the Armistead family see *W. & M. Quar.*, vi–ix, *passim*, and Keith, *Ancestry of Benjamin Harrison*.]

and by her had :

I   Miles, 1727, of Southampton, see p. 68,

II   Rebecca, 1728, m. 1747, Rev. Miles Selden, incumbent of Henrico parish from 1752 to 1776,

[Miles Selden was a grandson of Colonel Miles Cary² of Richneck. For the Selden family see *W. & M. Quar.*, v, 60, 264, vi, 234, and Hayden, *Virginia Genealogies*, 62 and 738.]

III   Anne, 1729?, m. 1743?, Captain Bennett Tompkins, of York,

[Miles Cary⁴ mentions in his will "my daughter Anne Tompkins." His widow Anne Cary names in her will "Mrs. Anne Tompkins wife of Capt. Bennett Tompkins." Mr. Tyler's record of the family of Tompkins of Pocoson parish, York (*W. & M. Quar.*, xvi, 96), shows this marriage and that the first child was born 1744, which justifies our conjectural dates, though it calls for an unusually early, but not unprecedented, marriage. Further proof is that Mary Tompkins, daughter of Bennett Tompkins, born according to Mr. Tyler's record 1749, married, as shown by York records, 1772, Richard Brown, of York; and his will, dated 1792 and proved 1795 (York *Will Book*, xxiii, 435), names his sons James Pride Brown, Richard Cary Brown and Bennett Brown as legatees and John Cary (presumably Col. John Cary⁵, of Back River) as an executor; all of which names tie in with the children of Miles Cary⁴.]

IV   Richard, 1730, of Peartree Hall, see p. 54,

V   ? Hannah,

VI   Mary, m. ? James Pride,

[Neither of the daughters Rebecca, Hannah or Mary is mentioned in their father's will and so they were probably dead before 1763.]

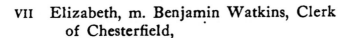

VII Elizabeth, m. Benjamin Watkins, Clerk of Chesterfield,

[For the distinguished descendants of this marriage, including Benjamin Watkins Leigh, see Bishop Meade, i, 450, and *Watkins Genealogy*. For a characterization of Benjamin Watkins, see Grigsby, *Virginia Convention of 1788*, i, 37.]

VIII John, 1745, of Back River, see p. 71,

IX Robert, 1746?–1807, m. Judith Ware, of Buckingham, *o.s.p.*

[The youngest child, he was not of age at the date of his father's will (1763), but was of age when his father died in 1766, as he proved the will and qualified as an executor. In 1785, his wife's grandmother, then the wife of Samuel Jordan, of Buckingham, conveyed lands to Robert Cary's wife which he inherited after the deaths, in 1788, of his wife and only child, an infant daughter. See *Ware* v. *Cary*, 2 Call, 222.]

2nd: The widow Anne [? Timson] Howard, of York, *s.p.*

SOURCES:

(1) The *Journals of the House of Burgesses* for the legislative service; various surviving official documents for the tenure of Miles Cary[4] as Clerk of Warwick; (2) Statement of Miss Susan Cary (1789–1873) made in 1868 in *W. M. Cary Notes* for tradition as to family history; (3) the *W. M. Cary Notes* for the will of Miles Cary[4], dated October 11, 1763, and proved December 11, 1766, in which he styles himself "the elder," extant in the form of a certified copy made from the Warwick records in 1844 (see *Appendix*); (4) the will of Anne Cary, widow of Miles Cary[4], dated January 26, 1768, and preserved in the York records of that year, speaks of "my late consort Major Miles Cary"; (5) the Southampton family Bible for the date of birth of the eldest son, thus fixing also the approximate date of the first marriage; (6) For confirmation of Miss Susan Cary's facts about the daughters of this generation, we have, in addition to the sources cited above, the will of their grandmother Rebecca Moss, second wife of their grandfather Major William Armistead, dated February 13, 1755 (*W. & M. Quar.*, vi, 228), and the will of their aunt Judith (Armistead) Robinson, dated March 6, 1768 (*W. & M. Quar.*, vi, 228).

V. Judge RICHARD CARY (*Miles⁴ of Peartree, Miles, Jr.³, Thomas², Miles¹*), 1730–1789, of Peartree Hall.

He was educated at William and Mary College (1758 in the catalogue) and admitted to the bar. Deputy King's Attorney for Warwick, 1760 (*W. & M. Quar.*, xx, 171). J. P. and High Sheriff of Warwick 1761. Succeeded his father as Clerk of Warwick and in residence at Peartree Hall in 1764. Clerk of legislative Committees for Religion and of Trade, 1766–1776. Signer of Association of 1774 (*W. & M. Quar.*, v, 98). Captain of Warwick militia, 1775 (*W. & M. Quar.*, xvi, 51). Revolutionary Committee of Safety for Warwick (*W. & M. Quar.*, v, 98, 250; *Va. Mag.*, xix, 385). Convention of 1776, where he was of the Committee, Archibald Cary, chairman, which framed the Declaration of Rights and the first State Constitution (*W. & M. Quar.*, vii, 2). Judge of Admiralty (and as such a member of the first Supreme Court of Virginia. See *W. & M. Quar.*, vii, 7), 1776–1788. Convention of 1788, where he voted against ratification of the Constitution of the United States. Judge of General Court, 1788–1789. A lay deputy in the first convention (1785) of the incorporated Episcopal Church (Hawks, *The Church in Virginia*, 1836). He had a pleasant taste for botany: there is in existence a letter he wrote in 1785 to "an old acquaintance" who had recently become an "excellency,"—Mr. Jefferson, then Minister in France,—forwarding tree seeds to be delivered to his scientific correspondents in France, and rehearsing with gusto his botanical conversations with the Italian physician Philip Mazzei, whose political indiscretion subsequently got Mr. Jefferson into serious difficulty. The family tradition is that a French decoration was conferred on Judge Cary in recognition of an essay on Virginia flora. See his obituary in the *Virginia Gazette*, November 19, 1789 (*Va. Mag.*, xx, 284), and the note on him in the preface to the first edition of Call's *Reports*. He is buried at Peartree Hall. In the *Virginia Census* of 1782 his household is listed for 10 whites and 30 blacks.

He m. 1759?, Mary, dau. of William Cole, of Warwick,

[Richard Cary and Mary Cole were both descendants of the immigrant Miles Cary; she through the Bassetts and Wills, her father being the grandson of the Colonial Secretary of State, Col. William Cole (1638–1694), of "Boldrup" (or "Bolthrope," as it is usually spelled), who was the immigrant Miles Cary's nearest neighbor and his successor as the leading man in Warwick. *W. &*

M. Quar., x, 173. For the Cole family, see W. & M. Quar., v, 177, xxi, 292, xxii, 62; Va. Mag., ii, 382.]

and by her had:

I   Richard, Jr., 1760, of Peartree Hall, see p. 55,

II   Miles, 1763, of Mulberry Island, see p. 57,

III   Polly, d. *ante* 1789, m. William Cary, of Windmill Point,

IV   Hannah, 1770–1803, m. Major William Dudley, of York,

V   Anne, 1776?–1809, m. 1796, William Wynne, of Warwick,

VI   Elizabeth, 1778–1805, unmarried,

[See her obituary in the *Virginia Gazette*, December 21, 1805, and her will in *Williamsburg Wills*.]

VII   Rebecca, d. 1799, unmarried.

SOURCES:

(1) The *Eggleston Notes* for Judge Cary's will, dated 1785. See *Appendix I;* (2) Statement of Miss Susan Cary, 1868; (3) Chancery records, *Cary v. Wynne,* 1807, and *Cary v. Sheild,* 1822, in *W. & M. Quar.,* xx, 67; there are complete copies in the *W. M. Cary Notes;* (4) Gleanings from public records and the *Virginia Gazette* in *W. M. Cary Notes.*

VI.   Captain RICHARD CARY, JR. (*Richard⁵, Miles⁴, of Peartree, Miles, Jr.³, Thomas², Miles¹*), 1760?–1800, of Peartree Hall.

William and Mary College. Served in dragoons in the Revolutionary army. "Commanding officer of the County of Warwick," 1793; Captain of Warwick militia at the array for the Whiskey Rebellion in 1794 (*Cal. Va. State Papers,* vi, 651; vii, 110) and of first battalion Sixty-eighth Virginia Regiment at mobilization for expected war with France, 1798 (*Cal. Va. State Papers,* ix, 40). It was the contemporary Captain Richard Cary, of the Massachusetts family, and not this Captain Richard Cary (nor his father the Judge, as stated by Grigsby), who was an aide-de-camp to General Washington (Ford, *Writings of Washington,* xiv, 432). Admitted to the bar, 1785. Commonwealth's Attorney for Warwick. House of Delegates for Warwick, 1785–1788. Senator for district comprising Elizabeth City, Warwick and York, 1792–1796. House of Delegates for Warwick, 1798–1800, dying in office. He was the fourth and last Cary of Peartree Hall, that house having been destroyed by fire during his life; and was undoubtedly buried in the Peartree Hall graveyard.

He m. Catherine, dau. of James Dudley, of York,

[She m. 2nd Thomas Pescud, of Warwick, *W. & M. Quar.,* xiv, 116, who succeeded also to Richard Cary's seat in the House of Delegates.]

and by her had:

    I   Richard, 1784?–*post* 1805, *o.s.p.,*
    II   Miles, 1785?, of Stone Run, see p. 56,
    III Catherine, unmarried.

SOURCES:

(1) Chancery papers, *Cary v. Wynne,* 1807; (2) Statement of Miss Susan Cary, 1868; (3) Gleanings from public records; (4) Swem and Williams, *Register,* p. 56.

VII. MILES CARY (*Richard6, Richard5, Miles4, of Peartree, Miles, Jr.3, Thomas2, Miles1*), 1785?–*post* 1827, of Stone Run.

William and Mary College. Lawyer. Sat in the House of Delegates for Warwick 1823–24, 1826–27. The site of his residence on Stone Run has not been identified, but it was probably on the tract of land below Richneck which the Carys are reputed to have conveyed to Warwick County, on which the existing clerk's office and court-house were built. See Judge Richard Cary's will in *Appendix I.*

He m. *ante* 1817, Ariana Digges, dau. of Henry Hill, of Petersburg, and by her had:

I   Miles, *o.s.p.*,

II   Henry, *o.s.p.*,

III   Catherine, m. James Powers, of York,

IV   Ariana, m. Frederick Cupar, of Canada,

V   Anna, unmarried.

SOURCES:

(1) Statement of Miss Susan Cary, 1868; (2) Chancery papers, *Cary v. Hill,* 1817, *W. & M. Quar.,* xx, 67; (3) Swem and Williams, *Register,* 1918.

VI. MILES CARY (*Richard⁵, Miles⁴, of Peartree, Miles, Jr.³, Thomas², Miles¹*), 1763–1798, of Mulberry Island.

He was for a time Deputy Clerk of York and afterwards Clerk of Warwick. His residence on Mulberry Island was the property called "Marshfield" in Judge Richard Cary's will.

He m.,

1st: Elizabeth, dau. of Thomas Jones, of Hampton, *s.p.,*

[This was the third marriage between the families. See *ante,* p. 41, and *post,* p. 138.]

and

2nd: 1797, Anne Moncure, 1775–1842, dau. of Anthony Robinson, of York,

[For the Robinson family see Hayden, *Virginia Genealogies,* 569.]

and by her had:

I   Miles, 1797, of Mulberry Island, see p. 58.

SOURCES:

(1) Statement of Miss Susan Cary, 1868; (2) For the second marriage, the Rev. Thomas Camm's certificate (*W. & M. Quar.,* xiv, 276); (3) Traditions and letters in Pecquet du Bellet, ii, 113.

VII. MILES CARY (*Miles⁶, of Mulberry Island, Richard⁵, Miles⁴, of Peartree, Miles, Jr.³, Thomas², Miles¹*), 1797–1849, of Mulberry Island and Richmond.

Planter. J. P. for Warwick. Removed to Richmond 1830. All of his sons were in the military service of the Confederate States.

He m. 1823, Harriet Staples, of Richmond, and by her had:

I   Anne, 1825–1879, m. Richard N. Hudson,
II   Sarah, 1828?, m. Wm. Elliott, of England, *s.p.*,
III   Anthony Robinson, 1830, see p. 58,
IV   Richard Milton, 1835?, of England, see p. 59,
V   Mary, 1837?, m. Dr. James A. Brown,
VI   Eleanor Josephine, 1840?–1899, unmarried,
VII   John Staples, 1842, see p. 60,
VIII   David Keeling, 1845–1863, *o.s.p.*, in the C. S. A. at battle of Gettysburg,
IX   Miles, 1848, see p. 61,
X   Roberta Robinson, 1849, unmarried.

SOURCES:

(1) Chancery papers, *Cary v. Wynne*, 1807; (2) M.I. of Miles Cary⁷ in Hollywood Cemetery, Richmond; (3) Statement of Colonel R. M. Cary in *W. M. Cary Notes;* (4) Statement of Mrs. Nora Doyle Levy⁹ of Louisa, 1918; (5) Gleanings from public records.

VIII. ANTHONY ROBINSON CARY (*Miles⁷, of Mulberry Island, Miles⁶, of Mulberry Island, Richard⁵, Miles⁴, of Peartree, Miles, Jr.³,*

Thomas², Miles¹), 1830–1898, of Chesterfield and Pulaski.

Quartermaster-Sergeant of Pegram's artillery battalion, C. S. A. Farmer in Chesterfield. Removed to Pulaski, where he died.

He m. Lucy Ellen Wood, and by her had:

I   Miles Davis, 1875–, of Glen Wilton, Va., unmarried,

II   Lucy Ellen, 1876, d. *infans,*

III   Lucy Ellenor, 1880, m. 1909, Alexander C. Stephens, of Washington, D. C.

SOURCES:

Statement of Mrs. Lucy Cary Stephens⁹, 1918.

VIII. Colonel RICHARD MILTON CARY

(*Miles⁷, of Mulberry Island, Miles⁶, of Mulberry Island, Richard⁵, Miles⁴, of Peartree, Miles, Jr.³, Thomas², Miles¹*), 1835–1886, of Richmond and London.

William and Mary College. Admitted to Richmond bar. Served in all grades from First Lieutenant to Colonel of Thirtieth Virginia Infantry, C. S. A. (*Cal. Va. State Papers*, xi, 149). Author of *Skirmishers' Drill and Bayonet Exercise as now used in the French Army*, Richmond, 1861. Went to England, 1865, and there established himself as a cotton and tobacco factor (Cary & McFarland). He lived in England the remainder of his life. As a consequence he played a part in reviving one of the most interesting educational traditions of Virginia. The modest fund created in 1742 by Mary Whaley, to endow a free school at Williamsburg in memory of her son Matthew (or "Mattey"), was in chancery in England from 1742 to 1865, when it was finally paid over, with its accretions, to Colonel R. M. Cary as agent for William and Mary College. Upon the proceeds ($8470) of this fund the College has since maintained its "Grammar and Mattey, Practice and Model School" on the site in Williamsburg where once stood the Governor's palace, not far from Mattey Whaley's grave in Bruton churchyard. See L. G. Tyler in *W. & M. Quar.* (1895), iv. 3.

He m.,

1st: Anna Parker Dunbar, of Richmond (d. 1876), and by her had:

  I Lelia, m. (in England) Parnell.

2nd: (in England) Lucy Wilson, and by her had:

  II Gladys, m. (in England) 1907, Walter Hall Rickards, of Berks.

SOURCES:

(1) Statement of Col. R. M. Cary 1866 in *W. M. Cary Notes;* (2) Gleanings from English newspapers in *W. M. Cary Notes.*

VIII. Major JOHN STAPLES CARY (*Miles[7], of Mulberry Island, Miles[6], of Mulberry Island, Richard[5], Miles[4], of Peartree, Miles, Jr.[3], Thomas[2], Miles[1]*), 1842–1895, of Petersburg.

Born at "Refuge" in Albemarle. Sergeant-Major in Pegram's artillery battalion, 3rd Corps, Army of Northern Virginia, C. S. A. Served later in militia as Captain, Petersburg Greys, and as First Major, 4th Va. Regiment. Merchant.

He m. 1869, Sara, dau. of Adrian Nicholas Bourdon and Sarah Obedience Moseley, his wife, and by her had:

  I Lily, 1871, d. *infans,*

  II Bourdon, 1872–, of Norfolk,

[He m. 1908, Ellen Hamilton McCarrick, of Norfolk, but has no children. He is an accountant.]

  III Howard Rutherford, 1874, d. *infans,*

  IV Anne Moseley, 1876, of Petersburg, unmarried,

  V Mary, 1879, of Petersburg, unmarried,

VI   Lily, 1881–1888,

VII   Sarah, 1884–1888,

VIII   Richard Milton, Jr., 1886–, of Petersburg.

[He m. 1916, Ida Louise Gill, but has no children. He is a
merchant.]

SOURCES:

Statement of Miss Mary Cary[9], of Petersburg, 1918.

VIII. Miles Cary (*Miles[7], of Mulberry
Island, Miles[6], of Mulberry Island, Richard[5],
Miles[4], of Peartree, Miles, Jr.[3], Thomas[2],
Miles[1]*), 1848–1912, of Richmond.

Served (before he was 17) in Crenshaw's battery of Pegram's
artillery battalion, C. S. A. Bookkeeper.

He m. 1876, Harriet Slaughter Beadles, and
by her had:

I   Harriet Wilson, m. *1st,* 1898, Sidney
Fowler Johnston; *2nd,* 1911, Dr. Wade
Hampton Carter, of Eggleston, Va.,

II   Miles, 1883–, of Welch, West Virginia.

[He m. 1912, Willie Gardner, and by her has a daughter, Virginia, born 1913. He is an electrical engineer.]

SOURCES:

Statement of Mrs. Harriet Cary Carter[9], 1919.

THE CHESTERFIELD BRANCH[1]

[1] The record of the Chesterfield Carys here given is admittedly
incomplete in the later generations. They have not maintained
traditions with any other branch of the family, but after the Revolution migrated in a body to the West, where trace of all but one
branch of them has been lost to their Virginia kin.

IV. THOMAS CARY, JR. (*Miles, Jr.³, Thomas², Miles¹*), 1698?-1755, of York and Chesterfield.

On June 16, 1727, he patents (*Va. Land Records,* xiii, 108) lands in King and Queen which had been "devised by John Pate dec'd to Capt. Miles Cary" (*i.e.* Miles, Jr.³), describing himself as "Thomas Cary, Jr., of Warwick County." By deed dated November 16, 1728, he acquired the plantation in York known as Essex Lodge (formerly belonging to the Bushrods), adjoining the lands of his father-in-law, Dr. Robert Philipson, and there lived most of his life. In 1753 he sold "the Lodge" to his brother, Major Miles Cary⁴, and when he died was living, as shown by his will, on a place known as "Pokashoch" in Chesterfield.

He m. 1722?, Dorothy, dau. of Dr. Robert Philipson, of York, and by her had:

I Robert, 1723?, of Chesterfield, see p. 62,

II Thomas, 1725?, of Chesterfield, see p. 63.

SOURCES:

(1) Gleanings from York records in *W. M. Cary Notes;* (2) The will of Thomas Cary⁴, dated August 12, 1754, and proved 1755, Chesterfield *Will Book,* I, 196; (3) The will of Dr. Robert Philipson, dated January 24, 1745/6, and proved in York March 17th of the same year; (4) The will of Dorothy Philipson Cary, 1761, Chesterfield *Will Book,* I, 548.

V. ROBERT CARY (*Thomas, Jr.⁴, Miles, Jr.³, Thomas², Miles¹*), 1723?-1782, of Chesterfield.

He m. Mary, dau. of ?William Jennings, of Amelia,

["She lived to be 92 years old and was remarkable for her good memory, good management and strength of character generally."]

and by her had:

I Miles, 1766?, of Chesterfield, see p. 64,

[62]

II Robert, 1768?, m. 1793, Mary, dau. of Edward Branch, of Chesterfield,

[See the will of Edward Branch, 1804, referring to his daughter Mary Cary and her children Samuel and Jane Cary (*W. & M. Quar.*, xxvi, 113). This Samuel Cary proved his mother's will in 1826 (Chesterfield *Will Book*, xi, 175) and subsequently lived in Richmond, where he is reputed to have left a daughter.]

III Wilson, 1770?, m. 1793, Judith Baker,

[He was an overseer for his kinsman Colonel Wilson Miles Cary, of Richneck. The tradition is that he moved to Kentucky and left a son, George H. Cary, who lived near Union City, Tenn.]

IV Anne,
V Dorothy,
VI Judith,
VII Elizabeth,
VIII Henry, m. Elizabeth Morrisette,

[He is reputed to have lived in Pocahontas County and subsequently to have moved to Kentucky.]

IX Nathaniel, *o.s.p.*,
X Thomas, m. Mary Grace Bagnall, *o.s.p.*

[She was of the Selden family. See *W. & M. Quar.*, v, 266.]

SOURCES:

(1) Papers on settlement of this Robert Cary's estate, 1782–1787, naming his children, then minors; (2) Other gleanings from Chesterfield records, including marriage certificates of the sons, in *W. M. Cary Notes;* (3) Traditions in Pecquet du Bellet, ii, 123; (4) Statement, 1869, of Mrs. Rhoda Cox Cary, of Louisville, in *W. M. Cary Notes.*

V. THOMAS CARY (*Thomas, Jr.⁴, Miles, Jr.³, Thomas², Miles¹*), 1725?–1784, of Chesterfield.

He m. Sally ? Kemp,

[See *W. & M. Quar.*, x, 209.]

and by her had:

I William,

[He is supposed to have moved to Tennessee and to have had nine children, including three sons.]

II Nathaniel, *o.s.p.*, 1789,

III John Philipson, m. 1786, Sally Loafman,

[The tradition is that he left sons Archibald and Richard, who died in Charlotte County, Va., without issue.]

IV Robert Philipson, m. Martha North,

[The tradition is that he moved to Tennessee and left a son Nathaniel in Missouri.]

V Kemp, m. 1790, Rebecca Butler,

[The tradition is that he moved to Tennessee and left sons Thomas and Aurelius in Howard County, Missouri.]

VI Edmund, m. 1793, Nancy Bowman,

[The tradition is that he died 1829 in Cumberland County, Kentucky, leaving a son and a daughter.]

VII Peter Minor, 1774, see p. 65.

SOURCES:

(1) The will of Thomas Cary[5], dated and proved 1784, Chesterfield *Will Book*, III, 487; (2) The will of his second son, Nathaniel, dated and proved 1789, Chesterfield *Will Book*, IV, 137; (3) Other gleanings from Chesterfield records, including marriage certificates and traditions, in *W. M. Cary Notes;* (4) Statement, 1869, of Mrs. Rhoda Cox Cary, of Louisville, in *W. M. Cary Notes.*

VI. MILES CARY (*Robert[5], Thomas, Jr.[4], Miles, Jr.[3], Thomas[2], Miles[1]*), 1766?–1813, of Chesterfield.

He m. 1791, Obedience Brummell, and by her had:

I   Nelson, 1791–*post* 1830, m. Anne Blount,

[He was a merchant in Richmond in 1830. It does not appear from any record that he left issue, but Pecquet du Bellet credits him with sons Robert Henry and John Pettus. None of this family is now extant in Chesterfield or Richmond.]

II   Edna,
III   Bidzey, m. 1828, William Walker,
IV   Milton, 1796, m. Phœbe Hancock.

[After 1834 he sold his property in Chesterfield and is believed to have moved to the West. The tradition that he established himself in Greenbrier County (now West Virginia) is apparently a confusion with the family of Carys who moved to Greenbrier from Frederick, Md., before 1830 (see *post*, p. 147). These Carys report diligent and unavailing search, about 1870, for the family of Milton Cary[7] in Greenbrier.]

SOURCES:

(1) Return by Nelson Cary[7] of appraisement of estate of his father, Miles Cary[6], 1813, Chesterfield, *liber* viii, 118; (2) Other gleanings from Chesterfield records in *W. M. Cary Notes;* (3) Pecquet du Bellet, ii, 123.

VI. Rev. PETER MINOR CARY (*Thomas[5], Thomas, Jr.[4], Miles, Jr.[3], Thomas[2], Miles[1]*), 1774–1852, of Chesterfield, and later of Kentucky.

He appears in the real estate records of Chesterfield and Prince Edward in various transactions prior to 1831, when he migrated to Jefferson County, Kentucky, and there died.

He m. 1795, Rhoda Cox, 1776–1872,

[She died in Kentucky, more than 96 years of age. In 1869 she made a lucid statement of the family tradition.]

and by her had:

[65]

I   Creed, 1799, *o.s.p.*,

II   Albert, 1802, m. Susan Hill,

[He was a farmer in Jefferson County, Ky., and had seven children, four daughters and three sons, Charles, Richard and William.]

III   Melia, 1805, m. Elizabeth Langford,

[He lived in Nelson County, Va., and there left two daughters and a son, Peter Minor.]

IV   George Hamet, 1811, of Louisville, see p. 66,

V   Christopher, 1814, m. Hattie Mason,

[He was a farmer in Jefferson County, Ky., and there left three daughters and a son, Edward Selden, Jr.]

VI   Edward Selden, 1817, m. Mary Seaton.

[He was a farmer in Jefferson County, Ky., and there left two sons, William Wirt and James Hamet.]

SOURCES:

(1) Gleanings from Chesterfield and Prince Edward records in *W. M. Cary Notes*; (2) Statement of George H. Cary[7], of Louisville, 1869, in *W. M. Cary Notes*.

VII. GEORGE HAMET CARY (*Peter Minor[6], Thomas[5], Thomas, Jr.[4], Miles, Jr.[3], Thomas[2], Miles[1]*), 1811–1886, of Louisville, Kentucky.

He was for many years established as a merchant in Louisville.

He m. 1840, Mary Elizabeth, 1820–1906, dau. of John H. Berryman,

[The Berrymans had migrated from Virginia to Woodford County, Ky.]

and by her had:

I   Arthur, 1841–, of Lexington, Ky.

Long a practising lawyer in Louisville, now retired.

He m.,

1st: 1876, Fanny Graddy, 1849–1878, of Versailles, Ky., and by her had:

I   Graddy, 1878–, of Louisville.

[Educated at University of Kentucky, and Center College, Kentucky, and, in law, University of Virginia, 1900. Now a practising lawyer in Louisville.]

He m. 1907, Marie, dau. of Henry Burnett, of Louisville, and by her has:

I   Arthur, 1911,
II   Henry Burnett, 1912.

2nd: 1895, Sydney Sayre, widow of D. D. Bell, of Lexington, Ky., *s.p.*

II   Alice, 1843–1899, m. 1867, Daniel Branch Price, of Versailles, Ky.,

III   John Berryman, 1846–, of Louisville, unmarried,

IV   Jane Railey, 1849–, m. 1876, Charles S. Tabb, of Louisville,

V   George Hamet, 1851–1895, of Versailles, Ky.

He m. 1887, Mary, dau. of James White, of Versailles, and by her had:

I   James White, 1888–,

[He graduated at the University of Kentucky as a mechanical and electrical engineer, and is now stationed at Lindsey, California. He m. 1917, Rena Louise, dau. of Sherman T. Pennebaker, and by her has a daughter, Barbara Worth, born 1918.]

[67]

  II Mary White, 1890–, m., in Atlanta, Ga.,

  III Mattie Virginia, 1891–,

  IV Elizabeth Robinson, 1893–.

VI Edward Humphrey, 1853–, of Louisville.

He carries on the tradition of his father's mercantile business in Louisville.

He m. 1879, Rebecca Wickliffe, 1854–1893, and by her had:

  I Hallie, 1882, m. 1910, Thomas S. Sneed,

  II Logan Wickliffe, 1884–,

[He is a Second Lieutenant of Infantry in the 89th Division, U. S. A., now (1919) in Germany.]

  III Rhoda, 1887, m. 1909, Edward C. Stevens.

VII Martha Woodson, 1855?–1885, m. Newton G. Crawford,

VIII Hallie, 1857–1878, unmarried,

IX Mary Clifton, 1866–, m. 1886, Brown C. Crawford.

SOURCE:

Statement of Graddy Cary[9], 1919.

THE SOUTHAMPTON BRANCH,
EXTINCT 1850

V. MILES CARY (*Miles[4], of Peartree, Miles, Jr.[3], Thomas[2], Miles[1]*), 1727–1766, of Southampton.

He succeeded his father as Clerk of the Committee on Public Claims, 1748. Licensed to practise law in York, 1748. Removed from Warwick to Southampton. Trustee, 1757, of Mrs. Elizabeth Smith's free school in Isle of Wight. (*W. & M. Quar.*, vi, 77.) Died *v.p.*

He m. 1752, Elizabeth, 1733–1774, dau. of Ethelred Taylor, of Southampton,

[For the Taylors of Southampton, see Hayden, *Virginia Genealogies*, 584, and *Va. Mag.*, xxiii, 104, 218.]

and by her had:

I   Elizabeth, 1753–1778, m. 1774, William Hay, 1748–1825, of Surry, Richmond city, and finally of Frederick,

[For the Hay family in Virginia, see *W. & M. Quar.*, xv, 85. The late Secretary of State, John Hay, was probably derived from this family. William Hay, *supra*, m. 1780, as his second wife, Elizabeth, youngest dau. of Bennett Tompkins, of York, like his first wife, a granddaughter of Miles Cary⁴, of Peartree Hall.]

II   Hannah, 1755–1781, of Chesterfield, unmarried,

III   Miles, 1757, of Southampton, see p. 69,

IV   Mary, 1760, unmarried,

V   Nathaniel, 1763–1767, *o.s.p.*

SOURCES:

(1) Family Bible of the Southampton family in *W. M. Cary Notes*; see also *W. & M. Quar.*, xv, 84; (2) Obituary of Miles Cary⁵ in the *Virginia Gazette*, September 19, 1766; (3) The will of Hannah Cary, dated 1781 and proved in Chesterfield; (4) Statement of Miss Susan Cary, 1868; (5) *Journals of the House of Burgesses*; (6) Gleanings from Southampton and York records in *W. M. Cary Notes.*

VI.   Captain MILES CARY (*Miles⁵, of Southampton, Miles⁴, of Peartree, Miles, Jr.³, Tho-*

[69]

mas², *Miles¹*), 1757–1807, of "Bonny Doon," Southampton.

Planter. J. P. for Southampton. It is related of him that he stipulated with his daughters that none of them should marry either a Stith or a Methodist preacher, because of the proverbial extravagance of the one and the poverty of the other. As soon as he died his eldest daughter married a Stith and the second a Methodist preacher, though, the tradition continues with evident intention of justification, the latter later became a clergyman of the Episcopal Church. Two of his own wives were heiresses, one of whom, probably the second, brought him "Bonny Doon."

He m.,

Ist: 1782, F. B. Petersen, *s.p.*

[The family tradition is that the first wife died within a few months of marriage. The name and date are supplied from Crozier, *Virginia Marriages,* sub Southampton County.]

2nd: 1785, Griselda Buxton, of Sussex, and by her had:

 I Nancy, 1787–1833, m. *Ist,* 1807, John Stith, of Petersburg,

[For the Stith family, see *W. & M. Quar.,* xxi, 193, 273.]

 and *2nd,* Belfield Starke, of Belfield, Greensville County,

 II Peggy, m. 1807, Rev. Lewis Taylor, 1784–1870, of Oxford, N. C.

3rd: Elizabeth, dau. of George Booth, of Gloucester, and widow of Colonel William Yates, of the Revolutionary army,

[For some notes on the Booths, of Gloucester, see Stubbs, *Descendants of Mordecai Cooke,* 1896.]

and by her had:

[70]

III Sally, d. 1821, m. Dr. Andrew Field, of Brunswick,

IV Patsey, d. *infans,*

V George Booth, 1803–1850, of "Bonny Doon" and Petersburg, *o.s.p.,*

[He m. the widow Martha (Blunt) Urquhart, of Southampton, and had an only daughter, Virginia Elizabeth, who died young. He was a lawyer, and sat as M. C. for the Petersburg district, 1842–43. With him the Southampton family became extinct.]

VI Charlotte Louisa, 1806–1852, m. 1827, Judge James Hervey Gholson; of Brunswick.

[She was famous as a beauty. For Judge Gholson and his family, see *Appletons' Cyclo. Am. Biog.*, ii, 634.]

SOURCES:

(1) Statement of Miss Susan Cary, 1868, and of Miss Jocasta L. Starke of Petersburg, 1903; (2) Gleanings from public records and newspapers in *W. M. Cary Notes.*

THE ELMWOOD BRANCH

V. Lieutenant-Colonel JOHN CARY (*Miles⁴, of Peartree, Miles, Jr.³, Thomas², Miles¹*), 1745–1795, of Back River, Elizabeth City County.

William and Mary College, 1760. If he was not included with his college contemporary Jefferson in Governor Fauquier's *"partie quarrée"* at the Palace, he did have the inspiration of Dr. William Small's teaching, and perhaps he had also the ruder exhilaration of taking part in the town and gown row into which, in 1760, the students were led by the fiery Welsh poet Owen, then master of the grammar school. (For the college life at this period, cf. Randall, *Jefferson*, i, 20 ff., and Tyler, *Williamsburg*, 147.) Inherited 1769 from his aunt Judith (Armistead) Robinson a plantation on Back River known as Bushenbrake, afterwards Elmwood, "reputed the richest and best improved farm in the lower parts of the County" (see *Virginia Gazette,* April 23, 1785). J. P., Captain and Lieutenant-Colonel for Elizabeth City. Member of Revolutionary Committee of Safety for Elizabeth City (*W. & M. Quar.*, v, 103). Senator for the district comprising Elizabeth City, Warwick and York, 1780-1781. He is buried at Peartree Hall.

He m.,

1st: 1765, Sally, 1750–1775, dau. of John Sclater, of York,

[For the Sclaters, see *post*, p. 89.]

and by her had:

I Anne Elizabeth, 1767, d. *infans,*
II Miles, 1771, of Campbell, see p. 78.

2nd: 1777, Susanna, 1753–1834, dau. of Gill Armistead, of New Kent,

[For the Armisteads, see *ante*, p. 52.]

and by her had:

III Hannah Armistead, 1778–1821, m. 1799, Horatio Whiting, of Gloucester,
IV Elizabeth Allen, 1779–1800,
V John, 1781, of Hampton, see p. 82,
VI Gill Armistead, 1783, of Elmwood, see p. 73,
VII Nathaniel Robert, 1784–1790, *o.s.p.,*
VIII Polly, 1786, d. *infans,*
IX Judith Robinson, 1787–1825, m. 1823, Colonel Harry Howard, of York,
X Susan, 1789–1873, unmarried,

[She was engaged to be married to her cousin Richard Cary[7], of Peartree Hall, grandson of the Judge, who died young, and she cherished his memory to a great age. These pages owe to her the preservation of much of the tradition they record. She is buried at Peartree Hall.]

COL. GILL ARMISTEAD CARY
OF ELMWOOD, BACK RIVER
1783–1843

XI   Richard, 1791, d. *infans,*

XII   Nathaniel Robert, 1792–1832, of Hampton, *o.s.p.,*

XIII   William Armistead, 1794–1798.

SOURCES:

(1) Elmwood family Bible, now in possession of T. Archibald Cary[8]; (2) Colonel John Cary's will, dated October 28, 1794, in Chesterfield records, July 23, 1795, naming his children then living; (3) Statement in 1868 of Miss Susan Cary[6]; (4) Gleanings from public records and newspapers in *W. M. Cary Notes.*

VI.   Colonel GILL ARMISTEAD CARY (*John[5], Miles[4], of Peartree, Miles, Jr.[3], Thomas[2], Miles[1]*), 1783–1843, of Elmwood and Hampton.

He saw service in the Virginia militia in 1812, when, like his kinsman Wilson Jefferson Cary[6], the exposure so affected his health as to color the remainder of his life. Generous, hospitable but proud and reserved, given to study and playing chess, he commanded the unfailing respect of his neighbors, but like many of his contemporaries of similar antecedents, never quite adjusted himself to the new "republican" world in which he found himself, and so took no part in public life, living quietly on his plantation. Like his older brothers, Miles and John, he was a vestryman of St. John's Church, Hampton. See Bishop Meade, *Old Churches,* etc., i, 236. He is buried at Peartree Hall, not at Richneck as stated in *W. & M. Quar.,* xiv, 166, where his M.I. is given.

He m. 1818, Sally Elizabeth Smith (1791–1879), dau. of Major James Baytop, of Gloucester, and by her had:

I   John Baytop, 1819, of Hampton and Richmond, see p. 74,

II   Nathaniel Robert, 1822, see p. 75,

III   Richard Miles, 1825, see p. 76,

IV   Gill Armistead, Jr., 1831, see p. 76.

SOURCES:

(1) Statements of Miss Susan Cary[6], 1868, and of T. Archibald
Cary[8], 1918; (2) Elmwood family Bible; (3) Tombstone of Gill
Armistead Cary at Peartree Hall (*W. & M. Quar.*, xiv, 166).

VII. Colonel JOHN BAYTOP CARY (*Gill Armistead[6], John[5], Miles[4], of Peartree, Miles, Jr.[3], Thomas[2], Miles[1]*), 1819–1898, of Hampton and Richmond.

William and Mary College, A.B. 1839, M.A. 1854, and later
Visitor. Last Principal (1847–1852) of the Syms-Eaton School,
Hampton, "the first free school in America," founded 1635 and in
1852 absorbed into the public school system of Virginia (*W. & M.
Quar.*, vi, 72, 76). Head-master, Hampton Military Academy,
which he founded 1852. "As a schoolmaster . . . worthy of a place
by the side of Arnold of Rugby." Major Thirty-second Virginia,
C. S. A., 1861. Promoted Lieutenant-Colonel at battle of Bethel,
1861. Inspector-General of the Army of the Peninsula on staff of
General Magruder. Had his horse shot under him at Yorktown
and again at Savage's Station, and, being disabled, was transferred
to pay department, where he served until Lee's surrender (*Cal. Va.
State Papers*, xi, 117). Ruined by the war, he began life anew in
middle age, and before he died had rebuilt his fortunes in business
in Richmond. There served in the Board of Aldermen, and as
Superintendent of Schools. In his honor his children founded the
chair known as the "John B. Cary Memorial School of Biblical
History and Literature" at the University of Virginia. See the appreciation of him by Charles A. Young, published by the Christian
Woman's Board of Missions, 1899, *The Power of a Noble Life*.

He m. 1844, Columbia, 1819–1902, dau. of
Colonel Thomas Hudgins of Gwynn's Island,
Mathews Co., who commanded the Sixty-sec-
ond Virginia Regiment, 1812,

[For the Hudgins family, of Mathews, see *W. & M. Quar.*, xxiv, 285.]

and by her had:

I   Gilliena, 1844, m. 1915, Colonel W. Gordon McCabe, of Richmond,

COL. JOHN BAYTOP CARY
1819–1898

II John Baytop, Jr., 1846–1860, *o.s.p.*,

[See his tombstone at Peartree Hall (not Richneck), *W. & M. Quar.*, xiv, 167.]

III Elizabeth Earle, 1848–1915, m. 1877, William Travers Daniel, of Orange,

IV Elfie May, 1853, m. 1879, John Lewis White, of Caroline,

V Sally Campbell, 1855–1891, m. 1884, Louis P. Knowles, of Pensacola, Fla.,

VI Thomas Archibald, 1858, see p. 77.

SOURCES:

Statement of T. Archibald Cary[8], 1918. Elmwood family Bible. See also *Reminiscences* of Benjamin W. Green in *W. & M. Quar.*, xv, 52.

VII. Dr. NATHANIEL ROBERT CARY (*Gill Armistead[6], John[5], Miles[4], of Peartree, Miles, Jr.[3], Thomas[2], Miles[1]*), 1822–1874, of Hampton.

William and Mary College, 1840. Captain, battalion Mississippi Rifles, U. S. A., in Mexican War. Major, C. S. A. (*Cal. Va. State Papers*, xi, 138). Physician. Died of yellow fever during epidemic while in charge of Quarantine Station at Pensacola, Florida. See his obituary in Richmond *Dispatch*, September 25, 1874.

He m. 1855, Susan, dau. of Miers W. Fisher, of Northampton County, and by her had:

I Sally Elizabeth Smith, 1858, m. 1883, William Samuel Graves, of Bedford;

II Juliet Fisher, 1860, m. 1885, Herbert Wellington Sitwell of Derbyshire, England,

[75]

III   Susan Armistead, 1862, m. 1885, George Samuel Nichols, of Bedford.

SOURCES:
Statement of T. Archibald Cary[8], 1918. Elmwood family Bible.

VII. RICHARD MILES CARY (*Gill Armistead[6], John[5], Miles[4], of Peartree, Miles, Jr.[3], Thomas[2], Miles[1]*), 1825–1898, of Hampton, Petersburg, and Pensacola, Fla.

William and Mary College, A.B. 1846. Severely wounded in C. S. A. before Petersburg, 1864. Schoolmaster.

He m. 1855, Hannah Elizabeth, dau. of John Cary Whiting, and by her had:

  I   Sally Baytop, 1857–1905, m. 1884, James Edwin Abercrombie,

  II   Martha Armistead, 1859, unmarried,

  III   Richard Miles, Jr., 1861, of Pensacola, Florida, see p. 78,

  IV   Lelia Page, 1864, m. 1889, Henry Hall, of Mobile,

  V   Clara Whiting, 1867, unmarried.

SOURCES:
Statement of T. Archibald Cary[8], 1918. Elmwood family Bible.

VII. Captain GILL ARMISTEAD CARY, JR. (*Gill Armistead[6], John[5], Miles[4], of Peartree, Miles, Jr.[3], Thomas[2], Miles[1]*), 1831–1880, of Hampton, and Montgomery, Ala.

Lieutenant Thirtieth Virginia Cavalry. Captain and A. A. G., C. S. A. Merchant in Montgomery.

LIEUT. GEORGE CARY, U.S.A.
1894–1918

He m. 1856, Jane Ladson Alston, dau. of John Rutledge Smith, of South Carolina, step-dau. of Dr. McCabe, of Hampton, and by her had:

    I   Isabella Gordon, 1859–1905, m. 1882, Gordon Cumming Macdonald, of Montgomery, Ala.,

   II Mattie Armistead, 1864, unmarried.

SOURCES:
Statement of T. Archibald Cary[8], 1918. Elmwood family Bible.

VIII. THOMAS ARCHIBALD CARY (*John Baytop*[7], *Gill Armistead*[6], *John*[5], *Miles*[4], *of Peartree, Miles, Jr.*[3], *Thomas*[2], *Miles*[1]), 1858–, of Hampton and Richmond.

Richmond College, 1873–76. Succeeded his father as Visitor of William and Mary College. Retired 1917 after many years in the insurance business.

He m. 1885, Maria Barry, dau. of Colonel George W. Abert, of Columbus, Mississippi, and by her has:

    I   John Barry, 1886, Lieutenant U. S. A., air service in France, 1918,

[He m. 1917, Katharine Roy, dau. of Dr. William S. Gordon, of Richmond.]

   II Patty Abert, 1888, canteen worker in France, 1918–19,

  III Archibald, 1890, d. *infans,*

  IV Sally Campbell, 1891,

   V George Abert, 1894–1918, Lieutenant U. S. A.; *o.s.p.,* in aviation service,

VI Maria, 1895–1899,
VII Thomas Archibald, Jr., 1899, U. S. M. C.,
1918.

SOURCES:

(1) Statement of T. Archibald Cary[8], 1918. (2) For the military service of the sons, see *Va. Mag.*, xxvii, 72.

VIII. RICHARD MILES CARY, JR. (*Richard Miles[7], Gill Armistead[6], John[5], Miles[4], of Peartree, Miles, Jr.[3], Thomas[2], Miles[1]*), 1861–, of Pensacola, Florida.

Born at "Round Hill," Isle of Wight County. Removed to Florida with his father. Captain, First Regiment, Florida Volunteers, in Spanish-American War, 1898. Now a merchant in Pensacola.

He m. 1903, Mary Ethel, dau. of George W. Wright, of Pensacola, and by her has:

I Richard Miles 3rd, 1905,
II Margaret Ethel, 1907,
III George Archibald, 1908,
IV Elizabeth Whiting, 1910,
V Henry Hall, 1917.

SOURCES:

Statement of R. M. Cary[8], 1919.

THE CAMPBELL BRANCH

VI. Captain MILES CARY (*John[5], Miles[4], of Peartree, Miles, Jr.[3], Thomas[2], Miles[1]*), 1771–1850, of "Buck Roe," Elizabeth City, and afterwards of Campbell County.

He acquired "Buck Roe" in 1802 with his second wife. (This interesting plantation, sometime the seat of a branch of the Armisteads, has been notable since 1621, when certain French vignerons were seated upon it to plant vines and feed silkworms, but soon took to worshiping the Virginia goddess *Tobo.*, or, as Governor Nicholson once pleasantly styled that alluring deity, Dulcinea del *Tobo.*, see Hening, i, 161; Tyler, *Cradle of the Republic*, 245 ff.; and, for Nicholson's witty despatch, *Cal. State Papers, Am. & W. I.*, 1704–05, 433.) Vestryman of St. John's, Hampton, 1810. Captain Sixty-eighth Virginia Infantry, 1812–1814. In 1816 removed to Campbell, where he died.

He m.,

1st: 1796, Martha, dau. of Captain John Sclater, of York, *s.p.*

2nd: 1802, Eliza King, dau. of Colonel Francis Mallory, of Elizabeth City, and widow of John Page, of Buck Roe,

[For Colonel Francis Mallory, and his death in action defending Elizabeth City during a British raid in 1781, see *Va. Hist. Reg.*, iv, 24. For the Mallory family, see *Va. Mag.*, xiii–xv.]

and by her had:

I   John, of Lynchburg, see p. 80,
II Sally Sclater, 1805–1847, m. Peter Carr Nelson, of Hanover and Lynchburg,
III Mary King, 1808–1812,
IV Eliza Mallory, 1810–1885, m. 1831, Benjamin Huntt, of Lynchburg and New York,
V   Miles, d. *infans,*
VI Mary King 2nd, 1813–1848, m. *1st,* 1834, James H. Everett, of Halifax; *2nd,* 1846, Captain Thomas Spencer of Charlotte,

VII   Virginia Jackson, 1815–1841, m. 1836, Edwin H. Jordan, of Albemarle.

SOURCES:

(1) Genealogical chart of John Cary[8], 1888; (2) For the first marriage, list of marriages by the Rev. T. Camm, President of William and Mary College (*W. & M. Quar.*, xiv, 175), will of John Sclater, 1796, in York records, June 19, 1797, naming his children, and deed of Richard Sclater, his son, reciting death of his sister Martha Cary (York *Deed Book*, 1809–19, p. 37); (3) Other gleanings from York and Elizabeth City records in *W. M. Cary Notes.*

VII. JOHN CARY (*Miles[6], of Campbell, John[5], Miles[4], of Peartree, Miles, Jr.[3], Thomas[2], Miles[1]*), 1802–1867, of Lynchburg and Richmond.

University of Virginia, 1826. As a schoolmaster he succeeded to, and for many years maintained, the high tradition of classical education at the boys' school which was established in the Masonic Hall of Lynchburg soon after the beginning of the nineteenth century. Mrs. Cabell testifies that he "exercised a powerful influence in this town." After 1856 he removed his school to Richmond.

He m.,

1st: 1831, Susan F. Lambeth, of Lynchburg, and by her had:

I   Eliza King, 1831–1901, m. 1863, Frederick A. Hoppe, of Charlottesville,

II   Susan Anderson, 1834–1854, unmarried,

III   Miles, 1836, of Richmond, see p. 81,

IV   John, 1839–1896, served in C.S.A. and was later of New York, *o.s.p.*,

V   George Lambeth, 1842–1911, of Richmond, m. 1902, Mary Virginia Nelson, *o.s.p.* He had served in the C.S.A.,

VI   Mary Virginia, 1845–1894, unmarried,
VII Francis Mallory, 1847–1896, of Rich-
     mond, *o.s.p.* He had served in the
     C.S.A.
2nd: 1852, Mrs. Martha A. Holmes, of
     Lynchburg, *s.p.*

SOURCES:

(1) Genealogical chart of John Cary[8] (*supra*), supplemented by statement of Alfred S. Cary[9], 1918. (2) Cabell, *Sketches and Recollections of Lynchburg*, 1858; Christian, *Lynchburg and its People*, 1900.

VIII. MILES CARY (*John[7], of Lynchburg, Miles[6], of Campbell, John[5], Miles[4], of Peartree, Miles, Jr.[3], Thomas[2], Miles[1]*), 1836–1896, of Richmond.

Merchant of the firm of Shields & Cary. See his obituary, Richmond *Weekly Times*, June 1, 1896.

He m. 1858, Mary, dau. of Samuel Schooler, of Caroline, and by her had:

I   Mary Conway, 1860–, m. 1882, John A.
     Upshur, of Richmond,
II   Shirley, dau., 1863–1918, m. 1888, James
     Melville Gentry, of Richmond,
III Alice, 1867–1869,
IV   Alfred Shields, 1870, of Richmond, see
     p. 82,
V   Miles, 1872, d. *infans.*

SOURCES:

Genealogical chart of John Cary[8], 1888, supplemented by statement of Alfred S. Cary[9], 1918.

IX. ALFRED SHIELDS CARY (*Miles³, John⁷, of Lynchburg, Miles⁶, of Campbell, John⁵, Miles⁴, of Peartree, Miles, Jr.³, Thomas², Miles¹*), 1870–, of Richmond.

Vice-President Eastern Coal and Export Corporation.

He m. 1895, Stuart Sidney, dau. of Algernon Sidney Bradley, of Richmond, and by her has:

 I Mary Katharine, 1897–,
 II Miles, 1903–,
 III Virginia Stuart, 1904, d. *infans.*

SOURCES:
Statement of Alfred S. Cary⁹, 1918.

THE PONTOTOC BRANCH, EXTINCT 1900

VI. JOHN CARY (*John⁵, Miles⁴, of Peartree, Miles, Jr.³, Thomas², Miles¹*), 1781–1822, of Hampton.

Deputy Collector of Customs at Hampton.

He m. 1808, Anne Wythe, dau. of George Sweeney, of Elizabeth City,

[For the Sweeney family and their connection with Chancellor George Wythe, see *W. & M. Quar.*, xvi, 237.]

and by her had:

 I John, 1809–1838, of Pontotoc, Miss., m. Anna Maria, dau. of Major John Cooper, of Elizabeth City, *o.s.p.*,
 II Jane, 1810, m. 1830, Thomas Gill Whiting,

III   Susan Martha, 1812–1829, unmarried,

IV   Anne Wythe, 1813–1817, unmarried,

V   Hannah Armistead, 1816, m. 1831, Colonel John F. Wray, of Hampton and later of Pontotoc, Miss.,

VI   Miles, 1817, of Pontotoc, Miss., see p. 83,

VII   Elizabeth Anne, 1819–1863, m. George Cooper, of Elizabeth City, then of Pontotoc, Miss., and finally of New Orleans,

VIII   Gill, 1821, d. *infans,*

IX   George, 1822, d. *infans.*

SOURCES:

(1) Statement of Miss Susan Cary[6], 1868; (2) Elmwood family Bible; (3) Statement, 1918, of Mrs. Thomas Lee[8], of York, a daughter of Hannah Armistead Cary Wray (*supra*).

VII. MILES CARY (*John[6], John[5], Miles[4], of Peartree, Miles, Jr.[3], Thomas[2], Miles[1]*), 1817–1868, of Pontotoc, Miss.

In 1835 his brother-in-law, Colonel John F. Wray, Patrick Henry Fontaine and Bolling Dandridge went together from Virginia to Mississippi, to take up Indian lands. Colonel Wray established himself at Pontotoc, Miss., and sent for his wife, who followed. With her, in 1836, went her brothers John and Miles and the Coopers. It was such a family migration to the Southwest as was typical in Virginia at the time. The journey was made in a caravan of 300 people, with slaves, wagons, pack-horses and cattle, much of the way over Indian trails, through primeval forests, and was arduous. On their arrival at Pontotoc, Mrs. Wray's first child was born in an Indian wigwam. John and Miles Cary set up as merchants, and Miles continued the business after his brother's early death. In the war between the States, although then a mature man, he served in the C. S. A., and died, soon after the war, of exposure then experienced. For the early life in Pontotoc see an extraordinary book, Lamar Fontaine, *My Life and My Lectures,* 1908.

[83]

He m. 1845, Sarah Jane Root, dau. of the
U. S. Indian agent at Pontotoc, and by her had:

I   Susan Wythe, 1846–1866, unmarried,
II   Johnette Roberts, 1848, d. unmarried,
III Annabel Lee, 1851–1892, m. B. B. Fontaine, of Memphis,
IV   Gillie Armistead, 1855, d. unmarried,
V   John Miles, 1860–1900, of Beeville, Texas, *o.s.p.m.*

[He m. 1888, Jennie Lee Burkett, of Okolona, Miss., and removed to Beeville, Texas, where he was a merchant. He left an only child, a daughter Mattie, who m. John Dowdle of Okolona, Miss.]

SOURCES:

Statements, 1868, of Miss Susan Cary[8], and, 1918, of Mrs. Thomas Lee, of York, and of B. B. Fontaine, of Memphis, the latter quoting Pontotoc family Bible.

CHAPTER FIVE

THE FOREST AND AMPTHILL

The immigrant's second son, Captain Henry
Cary, the builder, inherited and lived upon the
plantation in the interior of Warwick known as
The Forest.[1] His enterprising son of the same
name was one of the pioneers to take up wilderness lands in the upper valley of James River,
and, removing his own residence to the head of
navigation near the Falls, where the city of
Richmond was soon to grow, there built Ampthill House.[2]

[1] See *post*, p. 96, n. 1.

[2] AMPTHILL HOUSE, built by Henry Cary[3] in 1732, still stands on
the brim of the river valley about seven miles below Manchester,
on the Richmond-Petersburg turnpike. It looks over a characteristic
James River bottom which yields bountiful crops of corn, now cultivated by a single tractor instead of a troop of negroes. Some dis-
tance downstream, but within sight of the house, is the skeleton
of the mill which was erected during the nineteenth century on the
foundation of that of the eighteenth. Across the river, on the
Henrico shore, is the Randolph place, Wilton. While lacking re-
pair, the house is a notable example of Henry Cary's Flemish bond
brickwork, substantial timbering and oak paneling. Except Elmwood, it is the only Virginia house extant which was inhabited by
the immigrant Miles Cary's family in the eighteenth century. For
a century past it has been owned by the families of Temple and
Watkins, who crowd the two graveyards on the place.
   This Ampthill was apparently named immediately for a plantation of that name in Warwick which belonged to Henry Cary[3]
and afterwards to Miles Cary[4], of Peartree Hall: this in turn
was undoubtedly named by some former owner, doubtless a Bed-

II. Captain HENRY CARY (*Miles*[1]), 1650?–1720, of The Forest.

Named for his Hobson grandfather, he was devisee under his father's will of the Warwick plantation called The Forest, being the western half of Zachary Cripps patent, adjoining Richneck. J. P. and Captain for Warwick. He was a contracting builder and constructed, among other public buildings, the court-house of York County, 1694 (York records), the fort on York River, 1697 (*Va. Mag.*, xxiv, 401), the first capitol at Williamsburg, 1701–1703, William and Mary College (reconstruction after the fire of 1705), and the Governor's palace, 1705–1710, in which he lived during construction. (See *Hening*, iii, 226, 485, iv, 95; *Cal. Va. State Papers*, i, 125, 146.) His petition last cited is interesting evidence that bricks were burnt in Virginia as early as 1709, not *imported* as the tradition is in respect to so many eighteenth century houses. It is not known where he was buried.

He m. 1671, Judith, dau. of Edward Lockey, Jr., of York, merchant,

[There is evidence at once of the fact and the date of the marriage in a recital of it in proceedings in the General Court, May 24, 1671, for the settlement of the estate of Edward Lockey, Sr. (see MS. *Book of General Court Judgments*, 1670–1676, in library Virginia Historical Society and. *W. & M. Quar.*, viii, 203, 255). The Lockeys were London merchants resident in Virginia in the tobacco trade. Edward Lockey, Jr., was nephew of Edward Lockey, Sr., and son of John Lockey, of St. Botolph's, Aldgate, London, grocer, who died in Virginia. See P.C.C. *Admon. Act Book*, February 27, 1666, and *W. & M. Quar.*, iii, 278, viii, 202, 225.]

and by her had:

I   Judith, 1673?–*ante* 1716, m. Major William Barbar, of York,

fordshireman who brought with him to Virginia memories of the royal manor, famous for its park of ancient oaks and the fact that there the repudiated Queen Katherine of Aragon lived while her divorce was pending. (Cf. Shakespeare, *Henry VIII*, act iv, sc. 1.) The English Ampthill now belongs to the family of Russell, Dukes of Bedford, one of whom has derived from it the title by which he is known. There is another Ampthill in Virginia, the house built about 1790, on some of Archibald Cary's lands in Cumberland, by Randolph Harrison.

[86]

[For the Barbar family, see *W. & M. Quar.*, v, 195. Judith Barbar is mentioned in the will of Henry Cary[2] as "my late daughter."]

II   Anne, 1674?, m. *post* 1693, Stuckey,

[See the will, 1693, of Benjamin Reade, in York records, leaving legacy to "niece Anne Cary, daughter of Mr. Henry Cary" (*W. & M. Quar.*, iii, 40). Anne Lockey, sister of the wife of Henry Cary[2], married a Reade, presumably Thomas Reade (see Bruton parish register, 1712), who may have been the brother of this testator Benjamin Reade; in that case Benjamin might have called himself Anne Cary's uncle because his brother had married her aunt. In any event the Oxford Dictionary gives examples of the use of "niece" in the general sense of kinswoman. Anne Cary is called Anne Stuckey in her father's will, which is the only evidence for the marriage. Her husband has not been identified.]

III   Henry, 1675?, of Williamsburg, see p. 88,
IV   Elizabeth, 1678?, m. 1698?, Captain John Scarisbrook,

[This John Scarisbrook, or Scarsbrooke, as the name came to be spelled in Virginia, was captain of a merchant ship in service between Virginia and Liverpool and son of Lieutenant-Colonel John Scarisbrook, of York, merchant. (See *W. & M. Quar.*, xxiv, 200.) The Scarisbricks are an ancient family of Lancashire. In the seventeenth century a branch of them were merchants in Liverpool. (*Victoria County History, Lancashire*, iii, 265.) It seems probable then that the Virginia family were of the Liverpool Scarisbricks.

Three of the children of the immigrant Lieutenant-Colonel John Scarisbrook, of York, married descendants of the immigrant Miles Cary, viz.: Martha m. William Cary[2], Captain John *supra*, and Hannah m. Captain Miles Wills[3].]

V   Miles, 1680?–, *post* 1716, o.s.p.

[There is no record of him except in his father's will, where he is named as a legatee, but not as an executor. He must have died unmarried.]

SOURCES:

(1) The *W. M. Cary Notes* for a transcript from the original will of Henry Cary[2], dated January 27, 1716, and proved in Warwick, September 1, 1720; (2) Gleanings from York County records.

III. HENRY CARY, JR. (*Henry², Miles¹*), 1675?–1749, of Williamsburg, and later of "Warwick" in Henrico (Chesterfield).

Educated at William and Mary College, one of its earliest students. He carried on his father's business as a contracting builder and constructed the Brafferton Building 1723 (probably) and (certainly) the President's house and the chapel of William and Mary College 1729–1732 (*W. & M. Quar.*, i, 137, xi, 174) as well as a number of churches and court-houses, among others St. Paul's, Hanover, 1719, and St. John's, Hampton, 1727. (*W. & M. Quar.*, xx, 170; Tyler, *Cradle of the Republic*, 250.) In this construction of public buildings he was more fortunate than his father, as much of his work still stands to testify to his art, while successive fires have destroyed all identifiable monuments of his father. He was J. P. in Warwick County as late as 1727, but had moved to Williamsburg after his father's death and there was vestryman of Bruton Church (*W. & M. Quar.*, iii, 175, 180) and in 1726 Keeper of the Magazine. In 1730 he docked the entail and sold The Forest to Colonel Wilson Cary, of Richneck (*Hening*, iv, 307, vii, 440), acquiring in lieu of it 12,000 acres on Willis Creek, then in Henrico (afterwards Goochland and Cumberland). In 1736 he purchased from William Byrd 306 acres at the mouth of Falling Creek in Henrico (afterwards Chesterfield), and there, on the upland, established a flouring mill about which grew up a village which he called "Warwick." He had removed his residence to Henrico in 1727 and, though he lived later at Ampthill, usually described himself thenceforth as "of Warwick" or "of the parish of Dale." In 1733–34 he was High Sheriff of Henrico. He was doubtless buried at Ampthill, but no stone marks his grave. Many of his descendants, Bells, Randolphs, Pages and Harrisons, were long seated on his lands in Cumberland and Buckingham.

He m.,

1st: 1710? Sarah, 1695?–*ante* 1719, dau. of the Rev. James Sclater, incumbent of Charles River parish, York County,

[The Ampthill Bible has an entry in the hand of Archibald Cary, "Henry Cary, father of Archibald Cary, had by his first wife a daughter and two sons, who died before they came of age, vizt, Doyley Cary, b. July 3, 1712, and Henry Cary, b. November 3, 1714." The will of the Rev. James Sclater, dated 1721 (See *Ap-*

II, *Thomas Cary*

III, *Henry Cary*

IV *Archibald Cary*

AUTOGRAPHS OF THE AMPTHILL CARYS

The numerals indicate generations

pendix I), gives the clew to the name of the first wife in legacies to his two Cary grandsons. James Sclater was incumbent of Charles (formerly Pocoson) parish in York County from 1686 to 1724. His children are enumerated in his parish register, see *W. & M. Quar.*, iv, 138; in the lack of other record it appears from the known marriages of the other daughters that Henry Cary's wife was the fourth child Sarah. Col. John Cary[5], of Back River, and his son Captain Miles Cary[6], of Campbell, both married Sclaters of this family.]

and by her had:

I Mary, d. "a child,"

[The Bruton parish register shows that she was there buried in January, 1724.]

II Doyley, 1712–*ante* 1734, *o.s.p.*,

[The name Doyley is a puzzle. The Rev. Cope Doyley was incumbent of Hampton (Elizabeth City) 1687–1697, and of Bruton (Williamsburg) 1697–1702, when he died (Bishop Meade, i, 231, 149). He left young sons, Charles and Cope, who on their father's death were committed to the care of Henry Tyler, Sheriff of York, because they had no relations in Virginia (See York *O.B.*, September 24, 1702; *Va. Mag.* xii, 300). Cope Doyley was a landowner in Warwick (*Quit Rent Rolls*, 1704), and it is probable that Henry Cary or his Sclater wife had affectionate relations with him, but it does not appear why they should name for him their eldest son, born ten years after Mr. Doyley's death. Doyley Cary was witness to a deed from Richard Page to John Blair, dated July 31, 1730, which was recorded in York, and then disappears.]

III Henry, 1714–1734, *o.s.p.*

[The younger brother, Henry, died, 1734, leaving a will bequeathing his property to his father (see *Appendix I*), and his father's will names the two slaves which the Rev. James Sclater had bequeathed to Doyley and Henry, with remainder to the survivor, thus indicating what was the property his son Henry had to leave and his survivorship of his brother.]

2nd: 1719, Anne, dau. of John Edwards, of Surry,

[Henry Cary[3] testified, by an entry in the Ampthill Bible, that his second wife was Anne Edwards. The evidence for the foregoing identification of the mother of Col. Archibald Cary, establishing his kinship with his Revolutionary colleague Benjamin Harrison, is the will of John Edwards dated August 12, 1712, and proved May 20, 1713 (Surry *Will Book,* v, 147), naming, with other children, his third son Benjamin and his daughter Anne, then unmarried; followed by the will of this Benjamin Edwards dated November 6, 1721, and proved November 21, 1722 (Surry *Will Book,* vi, 422), the witnesses to which are Anne Cary, Henry Cary, and (Dr.) Archibald Blair, evidently Benjamin Edwards' sister, brother-in-law and physician.

John Edwards and William, his brother, who was Clerk of the General Court in 1688, and afterwards of the Council, were the third generation of a family of ancient planters, the first of whom was, before 1624, seated in Surry, where they still persist. See Keith, *Ancestry of Benjamin Harrison,* 50, and *W. & M. Quar.,* xv, 79.]

and by her had:

IV   Anne, 1720, d. *infans,*

[She was buried in Bruton Church, 1720.]

V   Archibald, 1721, of Ampthill, see p. 91,
VI   Judith, 1726–1798, m. 1744 David Bell, of Belmont on the James River, in Buckingham County.

[This marriage spread the Cary blood and name among a numerous progeny, Frys, Gists, Blairs, Langhornes, Wallers, Estes and others, in Virginia, Kentucky, Tennessee, Missouri and Maryland.]

VII   Sarah, 1729, m. 1748, Alexander Spiers,

[Alexander Spiers was a Scotch merchant and returned to his home in Glasgow in 1750, taking his wife with him. She never returned to Virginia, but is reputed to have died, *s.p.*]

3rd: 1741 ?, Elizabeth ? Brickenhead, *s.p.*

[She survived her husband and was living in Williamsburg in 1750, when she made a will which was proved in Chesterfield October 10, 1751 (*Will Book,* i, 149). By this she left legacies to "Mrs. Judith Bell," "Mrs. Sarah Spiers," "Anne, daughter of Archi-

AMPTHILL HOUSE
APRIL, 1919

bald Cary," and the bulk of her property to "John Brickenhead, Peruke maker in Old Street, near St. Luke's Church, London." This last may be a clue to her maiden name, of which no definite record remains.]

SOURCES:

(1) The Ampthill family Bible; (2) The will of Henry Cary[3], 1748 (see *Appendix*); (3) *Miller* v. *Page,* 6 Call, 28; (4) Gleanings from public records of York, Henrico and Chesterfield.

IV. Colonel ARCHIBALD CARY (*Henry³, Henry², Miles¹*), 1721–1787, of Ampthill in Chesterfield County.

Born in Williamsburg, he was probably named for his father's friend and physician, Dr. Archibald Blair, though not of kin. Educated at William and Mary College. When he came of age in 1742 his father vested him with the property known as "Buckingham," 4132 acres of land on Willis Creek, then in Goochland (*Deed Book,* iv, 95, and Hening, vii, 440), and there he entered public life; he was J. P. 1747 and sat as a Burgess for Goochland 1748–49. On the organization of Cumberland County, in 1749, to include his lands, he was in the first Commission of the Peace and a vestryman of Southam parish. Later, in 1750 he became "of Ampthill" on his father's death and removed to Chesterfield. He extended his father's manufacturing interests, maintained the flouring mills at "Warwick," established a ropery, developed the deposits of limonite iron ore on his lands in Buckingham, and set up a furnace and foundry at Falling Creek, where in 1622 the first such venture had been made in the colony. (Brock, Va. Hist. Soc. *Collections,* vii, 51, says that in 1876 he identified the sites of both furnaces, that of 1622 as well as that of 1760, by remnants of slag in the soil. This was an archæological achievement worthy of Layard or Schliemann, but is not to be matched forty-three years later.) In local community affairs he was progressive; as J. P. (long Presiding Magistrate and County Lieutenant) he advocated the construction of roads and bridges; privately he imported pure-bred cattle, which found their way into the Valley of Virginia and in time into Kentucky, carrying with them the name "Cary's Stock" (*W. & M. Quar.,* xxvi, 167). An uncompromising member of the Established Church, as a magistrate he prosecuted the Baptists (*Va. Mag.,* xi, 416); and after disestablishment was, with his kinsmen Colonel Wilson-Miles Cary and Judge Richard Cary, a delegate to the convention of 1785 which organized the incorporated

[91]

Episcopal Church in Virginia. In 1756 he succeeded to the seat
in the Assembly for Chesterfield which had been held by Richard
Eppes since the creation of the county, and at once took active
part in the organization of the colony against the French in-
vasion then expected. Thenceforth until his death he represented
Chesterfield continuously. By 1762 he had taken the place in
the Assembly of his great-uncle Miles Cary[2], being Chairman
of the Committee of Public Claims, a post he held during the
remainder of the colonial period. In 1764 he was one of the committee of nine which prepared the memorials to the King, the Lords
and the Commons against Grenville's determination to impose
stamp taxes, but in 1765 he voted with the conservatives against
Patrick Henry's fiery resolutions. He took a leading rôle in the
Revolution in Virginia; he signed the Associations of 1769, 1770
and 1774; in 1773 he became a member of the Committee of Correspondence; was in all the Conventions of 1775; in the Convention of 1776 he was Chairman of the Committees, so that "it was
from his lips that the words of the resolution of independence,
of the declaration of rights, and of the first constitution of Virginia
first fell upon the public ear"; at home he was Chairman also of
the county committee of safety for Chesterfield (*W. & M. Quar.*,
v, 102). On the organization of the State government he became
Speaker of the Senate, and died holding that office. He had subscribed liberally to the Revolution in money as well as influence.
Thus in January, 1781, he calls the Governor's attention (*Cal. Va.
State Papers,* i, 471) to the fact that there is due him by government £40,000 on one account and £18,000 on another, while he
is faced with the obligation to provide £16,000 "for my proportions
towards raising the 3000 men." While these figures were in Virginia depreciated currency, not sterling, they represented large
values. In this situation, on April 30 of that year his mills at
Warwick and Falling Creek were destroyed by Benedict Arnold
(see Arnold's report of May 12, 1781, to Sir Henry Clinton, in
Tarleton, *Campaigns in North America* (1787), 337). Although
a large landholder (according to the land and tax books he died
seized of 2180 acres in Chesterfield, with 36 slaves; 4992 acres
in Cumberland, with 189 slaves; and 7000 acres in Buckingham,
with 41 slaves), yet, as a consequence of his sacrifices, he found
himself in straitened circumstances at the end of his life. By
tradition he is called "Old Iron," but whether with reference to
his furnace or his character does not appear. He had indeed developed a peremptory disposition, as witness his celebrated message
to Patrick Henry in 1776 (Wirt, *Life of Patrick Henry* (1836), 223)
and the subsequent familiar description of him as "the old bruiser"
(Rowland, *George Mason,* i, 334; Greene, *Nathaniel Greene* (1871),
iii, 506); but, on the other hand, General Washington, though

eleven years his junior, maintained an affectionate relation with
him, calling him "Archy" (Ford, *Writings of Washington*, ii, 428) ;
and the Saratoga convention prisoner, Lieutenant Anburey, testifies
(*Travels through . . . America* (1791), ii, 312) to his courtesy and
genial hospitality. His reputation being confined to Virginia, the
immediate memorial of his fame was his name given to a street in
Richmond, and, what would, perhaps, have given him greater satisfaction, to a noble stake-horse and sire, "The Godolphin Arabian
of America," Sir Archy, foaled 1805, by imp. Diomed out of imp.
Castianira (Anderson, *Making the American Thoroughbred*
(1916), 39). No stone marks his grave; indeed the place of burial
is not known. Tradition has it that he was buried in the cellar of
Ampthill House, where his "hant" is still seen by the negroes. For
him, see the eloquent appreciation in Grigsby, *Virginia Convention of 1776*, 90, and a brief notice in *Appletons' Cyclo. Am. Biog.*,
i, 548. His correspondence and personal papers were destroyed,
so that material is lacking for a "Life." There is in existence a
pleasant portrait of him by the elder Peale.

He m. 1744, Mary, 1727–1781, dau. of Colonel
Richard Randolph, of Curles (and of Jane, dau.
of the first John Bolling, of Cobbs, through
whom Archibald Cary's descendants derive their
infusion of the blood of Pocahontas),

[See Robertson, *Pocahontas and Her Descendants*, 1887.
For the Bolling family, see *Memoirs of the Bolling Family*, ed.
Wynne, 1868, and Stanard, *Va. Mag.*, xxi and xxii *passim*.
For the Randolph family, see Slaughter, *Bristol Parish*, 212, and
Stanard in *W. & M. Quar.*, vii–ix, *passim*.]

and by her had:

I Anne, 1745–1789, m. 1761, Colonel
Thomas Mann Randolph, 1741–1794,
of Tuckahoe,

[It was through this marriage (see *W. & M. Quar.*, viii, 119)
that the Carysbrook family united the blood of Henry Cary[2] and
Miles Cary[2]; and that the Cary blood and name were carried
among the Coolidges of Boston, who now (1919) own Tuckahoe.]

II Mary, 1747, d. *infans*,

[93]

III   Jane, 1751–1774, m. 1767, Thomas Isham Randolph, of "Ben Lomond" in Goochland, son of Colonel Isham Randolph, of Dungeness,

[From this marriage descended the Harrisons of "Clifton" and the Hutchinsons of St. Louis. It was the older sister of this Thomas Isham Randolph who was the mother of Thomas Jefferson. See *W. & M. Quar.,* viii, 122, 263.]

IV   Sarah, 1753–1773, m. 1770, Archibald Bolling, of Goochland, a younger son of the second John Bolling, of Cobbs, and a grandson of Archibald Blair,

[Sally Cary was the first of his four wives. See the lively notice of him in Robertson, *Pocahontas and Her Descendants,* 1887.]

V   Eliza, 1755, d. *infans,*

VI   Henry, 1758, d. *infans,*

VII   Mary, 1766–1797, m. 1782, Major Carter Page, of "The Fork," Cumberland County,

[For the descendants of this marriage, and Dr. Mann Page's amusing correspondence about the "Cary fortune," see Page, *Genealogy of the Page Family,* 1893, pp. 108 and 120. Most of the Ampthill heirlooms passed to the Pages.]

VIII   Elizabeth, 1770?, m. 1787, Robert Kincaid, of Manchester.

[This Elizabeth, or Betsy, was not entered in the Ampthill Bible. After her mother's death and the marriage of her next older sister she assumed, though still a child, the management of her father's household and thereby won his warm affection, as appears by his will. The codicils disclose, however, that her father strongly disapproved of her intended marriage to Robert Kincaid and sought to prevent it. A notice in the *Virginia Gazette* shows that the

JUDITH CARY
MRS. DAVID BELL
1726–1798

marriage took place a few weeks after Colonel Archibald Cary's death. There were Kincaid and Irving descendants.]

SOURCES:

(1) The Ampthill family Bible; (2) The will of Archibald Cary, 1787 (see *Appendix*).

NOTE. *At the death of Colonel Archibald Cary, of Ampthill, the male line of the second son of the immigrant became extinct; but the descendants of the marriage of his granddaughter Virginia Randolph, dau. of Thomas Mann Randolph, of Tuckahoe, with Wilson Jefferson Cary, of Carysbrook (see post, p. 113), carry on the blood of this line in the Cary name.*

CHAPTER SIX

RICHNECK, CEELYS, CARYSBROOK,
AND OAKHILL

To his third son, the surveyor, the immigrant
assigned as a portion the eastern half of the
Warwick lands he had purchased from Zachary
Cripps: this property, adjoining The Forest,
came to be known as Richneck [1] and like the lean

[1] *The Richneck estate.* Zachariah Cripps, "gent.," came to Virginia in 1621 (*Va. Mag.*, ii, 77) and in 1625 was living over the river from Jamestown in the only stone house in the colony (Brown, *The First Republic*, 626). In 1628 he patented 100 acres at the south end of Mulberry Island (*i.e.,* Joyles Neck, subsequently devised by Miles Cary to his kinsman Roger Daniel) and in 1629, 1633 and 1639 represented that community as a Burgess (Stanard, *Colonial Virginia Register*). In 1637 and 1645 he patented 1050 acres on Back Creek (now Stone Run) in the interior of Warwick, bounded by "the Mill Land" and "Thomas Taylor's land," *i.e.,* Magpie Swamp, and apparently called the part which he seated "The Forest," as it is named in Miles Cary's will. It appears from that will and subsequent patents that the immigrant Miles purchased all of Zachariah Cripps' lands in Warwick, and divided the inland 1050 acre tract between his sons Henry and Miles. (See their confirmatory patents, April 23, 1681, and November 20, 1682, *Va. Land Register*, vii, 87 and 201.) Miles[2] called his portion "Richneck" in reference to its situation between the forks of Stone Run. There he built a house which survived until 1865, but is identified now only by the cavities of the cellars; there the Committee on Public Claims of the Assembly sat in March, 1692/3 (*Journals of the House of Burgesses 1659–1693*, p. 419), and there also was long the seat of the County Court and of the Clerk's office. His inheritance being about 500 acres, Miles[2] paid quit-rent on Richneck, in 1704, for 1960 acres. His son Wilson[3] acquired The Forest and other adjacent lands, so that at his death, in 1772, the Richneck

kine of Pharaoh's dream, ultimately swallowed
most of the other Cary properties in Warwick.
While retaining Richneck until the end of the
eighteenth century, the descendants of this second
Col. Miles Cary lived also for three generations
on the shore of Hampton Roads in Elizabeth
City, at Ceelys,[1] the handsome house they had

estate comprised some 4000 acres, stretching from Magpie Swamp
on the east to the Warwick River on the west, and from the "Claiborne Neck dams" on the north down Stone Run to the present
site of Warwick Court House where it joined Judge Richard
Cary's Peartree Hall lands: the property is now bisected by the
railroad from Richmond to Newport News. The tradition is that
Ampthill House was a substantial reproduction of the house at
Richneck, so that we can reconstruct the latter in imagination.
Four generations of Carys called this place home and there were
born and buried. Like his father, Colonel Wilson-Miles Cary[4]
eventually established himself at Ceelys, and soon after (in 1788)
offered Richneck for sale. In 1793, after the death of Wilson[5],
who lived out his life at Richneck, a sale was effected to "The
Richneck Company" formed by William Hylton, Dr. Fouchee and
others, after negotiations with the French minister citizen Genet,
with the intention of supplying lumber for the French navy. The
failure of this project was one of the principal causes of "the old
Colonel's" financial embarrassment. The property has remained
in corporate hands and in 1919 belongs to the Old Dominion Land
Company. Despite its name, the land, a flat undrained sandy
loam, is not naturally available for profitable agriculture and so
stands to-day as it did in the seventeenth century, largely under
forest growth; the original white oak which gave the place its value
has been cut out, the present cover being principally scrub oak, pine
and gum. The drained areas, like the upland clearing about the
site of Richneck House (a mile northeast of the railroad station
known as Oriana), still respond smilingly to cultivation. This Cary
Richneck must be distinguished from the earlier plantation of the
same name on Archers Hope Creek, originally of George Menefie
and later of Secretary Ludwell.

[1] *Ceelys.* On December 1, 1624, John Bush, "gentleman," who
had come to Virginia in 1618, patented 300 acres in the parish of
Kiccoughtan adjoining the lands of Lieutenant Albino Lupo "bor-
dering on the main river" James. (*Va. Mag.,* i, 194.) This and

inherited from the Wilsons: they maintained
residences also in Hampton and Williamsburg.

other lands on the west extending to Salfords (since corrupted to
Salters) Creek, originally grouped with the Warwick River settlements, was later acquired by Thomas Ceely who resided there in
1639, when he sat as a burgess for Warwick River (Tyler, *Cradle
of the Republic,* 244); he had apparently formerly resided on the
Matthews land, Denbigh, which he represented in the Assemblies
of 1629–30. Another Thomas Ceely conveyed this property to
Colonel William Wilson (then Major) by two deeds dated January, 1691, and July, 1695. This purchase was the nucleus of an
estate of 2000 acres for which Colonel Wilson continued the name
Ceelys. It would be pleasant to know that these Thomas Ceelys
were descendants of the Bristol merchant Thomas Cely, who in 1588
commanded the *Elizabeth Drake* in the fight against the Armada.
(See his letter in Laughton, *The Defeat of the Spanish Armada,*
1895.)

The large brick house, which the Carys subsequently inhabited
for two generations, and which was a centre of hospitality during
the time of Colonel Wilson Cary, had been built in 1706 by Colonel
William Wilson. There Colonel Wilson Cary collected his interesting library (see *Sally Cary*) and there he imported and used
the notable service of table silver, of which some items still survive
in inheritance: it was this plate which inspired the jocular transla-
tion of the motto on Colonel Wilson Cary's arms, thereon engraved,
Cari deo nihil carent, as "The Carys, by God, want nothing." Sold
in 1799 by Colonel Wilson-Miles Cary, Ceelys House was dilapi-
dated, during the war between the States, by Butler's "contra-
bands," who camped on the spot and used the bricks for the chim-
neys of their huts (*Va. Mag.,* ix, 105). In 1919 the site is marked
by what remains of a grove of ancient trees, in the shade of which
has grown up a settlement of modern suburban villas known as
Kecoughtan, the Indian name of Hampton. In front, where once
was a notable falling garden reaching to the water's edge, now
runs the Boulevard trolley line between Newport News and Hampton; but the noble prospect of Hampton Roads is still the same as it
was in Colonel Wilson Cary's day, for all that, instead of the ships
of H. M. Navy, it has recently been illustrated by American
dreadnoughts, aëroplanes and camouflaged transports laden with
victorious homeward bound "Anzacs." On the opposite shore the
skeletons of two giant coal piers now loom above the pine trees
which have been characteristic of the landscape since the days of
Captain Christopher Newport.

At the beginning of the nineteenth century these Carys migrated definitely to their up-country plantation, Carysbrook in Fluvanna.[1] A portion of this property cut off as the inheritance of a junior branch was subsequently called Oakhill.

[1] The first patent for CARYSBROOK was taken out in 1725, by Mary Blair for her son Miles Cary[3] of Ceelys, then under age. It was 1600 acres in Goochland (afterwards Fluvanna) lying on both sides of the Rivanna, where it received the stream which then took the name Cary Creek, by which it is designated in the patents and on Fry and Jefferson's map of Virginia, 1755. After he became of age Miles Cary[3] took out a new patent in 1737 (*Va. Land Register,* xvii, 389), by which he enlarged the boundary to 4000 acres. The plantation house at Carysbrook was a rambling unpainted frame structure to which many misfit additions had been made, always with the expectation that they were temporary and that a permanent brick house was to be built. It was originally used as a summer lodge in the wilderness by Miles Cary[3], and afterwards by his brother and nephew, but remained practically a "quarter" in charge of an overseer until 1810, when Wilson Jefferson Cary and his family there established themselves, removing from his grandfather's house in Williamsburg to secure domestic independence. The house was destroyed by fire in 1826: with it disappeared all the family papers and many of the other heirlooms which had accumulated at Richneck and Ceelys. One who has heard the glittering details of this loss, as refracted through tradition, and has also read eighteenth century inventories of similar Virginia households, is tempted affectionately to recall the philosophy of the ingenious Caleb Balderston "this fire will be a creditable apology for the honour of the family for this score of years to come, if it is well guided . . . where's the tapestries and the decorements, beds of state, twilts, pands, and testors, napery and broidered work? —the fire, the fire, the fire." The plantation is a conspicuously rich river bottom in a notoriously poor county: "the state of Flu" has always been something of a byword in Virginia. After it was sold by the Carys in 1831, Carysbrook passed to the Harrisons and later to the Bryans, and now (1919) belongs to C. E. Jones, who has developed out of it one of the most prosperous farms in the State. The place is what it always was, remote, and will so remain until the construction of the proposed State highway system which promises to put it on a main north and south road.

II. Colonel MILES CARY (*Miles¹*), 1655?–1709, of Richneck.

He was educated in England, where he was at school when his father made his will. Apparently he was the only one of the immigrant's sons who had this advantage, which is evident throughout his career. He began life as a surveyor and prospered progressively in various business ventures carried forward contemporaneously with his public service. He was J. P. for Warwick as early as 1680. Captain 1683, Lieutenant-Colonel and Commander in Chief in Warwick 1699 (*Va. Mag.*, x, 215). Colonel and County Lieutenant for Warwick 1705. Clerk of the General Court 1691 (*Va. Mag.*, xx, 118; *Cal. Va. State Papers*, i, 27), Register of the Vice-Admiralty Court 1697–99 (*Va. Mag.*, xxi, 74; *W. & M. Quar.*, v, 129). In 1693 he was in New York as commissioner on behalf of Virginia to treat concerning the "quota" which the English government sought (in vain) to have contributed by each of the colonies for the war with Frontenac and the French in Canada: by his recommendation in accordance with the far-sighted plan of the home government he then incurred the disapprobation of those of his colleagues in the Assembly who maintained the characteristic colonial attitude of ostrich-like selfishness; but Governor Andros saw to it that he was well paid for his trouble. (See Governor Benjamin Fletcher's dispatches from New York, August and October, 1693, in O'Callaghan, *Documents Relative to the Colonial History of New York*, iv, 37 and 56; *Journals of the House of Burgesses 1659–1693*, pp. lxxii, 485, 488; *Cal. Va. State Papers*, i, 47; *Va. Mag.*, xxiv, 400.) Burgess 1683–1706. Chairman of Committees on Privileges and Elections, Public Claims, etc. Senior Burgess of Committee to revise laws 1699–1704. (Hening, iii, 181. The important work of this Committee was the *Revisal of 1705*, which appears in Hening, iii, 229 ff.; incidentally it was charged with the supervision of construction of the first capitol at Williamsburg (*W. & M. Quar.*, x, 78), Miles² being paymaster, while his brother Henry was overseer of the work. The journal of this Committee has recently been printed in McIlwaine, *Legislative Journals of the Council*, iii, Appendix.) Charter Trustee William and Mary College 1693, and Rector 1705–06. (*Cal. State Papers, Am. & W. I.*, 1704–05, No. 924, p. 427.) Surveyor General 1699–1709. (*Cal. State Papers, Am. & W. I.*, 1700, No. 523, li, p. 321.) Naval Officer and Receiver of Virginia duties for York River 1699–1709. (*Cal. State Papers, Am. & W. I.*, 1700, No. 1055, p. 766; Hunsdon peerage case 1707, *Harl. MS.* 6694.) He died intestate. In 1699 he had been a candidate to be Speaker, when Robert Carter was elected over him after two days' balloting during which the Assembly steadily divided twenty and twenty. (McIlwaine, *Jour-*

COL. MILES CARY
OF RICHNECK
1655–1709

nals of the House of Burgesses 1695–1702, p. 132.)[1] A staunch supporter of Gov. Nicholson in his quarrel with Commissary Blair, and so involved in the bitter partizan politics of the time, the Blair faction succeeded also in keeping him out of the seat in the Council for which both Andros and Nicholson recommended him. There is in existence an interesting portrait of him.

He m.,

   1st: 1683?, Mary, 1667–1700, dau. of Lieutenant-Colonel Thomas Milner, of Nansemond, *s.p.*

[For the Milners of Nansemond, see *ante* under Thomas Cary[2]. Colonel Thomas Milner was a conspicuous figure in Virginia at the end of the seventeenth century, Clerk of the Assembly during its contest with Lord Howard of Effingham, and their agent to present grievances to the King in 1685. For this the Governor turned him out of all his profitable and honorary employments, but under Nicholson and Andros he was reinstated in the commission of the peace, was elected a burgess, and in 1691–93 was Speaker at the time his son-in-law was beginning his legislative career. Like his son-in-law, he was a surveyor, and one of the founders of William and Mary College. See *Va. Mag.*, iv, 168.]

   2nd: 1702, Mary, 1675–1741, dau. of Colonel William Wilson, of Ceelys,

----

[1] *Dr. McIlwaine says* (ibid., *Introduction, p. xxx*) *that the defeated candidate for Speaker in 1699 was "probably Mr. Philip Ludwell." This conjecture ignores the testimony of the Journal itself. While the names of, and votes for, the several candidates were not recorded, it was the courteous custom of the age that when there was a contest the defeated aspirant should serve as Chairman of the Committee to notify the Governor of the election. See, e.g., 1692 and 1693, when Thomas Milner was elected Speaker over Samuel Swann and William Fitzhugh, respectively; 1696, when Robert Carter was elected over Benjamin Harrison; 1698, when William Randolph was elected over Robert Carter, and 1702, when Peter Beverley was elected over William Leigh. In 1699 Miles Cary was Chairman of this committee (Journal, p. 133), and, moreover, throughout the session always occupied the chair when the Assembly sat in Committee of the Whole House. At the end of the seventeenth century, as at all other times, partizan politics ran high in Virginia over so rich a prize as the Speakership, but in the purely honorary employments the amenities were recognized.*

[The origin of this Wilson family in England has not yet been established; they were possibly from Bristol (*W. & M. Quar.*, vii, 225), or they may have been derived from the Rev. John Wilson, incumbent in 1637 of Elizabeth River parish, Norfolk County (Bishop Meade, i, 271, and Brock in *Spotswood Papers*, i, 30). The curious and unidentified arms they bore, *e.g.* on Colonel Wilson's seal attached to a surviving paper (*Cal. Va. State Papers*, i, 136) and in his M.I. reproduced *infra*, which was long legible in the churchyard of St. John's, Hampton (McCabe, in the *Church Review*, 1853, vi, 125), but is now gone, indicate a pious ancestor. For what is known of some of them in Virginia, see *W. & M. Quar.*, xx, 188, and Richmond *Critic*, June 14, 1890. Colonel William Wilson (1646–1713) was a successful merchant at Hampton, and accumulated a large estate. He was Burgess, J. P. and County Lieutenant for Elizabeth City and Naval Officer for the Lower James River district from 1699 to 1710; all the posts subsequently held by his Cary descendants. His M.I. read:

ARMS OF WILSON

[As described in Burke, *General Armoury*. "Sa. on a cross engr. between four cherubim or, a human heart of the first, wounded on the left side ppr. and crowned with a crown of thorns vert."]

UNDER THIS STONE LYES THE BODY OF CAPT. WILLIS WILSON, WHO DEPARTED THIS LIFE THE 19TH DAY OF NOVEMBER, IN THE YEAR 1701: IT BEING THE 28TH YEAR OF HIS AGE. THE MEMORY OF THE JUST IS BLESSED. PROV. 10. MAY HIS MEMORY BE RECORDED IN EVERLASTING REMEMBRANCE.

UNDER THIS ALSO LYES THE BODIES OF COLONEL WILLIAM WILSON & OF JANE, HIS WIFE, PARENTS OF THIS BEFORE-MENTIONED CAPT. WILSON. THE SAID COLONEL WILSON DIED JUNE 17, 1713, AGED ABOUT 67 YEARS, & HIS SAID WIFE, MAY 5, 1713, AGED ABOUT 58 YEARS, & LEFT AN ONLY DAUGHTER SURVIVING.

Mary, this "only daughter surviving" (but see *W. & M. Quar.*, ix, 125), was evidently a charmer. By her coquetry in 1702, when she was first a widow and was about to marry Colonel Cary, she provoked a fire-eating Scot, Captain James Moodie, commanding H.M.S. *Southampton*, then stationed in Virginia, to threaten her father's life and to challenge Cary to a duel; the record of which proceeding, preserved in the York Court *Order Book* for 1702, is a curious chapter in the history of the code of honor in Virginia, and would have astonished the "Sir Lucius O'Triggers" of later generations. (See also Colonel Robert Quarry's dispatch to the

II. *Miles Cary*

III. *Wilson Cary*

Miles Cary

IV. *Wilson Miles Cary*

V. *Wilson Cary*

VI. *W. J. Cary.*

VII. *Wilson Miles Cary*

Archd Cary

VIII. *W. Miles Cary*

Jno. B Cary

Clarence Cary

IX. *Wilson M. Cary*

Fairfax Cary

X. *W. Miles Cary, Jr.*

AUTOGRAPHS OF THE RICHNECK CARYS

The numerals indicate generations

Lords of Trade, June 16, 1703, O'Callaghan, *Documents relating to the Colonial History of . . . New York*, iv, 1056.) Mary Wilson had three husbands, William Roscow, of Blunt Point, Miles Cary and Archibald Blair. There might be paraphrased for her the inscription on the portrait of the second wife of Sir Henry Cary, of Cockington, also thrice wed:

> Thrice happy Mary
> Blair, Roscow, Cary.

Surviving them all, she elected to be buried with her first husband at Blunt Point. See her M.I. in *W. & M. Quar.*, xiv, 163.]

and by her had:

I   Wilson, 1702, of Richneck and Ceelys, see p. 105,

II   Mary, 1704–1775, m. Joseph Selden (d. 1727), of Hampton,

[For the Seldens and their second intermarriage with Carys see *ante, p. 52.*]

III   Anne, 1706–*ante* 1749, m. . . . Whiting, of Gloucester,

[Called "Ann" on her father's tombstone, she is named "my sister Anne Whiting" in the will of her brother Wilson, 1772, in terms to suggest that she had then been long dead, but having reference to Colonel Henry Whiting. Colonel John Bolling, of Cobbs, also mentions her in his will, 1749, as dead, so that we may carry back her date at least that far. As no mention of any Whiting is made in the 1752 will of the bachelor Miles[3], of Ceelys, who provided legacies for all his nephews and nieces, it is improbable that Anne Whiting had any surviving children. The loss of the Gloucester records has left the earlier portions of the Virginia pedigree of the Whitings in much uncertainty: it has not been possible to determine which of them married Anne Cary. See *Va. Mag.*, ix, 109; xviii, 356. For the later Whitings, several of whom married Carys, see Hayden, *Virginia Genealogies*, 479, and Horner, *History of the Blair, Banister and Baxter Families*, 176.]

IV   Miles, of Ceelys and Carysbrook, 1708–1756, *o.s.p.*

[He was educated at William and Mary College and inherited Ceelys from his mother. Carysbrook, then in Goochland, was patented for him in 1725 and he was, in consequence, J. P. for Goochland, in the commissions of 1737 and 1741. He died a bachelor, leaving the bulk of his estate to his brother Wilson under an elaborate will, dated 1752, now of genealogical value, as he mentioned most of his immediate family. See *Appendix*.]

SOURCES:

(1) The authorities for the immigrant; (2) Gleanings from public records in *W. M. Cary Notes;* (3) The M.I. on Miles Cary's tombstone at Richneck, reproduced *infra,* for the first marriage and the names of the children; (4) the surviving marriage bond (*W. & M. Quar.*, v, 58) for the date of the second marriage; (5) the record of the matriculation of Wilson Cary[2] at Trinity College, Cambridge, for his birth date; (6) the will of Miles Cary[3], dated October 11, 1752, in *Appendix* for the other children.

TOMBSTONE OF MILES CARY, THIRD SON OF THE IMMIGRANT, AT RICHNECK, WARWICK COUNTY, VIRGINIA.

ARMS OF MILNER, CO. LINCOLN.
[Sa. a chev. betw. three snaffle bits or.
Crest: A horse's head, couped, bridled and maned or.]

HERE LYETH Y^E BODY OF MARY THE WIFE OF MILES CARY & DAUGHTER OF THOMAS MILNVR AND MARY HIS WIFE, LATE OF NANZEMOND COUNTY, DEC'D. SHEE WAS BORN THE 6TH OF AUGUST 1667 AND DIED THE 27TH OF OCTOBER 1700 IN THE 34TH YEAR OF HER AGE. IſSUELEſS.

ALSO THE BODY OF COL^O MILES CARY, HUSBAND OF THE SAID MARY, WHO DIED FEB'RY 17TH 1708 & LEFT 2 SONS, WILSON & MILES, AND 2 DAUGHTERS MARY & ANN BY MARY, Y^E DAUGHTER OF COL. WM. WILSON OF HAMPTON.

NOTE. *The inscription was copied in 1868 by Captain Wilson Miles Cary, and again by Dr. Lyon G. Tyler (see* W. &. M. Quar., *xiv,* 167). *It is given also, from another copy, in* Va. Mag., *viii,* 264, *but with a misreading of the defaced date of Colonel Cary's death. See the correction, and proof of the date as here printed, in* Va. Mag., *ix,* 213. *The year is, of course, recorded on the inscription in old style.*

The inscribed ironstone slab surmounted a brick altar tomb, like that at Windmill Point. On either side of it were later constructed arched brick vaults in which were interred the two succeeding

THE CEELYS PLATE

*generations of the Richneck and Ceelys family. When in 1855
Bishop Meade visited Richneck (Old Churches, etc., i, 242), the
graveyard was already a neglected ruin, as it still is in 1919, lying
unfenced in an open field, but fortunately covered by a decent
mantle of jonquils. The two brick vaults have now collapsed and
the tombstone of Mary Milner and Miles Cary[2] is in fragments,
but these can still be pieced together so as to make out most of the
inscription.*

III. Colonel WILSON CARY (*Miles[2], Miles[1]*), 1702–1772, of Richneck and Ceelys.

William and Mary College 1719. Trinity College, Cambridge,
1721–1723, where the record of his matriculation reads, "Admissus
Wilson Cary, pens[r], June 30, 1721, an. nat. 18, filius Miles Cary
de Virginia in India occidentali, e Collegio Gulielmi et Mariæ
in eadem terra." On his return from college in England, he lived
at Richneck and there founded the collection of books since known
as the Ceelys Library, as shown by his first book-plate (see *Sally
Cary, Appendix III*). Naval Officer and Collector of Virginia
duties for Lower James River 1726–1760. J. P. for Warwick and,
after 1726, for Elizabeth City (*W. & M. Quar.*, xx, 169), when,
on his appointment as Naval Officer, he acquired a house in Hampton, where he lived much of his time until, after inheriting Ceelys
from his bachelor brother in 1756, he removed thither. Colonel and
County Lieutenant for Elizabeth City 1751 (*Cal. Va. State Papers,*
i, 247). There is an amusing glimpse of him in his old age in a
letter of George Mason (Rowland, *George Mason*, i, 296). He is
buried at Richneck. See his obituaries in *Virginia Gazette*, December 3, 1772, and Rind's *Gazette*, No. 344, December 10, 1772, and
Wilson Cary of Ceelys and His Family (*Va. Mag.*, ix, 104). His
portrait was destroyed in the fire which consumed the house at
Carysbrook in 1826.

He m. 1728?, Sarah, 1710?–1783, daughter of John Pate, of Gloucester.

[That her name was Sarah is evidenced by a number of surviving signatures as well as a deed, in York records, by Wilson
Cary and Sarah his wife, dated January 20, 1728, O.S. (which fixes
also the approximate date of the marriage), but her extraction long
eluded discovery. Among the remnants of the Ceelys library are
several books (*e.g.*, Dryden's *Miscellany Poems*, iii, 1693, and v,
1703; Echard's *Ecclesiastical History*, 1702) bearing on the title-
page the signature of "John Pate," the last with the date 1706 ap-

pended. Moreover, Colonel Wilson Cary by will disposed of lands lying on Poropotank Creek in Gloucester and King and Queen, the acquisition of which was not readily explainable except on the assumption of inheritance. It appears also from casual mention in the York records that Miles Cary[2] was administrator of the estate of Edward Pate and that a Miles Cary (probably Miles, Jr.[3], of Potash Creek) was executor of John Pate under a will, now lost with the Gloucester records; while John Pate appears on the *Virginia Quit Rent Rolls* of 1704 as the owner of lands on Poropotank in Gloucester and King and Queen. These facts long persuaded Captain W. M. Cary that the wife of Colonel Wilson Cary was daughter to John Pate, but he could not prove it. (See his notes of 1901 in *Va. Mag.*, ix, 107.) In 1913, while working among the MS. sources of Virginia history in Richmond, he came upon confirmatory evidence, upon which he triumphantly announced to the present Editor, as to others, that he had established the last unproved fact in his own pedigree,—that Sarah Cary was Sarah Pate, of Gloucester. After Captain Cary's death I searched his papers for the evidence of this proof, but, by a perversity of fate, have not yet been able to turn up the note. The John Pate who is identified as the father of Wilson Cary's wife was the eldest of the sons, named in the Abingdon parish register, of Major Thomas Pate, at whose house Bacon the Rebel died. For what little is known of the Pate family, see *W. & M. Quar.*, v, 279.]

and by her had:

I   Sally, 1730–1811, m. 1748, George William Fairfax, 1724–1787, of Belvoir, Fairfax County,

[See *Sally Cary*, 1916.]

II   Mary, 1733–1781, m. 1754, Edward Ambler, 1722–1767, of Jamestown,

[She was the Mary Cary who is celebrated with romantic details by Washington Irving and Bishop Meade as George Washington's "first sweetheart." The foundation of the legend seems to have been Washington's letter (Ford, *Writings of Washington*, i, 7), written in 1749 from Belvoir to his "Dear Friend Robin," describing how there he "might, was my heart disengaged, pass my time very pleasantly, as there's a very agreeable young lady lives in the same house (Colonel George Fairfax's wife's sister)." But see *Sally*

SALLY CARY
MRS. GEORGE WILLIAM FAIRFAX OF BELVOIR
1730-1811

Cary. For the Ambler family see Bishop Meade, *Old Churches,* etc., i, 103, and *W. & M. Quar.,* v, 50.]

III Wilson-Miles, 1734, of Richneck, Ceelys and Carysbrook, see p. 108,

IV Anne, 1735–1786, m. 1752, Colonel Robert Carter Nicholas, 1728–1780, of Williamsburg,

[See, in Bishop Meade, i, 184, her admirable letter of 1784 to her son Wilson Cary Nicholas on his entry into public life. The original lies before me as I write: it is as beautiful in MS. as it is inspiring in sentiment. For Robert Carter Nicholas, his sons, and other descendants of Anne Cary, see Edmund Randolph's MS. quoted in *Letters and Times of the Tylers,* i, 57; Grigsby, *Virginia Conventions of 1776 and 1788; Appletons' Cyclo. Am. Biog.* (1894), iv., 511; *Harper's Encyc. U. S. Hist.* (1902), vi, 465; *W. & M. Quar.,* xxvii, 132.]

V Elizabeth, 1738–1778, m. 1759, Bryan Fairfax, 1736–1802, of Towlston, Fairfax County.

[For Bryan Fairfax (afterwards eighth Lord Fairfax) and his family in Virginia, with their several infusions of Cary blood, see *Catlett v. Marshall,* 10 Leigh (Va.), 79; Minutes of evidence *Fairfax Peerage claims,* 1800 and 1908, in House of Lords; *The Formation . . . of Fairfax Lodge No. 3255,* Guiseley (Bradford), Yorkshire; privately printed 1909, with portraits of all twelve of the Lords Fairfax and others of the family; Burnaby, *Travels Through North America,* 1798, Appendix 4; Washington Irving, *Life of George Washington* (1855), i, 25 ff.; Bishop Meade, *Old Churches,* etc., 1857, ii, 106, 256, 281; Sabine, *Loyalists of the American Revolution,* 1864, i, 408 ff.; Neill, *The Fairfaxes of England and America,* 1868; Markham and Skaife, *Genealogies of the Fairfaxes* in J. G. Nichols, *Herald and Genealogist,* vi (1870) and vii (1871); C. C. Harrison, *A Little Centennial Lady* (1876), and *My Lord Fairfax of Virginia* (1879), in *Scribner's Monthly,* xii, 301, and xviii, 715; Brockett, *The Lodge of Washington,* 1876; Dr. Philip Slaughter, Appendix to *Memoir of Randolph Fairfax* (3rd ed., 1878); Ford, *Writings of George Washington,* 1889–1893, *passim;* Hamilton, *Letters to Washington* (Colonial Dames ed.), 1898; R. H. Spencer, *The Carlyle Family* (of Alexandria), 1910;

C. C. Harrison, *Recollections Grave and Gay*, 1911; Callahan, *Washington, the Man and the Mason*, 1913; *Sally Cary*, 1916.]

SOURCES:

(1) Ceelys family Bible; (2) the wills of Miles Cary[3] of Ceelys, 1752, and of Colonel Wilson Cary himself, in *Appendix*. Colonel Wilson Cary's will is printed at length in *Va. Mag.*, ix, 189; (3) Fairfax family records, MSS.; (4) Gleanings from public records, *Virginia Gazette*, etc.

IV. Colonel WILSON-MILES CARY (*Wilson[5], Miles[2], Miles[1]*), 1734–1817, of Richneck, Ceelys and Carysbrook.

Born at Richneck, where, and at Hampton, he lived from his marriage, 1759, until the Revolution: his mother occupied Ceelys until her death, 1783. William and Mary College 1752–55 (*W. & M. Quar.*, xxvii, 133). J. P. for Warwick and later for Elizabeth City, where he was long Presiding Magistrate. He was on the bench at the hearing of the Parson's Cause in Elizabeth City in 1763. (*W. & M. Quar.*, xx, 172.) Served in all grades of Elizabeth City militia from Lieutenant (1762) to Colonel and County Lieutenant. Burgess and Delegate for Elizabeth City, Warwick and Fluvanna at intervals, 1765–1796. Signer of the Association of 1774: his name is on the monument to those who met at the Raleigh Tavern for that purpose, which stands on the site of the old Capitol at Williamsburg (*W. & M. Quar.*, xiii, 65). Committee of Safety for Elizabeth City 1775 (*W. & M. Quar.*, v, 253). Convention of 1776. Thirty-one years later, at the celebration in 1807 of the second centenary of Jamestown, he was chaired as one of the three survivors of this convention (Tyler, *Cradle of the Republic*, 92). Naval Officer and Receiver of Virginia duties for Lower James River 1760–1776, when he resigned to espouse the patriot cause. He was in consequence a mark for plunder by the British during the war; thus twenty-four of his slaves were carried off from Richneck and Ceelys on one occasion and Carysbrook was raided on another. See the picturesque story of his thoroughbred stallion captured by Tarleton at Carysbrook and subsequently recovered at Yorktown (Burk (Girardin), *History* of *Virginia*, iv, 504). Visitor of William and Mary College 1800, etc. Delegate to Conventions of the Episcopal Church from its incorporation in 1785 until 1797 (see President Madison's pleasant anecdote about him in Bishop Meade, *Old Churches*, etc., i, 50). Inherited a large fortune and broad acres (*e.g.*, as late as 1782 he is listed in the *Virginia Census* as the owner of what was, at the time, an

COL. WILSON-MILES CARY
OF CEELYS AND CARYSBROOK
1734–1817

unusual number of slaves, viz.: at Scotchtown, 80; at Carysbrook, 200; at Richneck, 1, with the Elizabeth City list, which included Ceelys, missing), but by profuse hospitality steadily diminished his patrimony in the economic depression which followed the Revolution in Virginia. During the Revolution he acquired an estate in Hanover, known as Scotchtown, and there resided in a pleasant colony of refugee kinsmen, Amblers, Nicholases, and Nelsons (see Bishop Meade, i, 109). After Yorktown he established himself at Ceelys, but abandoning that residence after his first wife's death in 1799, lived for some years in Williamsburg and finally removed to Carysbrook in Fluvanna, where he had been first in the Commission of the Peace on the organization of the county in 1777. There he died and was buried, leaving in his will an abiding mirror of his character. See his obituary in the Richmond *Enquirer* newspaper of December 4, 1817, for evidence of the respect and esteem in which he was held in the new world into which he had lived. There is a portrait of him in his old age—a venerable figure.

He m.,

1st: 1759, Sarah, 1738–1799, dau. of John Blair, President of the Council,

[For the Blair family and the lively letters of Anna Blair (Mrs. John Banister of Battersea) to her sister Mary Blair (Mrs. George Braxton of Newington), with glimpses of the family of their sister Sarah (Mrs. Wilson-Miles Cary), see Horner, *History of the Blair, Banister and Braxton Families,* 1898.]

and by her had:

I   Wilson, 1760, of Richneck, see p. 111,

II Sally, 1762–1779, m. 1778, Captain Thomas Nelson, Jr., of Yorktown, afterwards of Hanover,

[She was mentioned in the will of her grandfather Wilson Cary for two legacies, one of books, when she was 10 years of age. Esteemed a beauty, she married at sixteen and died in childbed at Ceelys a year later. Her son, Thomas Cary Nelson, survived: from him descend a numerous issue including Nelsons, Pages and Newtons. Her husband was a son of the Secretary; there survives a friendly letter from General Washington (who knew the charm of Cary women) permitting him to resign from the army in order to marry. For the Nelson family, see Page, *Genealogy of the Page Family,* 1893.]

III   Mary Monro, 1764–1836, m. 1787, Wm. Samuel Peachy, of Williamsburg and Flower de Hundred,

[For the Peachy family, see *W. & M. Quar.,* iii, 111.]

IV   Miles, 1766–1774, *o.s.p.,*

[See his obituary in the *Virginia Gazette,* April 21, 1774.]

V   Elizabeth Blair, 1770–1822, m. 1796, Ferdinando Fairfax, 1769–1820, of Fairfax County.

[Ferdinando Fairfax was third son of Bryan, eighth Lord Fairfax, and of Elizabeth Cary⁴. For him and his children see Brockett, *The Lodge of Washington* (1876), 118.]

2nd: 1802, Rebecca, 1755–1823, dau. of the Rev. Thomas Dawson, *s.p.*

[Mr. Dawson was "one of His Majesty's Honourable Council, Commissary for the Lord Bishop of London, President of the College of William and Mary, and minister of Bruton Parish, a man eminently adorned with moderation, meekness, forgiveness, patience and long-suffering" (see his obituary, probably written by his friend Governor Fauquier, in *W. & M. Quar.,* vi, 216; and for a more human picture of him, Tyler, *Williamsburg,* 147.) Commissary Dawson's wife was Priscilla Bassett, of the Eltham family, so that Rebecca Dawson was a descendant of the immigrant Miles Cary.]

SOURCES:

(1) Ceelys family Bible; (2) The *Carysbrook Memoir MS.;* (3) the will of Colonel Wilson-Miles Cary, in *Appendix;* (4) Other family papers and correspondence of that generation in *W. M. Cary Notes;* (5) Gleanings from public records, newspapers; Bishop Meade, *Old Churches,* etc.; Hawks, *The Church in Virginia,* 1836, etc.

WILSON JEFFERSON CARY
1784–1823

V. WILSON CARY (*Wilson-Miles⁴*, *Wilson³*, *Miles², Miles¹*), 1760–1793, of Richneck.

William and Mary College 1775. He lived out his life at Richneck and was J. P. 1785–1793 and High Sheriff for Warwick 1792. He sat in the House of Delegates 1786–87 and, never of robust health, died prematurely, at the beginning of what promised to be a useful career, as he was reputed a man of unusual parts and scholarship, bred by close and constant study.

He m. 1782, Jean Barbara, 1766–1840, dau. of Dabney Carr, of Louisa, and of Martha Jefferson, sister of Thomas Jefferson,

[It was her father who moved, in 1773, the resolutions for the appointment of inter-colonial Committees of Correspondence, one of the first overt acts of the American Revolution. Thomas Jefferson, who loved him, prepared the inscription which in recent years has been placed on his tomb at Monticello. For the Carr family, see *Va. Mag.*, ii, 221, and *W. & M. Quar.*, vi, 106, 130. There is copious material for a genealogy of the Carrs in the *W. M. Cary Notes.*]

and by her had:

I   Wilson Jefferson, 1784, of Carysbrook, see p. 112,

II   Miles, 1786, d. *infans,*

III Sally, 1788–1841, m. 1806, William Newsum, 1785–1828, of Norfolk,

[William Newsum was a brilliant student at William and Mary College and began his career at the Norfolk bar, and in the House of Delegates for Norfolk borough 1806–1808. In 1812 he served as Captain, U. S. A., subsequently establishing himself on Cary lands, at "Greenwood" in King and Queen County, whence again he went to the House of Delegates in 1816. Finally in 1823 he migrated with his family to the Southwest and set up, in the Virginia tradition, a plantation known as "Longwood" in Maury County, Tenn. As happened so often in such migrations at the time, the cultivation of new land bred fevers which, almost at once, swept away most of his children and soon claimed him. His wife, and her mother, who had gone out to join them, survived at Long-

wood many years. There are Skipwith and other descendants of
this family in the Southwest. For the Newsum immigrant see
Va. Mag., iv, 429.]

IV   Miles, 1789, of Oakhill, Fluvanna
County, see p. 121,

V   Jane Blair, 1791–1805, unmarried,

[See her obituary in the *Virginia Gazette*, July 24, 1805.]

VI   Martha Carr, 1792, d. *infans.*

SOURCES:

(1) Ceelys family Bible; (2) The *Carysbrook Memoir MS.;* (3)
Gleanings from contemporary public records, correspondence, newspapers, etc., in *W. M. Cary Notes.*

VI. WILSON JEFFERSON CARY (*Wilson⁵, Wilson-Miles⁴, Wilson³, Miles², Miles¹*), 1784–1823, of Carysbrook.

He was born at Richneck; educated at William and Mary College, 1803; studied law at Richmond in the office of his kinsman
the brilliant and unfortunate Edmund Randolph, and was admitted
to the bar. He undermined his health by exposure at a military camp
during the War of 1812, and succeeded to his grandfather's estate
in 1817 under a heavy burden of inherited debt, all of which colored his life. Having a certain characteristic aloofness from popular
contact, he eschewed public life, although he was the largest landholder in Fluvanna and bred in the tradition of such occupations.
He went to the Assembly much against his will for two terms,
1821–23, at the request of his uncle Mr. Jefferson, to assist in pro-
moting legislation in aid of the University of Virginia. He was at
all times a staunch supporter of Mr. Jefferson's politics, despite his
grandfather's disapproval, and in 1815 engaged in a political con-
troversy with his kinsman John Randolph of Roanoke which was
expected to result in an affair of honor. See his spirited card in
the Richmond *Enquirer* newspaper, April 1, 1815. He and his
brother Miles were the pillars of the Episcopal Church in Fluvanna
(Bishop Meade, *Old Churches,* etc., ii, 40). An enlightened and
progressive agriculturist, he was an active member of the Albemarle
Agricultural Society and diligently sought, by experiments in stock-
breeding, to combat the economic depression into which Virginia
tobacco and grain farming had fallen in his day; but in that re-

PRIVATE RANDOLPH FAIRFAX, C.S.A.
1842–1862

spect he was in advance of his generation. He was J. P. for
Fluvanna until his death, and conscientiously sat in the County
Court. He died prematurely from a malady contracted in the
course of that duty, and is buried in the Jefferson graveyard at
Monticello, beside his maternal grandfather Dabney Carr.

He m. 1805, Virginia, 1786–1852, youngest
dau. of Colonel Thomas Mann Randolph, 1740–
1793, of Tuckahoe (a granddaughter of Archibald Cary⁴),

["She was a lady of superior intellect, and many of her produc-
tions both in prose and verse have had extensive circulation during
the last thirty years." See her obituary in the *National Intelli-
gencer*, May 5, 1852. Her best known book was *Letters on Female
Character*, 1828, but she was the author also of two novels, *Mutius*
and *Ruth Churchill*, as well as a *Christian Parent's Assistant*.
Her father played a leading part in the Revolution in Virginia as
member of the Convention of 1776 and the Colonial Committee of
Safety. For him, his son and grandson in public life see *Appletons'
Cyclo. Am. Biog.*, v, 173, and, in relation to Thomas Jefferson,
Randolph, *Domestic Life of Thomas Jefferson*, 1871.]

and by her had:

I Wilson Miles, 1806, of Baltimore, see
    p. 115,

II Jane Blair, 1808–1888, m. 1831, Rev.
     Edward Dunlap Smith, of New York,

[Dr. Smith was a native of Philadelphia, and met his wife while
a student at the University of Virginia. As a preacher he created
a sensation in Virginia: tradition described him as "a vivid pulpit
orator." A congressional chaplain for some years in Washington,
he removed to New York in 1853 and became pastor of the Chelsea
Presbyterian Church in West Twenty-second Street, and there his
wife lived the remainder of her life. One of her sons, Archibald
Cary Smith (1837–1911), was distinguished as a marine architect
and designer of racing yachts. See the memoir of him in the New
York *Sun*, December 9, 1911.]

III Mary Randolph, 1811–1887, m. 1829,
      Dr. Orlando Fairfax, 1806–1882, of
      Alexandria and Richmond,

[113]

[Orlando Fairfax was brother to the wife of his own wife's brother, Archibald Cary. Mary Randolph Cary's eldest son, Randolph Fairfax (1842–1862), was killed in action at the battle of Fredericksburg, a private in the Rockbridge Artillery of the famous "Stonewall Brigade" C. S. A., which, with other students at the University of Virginia, he had joined in August, 1861. Dr. Philip Slaughter then wrote a memoir of him, based on his letters to his mother from the field, of which 10,000 copies were distributed through the Confederate army at the expense of General R. E. Lee, General J. E. B. Stuart, General Fitzhugh Lee and other officers, in two editions, as a stimulating tract upon the Christian soldier; this was enlarged and republished in 1878. It contains unusual testimonies to his moral force by Randolph Fairfax's comrades and officers. Speaking of the descendants of William Randolph of Turkey Island, a company which includes Thomas Jefferson, Edmund Randolph, John Marshall and Robert E. Lee, Dr. Slaughter said later (Wyndham Robertson, *Pocahontas and Her Descendants*, 1887) that Randolph Fairfax "was (considering the brevity of his career) morally and physically one of the most beautiful branches of this remarkable family tree." He is the eponymous hero of the Fairfax Society at the Episcopal High School, Alexandria, Va.]

IV   Anne Martha, 1813–1822, unmarried,

V   Archibald, 1815, of Cumberland, Md., see p. 119,

VI   Ellen Randolph, 1817–1901, unmarried,

VII   Patsey Jefferson, 1820–1873, m. 1842, Gouverneur Morris, 1813–1888, of Morrisania, New York,

[This Gouverneur Morris was the son of the Revolutionary statesman of the same name (1752–1816) who had married, 1809, Anne Cary Randolph, daughter of Thomas Mann Randolph, of Tuckahoe, and sister of Virginia Randolph Cary. For the Morris family see *Appletons' Cyclo. Am. Biog.*, iv, 414; Sparks, *Memoirs of Gouverneur Morris*, 1832; Theodore Roosevelt, *Gouverneur Morris*, 1888; Anne Cary Morris, *Diary and Letters of Gouverneur Morris*, 1888.]

VIII   Sally Newsum, 1822, d. *infans,*

IX   Louisa Hartwell, 1823, d. *infans.*

WILSON MILES CARY
OF BALTIMORE
1806–1877

SOURCES:

(1) The *Carysbrook Memoir MS.* by his eldest daughter; (2) The will of Wilson Jefferson Cary in *Appendix* and the papers on the settlement of his estate in Fluvanna records.

VII. Colonel WILSON MILES CARY (*Wilson-Jefferson6*, *Wilson5*, *Wilson-Miles4*, *Wilson3*, *Miles2*, *Miles1*), 1806–1877, of Carysbrook and Baltimore.

Born at Williamsburg, he went from Hampden-Sidney to William and Mary College, 1824, and thence to the first session of the University of Virginia, 1825, where his career was cut short by an affair of honor with one of the instructors. He subsequently studied law at Chancellor Henry St. George Tucker's law school at Winchester. Captain of militia in Fluvanna. After his marriage he lived for some years in Charlottesville, where he practised law and, like his father a staunch Democrat of the Jefferson School, edited the *Virginia Advocate* newspaper, opposing the current political doctrine of nullification (*Va. Mag.*, viii, 339, and ix, 132). When Carysbrook was sold some years after his father's death he removed to "Haystack," Baltimore County, Md., 1835, and sat in the Maryland State Senate 1846–1852. Later he was for a time Clerk of the Court of Common Pleas, and of the County Court for Baltimore County, etc. His wife and daughters maintained for many years the Southern Home School in Baltimore.

He m. 1831, Jane Margaret, 1809–1903, third dau. of Peter Carr, of Albemarle,

[She was a great-niece of Thomas Jefferson and grew up at Monticello, under the education of the ex-President, whose methods of training children she projected, during more than sixty years, upon the girls who attended her school; but it is clear that her own strong and sweet character was the potent and enduring influence. For her father, Peter Carr, and his brothers in Albemarle see Kennedy, *Life of William Wirt* (1849), i, 69 ff., and Randall, *Life of Thomas Jefferson* (1857), i, 84, 435.]

and by her had:

1 Sarah Nicholas, 1832–1893, m. 1855, James Howard McHenry, 1820–1888,

of "Sudbrook," Baltimore County, Md.,

[James Howard McHenry was grandson of (1) James McHenry (1753–1816), an immigrant from the north of Ireland to Philadelphia, afterwards of Baltimore, who served in the Continental Army as surgeon and later as Secretary to General Washington, and in 1796 was Secretary of War in Washington's Cabinet; Fort McHenry in Baltimore harbour is named for him; and (2) of that sterling soldier Colonel John Eager Howard (1752–1827) of Maryland, who won a Congressional medal of honor at the battle of Cowpens, 1781. For them see *Appletons' Cyclo. Am. Biog.,* iv, 121, and iii, 277.]

II   Virginia, 1833, d. *infans,*
III Hetty, 1836–1892, m. *1st:* 1865, General John Pegram, 1832–1865, C. S. A.

[She was a brilliant figure in the society of Richmond during the Confederacy, about whom many traditions and anecdotes survive. See the contemporary memoirs, as cited *infra* for her cousin and companion Constance Cary, and her own obituary in the Baltimore *Sun* newspaper, September 29, 1892. For General Pegram and the Pegram family, see Hayden, *Virginia Genealogies,* 314.]

2nd: 1879, Professor H. Newell Martin, 1848–1897, of Johns Hopkins University.

[For him, see *Proceedings of the Royal Society,* vol. 60, xx.]

IV   Virginia Randolph, 1837, d. *infans,*
V   Wilson-Miles, 1838–1914, of Baltimore, *o.s.p.,*

[Born at "Haystack," Baltimore County, Md., he was educated at the University of Virginia, 1857; Captain and Major in the Quartermaster Department, C. S. A. Admitted to the Baltimore bar after the war between the States, he served for some years as Clerk of the Criminal Court of Baltimore, but soon became a professional genealogist, the *W. M. Cary Notes* on his own family being but one of many such monuments of his industry and ingenuity in re-

HETTY CARY

MRS. JOHN PEGRAM

RICHMOND, 1865

search. Much of his best work was done in England. He never married. See a sympathetic notice of him in *Va. Mag.*, xxiii, 33. He is buried with his father and mother at St. Thomas Church, Garrison Forest, Baltimore County, Maryland. The M.I is:

> ### WILSON-MILES CARY
> eldest son of Wilson-Miles Cary
> and of Jane Margaret Carr, his wife,
> Born December 12, 1838,
> Died August 28, 1914.
> A native of Maryland, of Virginian lineage,
> he commenced life a Confederate soldier,
> and ended it a ripe and learned scholar.
> *"Esse, quam videri, bonus malebat."*]

VI   John Brune, 1840, of Baltimore, see p. 117,

VII   Jane Margaret, 1843–, unmarried,

[She it was who wedded the words of Randall's "Maryland, My Maryland" to the old college air of "Lauriger Horatius" and first sang before the Army of Northern Virginia a war song whose echoes have not died. As an educator in the Southern Home School in Baltimore she was an able second to her mother.]

VIII   Sydney Carr, 1845, of Baltimore, see p. 118.

SOURCES:
(1) The Haystack family Bible; (2) The *W. M. Cary Notes.*

VIII.   JOHN BRUNE CARY (*Wilson-Miles[7], Wilson-Jefferson[6], Wilson[5], Wilson-Miles[4], Wilson[3], Miles[2], Miles[1]*), 1840–1917, of Baltimore.

Born at "Haystack," Baltimore County, Md., he began life with service in the First Maryland Cavalry, C. S. A. Merchant in Richmond and Baltimore, with interludes of ranching in Colorado and of town development at Middlesboro, Kentucky. He maintained in a modern world the traditional dignity of the Old Virginia Gentleman. His sterling character, his sweetness and gentleness of disposition made him beloved by all who knew him. He is buried with his family at Garrison Forest, Baltimore County, Md.

[117]

He m. 1867, Frances Eugenia, 1841–1909, youngest dau. of William S. Daniel, of Jefferson, and by her had:

I   Jane Margaret, 1869, d. *infans,*

II   Hetty, 1871–, m. 1894, Fairfax Harrison, of Belvoir, Fauquier County, Va.,

III   Katherine Daniel, 1874–, m. 1895, J. A. Ulman, of Baltimore,

IV   Ellen Buchanan, 1876–, m. *1st:* 1902, F. M. Burbank, of Baltimore, and *2nd:* Dr. Philip Kingsnorth Gilman, of San Francisco,

V   Jane Margaret, 1878–, m. 1899, Charles Ridgely White, of Baltimore,

VI   Wilson-Miles, 1880, of Baltimore, see p. 119,

VII   Frances Daniel, 1884–, m. 1912, William Hamilton Lawrence, of Manila, P. I.

SOURCES:
The *W. M. Cary Notes.*

VIII. SYDNEY CARR CARY (*Wilson-Miles[7], Wilson-Jefferson[6], Wilson[5], Wilson-Miles[4], Wilson[3], Miles[2], Miles[1]*), 1845–1896, of Baltimore.

Merchant in Baltimore.

He m. 1885, Pauline, d. 1887, dau. of William H. Playford, of Uniontown, Pa., and by her had:

CAPTAIN WILSON-MILES CARY, C.S.A.
1838–1914

I   Gwendolen, 1887–, m. 1907, Francis Potter, of New York.

SOURCES:
The *W. M. Cary Notes.*

IX. WILSON MILES CARY (*John Brune[8]*, *Wilson-Miles[7]. Wilson-Jefferson[6],Wilson[5],Wilson-Miles[4], Wilson[3], Miles[2], Miles[1]*), 1880–, of Baltimore.

Manufacturer in Baltimore.

He m. 1903, Helen Snowden Lanahan, of Baltimore, and by her has:

I   Anne Snowden, 1904–,
II Wilson Miles, 1906–.

SOURCES:
The *W. M. Cary Notes.*

THE CUMBERLAND BRANCH

VII. ARCHIBALD CARY (*Wilson-Jefferson[6], Wilson[5], Wilson-Miles[4], Wilson[3], Miles[2], Miles[1]*), 1815–1854, of Cumberland, Maryland.

Born at Carysbrook, he was educated at the University of Virginia 1835, and subsequently renewed his study of law at Transylvania University (Lexington, Ky.). He early reverted from the Democratic politics of his father and brother to the Federal principles of his great grandfather, as developed in the "American System." Practised law at Port Gibson, Miss., where he edited the *Port Gibson Correspondent* newspaper. Returned to Virginia to recuperate from yellow fever 1844, and engaged in literary campaigning for Henry Clay and the Whig party. Removed to Cumberland, Maryland, and there edited the *Civilian* newspaper until his death. He was the author of a number of serious studies in criticism and history, in addition to the steady grind of writing "leaders" for his newspapers. He is buried with his wife's family at Ivy Hill Cemetery, near Alexandria, Va.

He m. 1838, Monimia, 1820–1875, youngest dau. of Thomas, ninth Lord Fairfax, of Vaucluse, Fairfax County,

[This was the fifth recorded marriage between these two families —one in England, four in Virginia. For Thomas, Lord Fairfax, eldest son of Bryan and of Elizabeth Cary⁴, see his obituary in the *London Magazine*, 1846.]

and by her had:

I Falkland, 1840–1856, *o.s.p.,*

[Like his cousin Randolph Fairfax, Falkland Cary was a youth of distinguished physical beauty and unusual precocity of character, and, like him again, died prematurely.]

II Constance, 1843–, m. 1867, Burton Norvell Harrison, 1838–1904, of New York,

[For her part in the Confederacy, see John S. Wise, *The End of an Era;* Mrs. Clay, *A Belle of the Fifties;* Mrs. Chesnut, *A Diary from Dixie;* Cooper de Leon, *Belles, Beaux and Brains of the Sixties,* and her own *Recollections Grave and Gay.* For the record of her fertile literary production from 1880 to 1911, see *Who's Who,* 1916. For Burton Harrison and his family in Virginia and New Orleans, see *The Harrisons. of Skimino,* 1910.]

III Clarence, 1845, of New York, see p. 120.

SOURCES:

(1) Archibald Cary's entries in his MS. *Cary Book;* (2) His will (in *Appendix*), diaries and correspondence; (3) His daughter's *Recollections Grave and Gay,* 1911.

VIII. CLARENCE CARY (*Archibald⁷, Wilson-Jefferson⁶, Wilson⁵, Wilson-Miles⁴, Wilson³, Miles², Miles¹*), 1845–1911, of New York.

[120]

ARCHIBALD CARY
OF CUMBERLAND, MD.
1815–1854

Born at his maternal grandfather's house, "Vaucluse," Fairfax County, Va., he was at 16 present at the first battle of Bull Run as a "marker" for a Virginia regiment; later he was commissioned Midshipman, C. S. N., and saw adventurous deep sea service in the Confederate cruiser *Chicamauga,* blockade running and commerce destroying; later, while attached to the *Palmetto State* ironclad, he was cited for gallantry at the defense of Fort Fisher, N. C., January, 1865. Removed to New York, 1867, and there practised law the remainder of his life, with excursions of extended travel. He had a genius of friendship. His diversions were the production of occasional verse, and the study of languages, in the course of which he published two essays in elucidation of Horace. He was the author also of two economic studies growing out of his professional employments in the Orient, viz.: *China's Present and Prospective Railways,* 1899, and *The Trans-Siberian Route,* 1902. He is buried with the Fairfaxes at Ivy Hill Cemetery, Alexandria, Va.

He m. 1878, Elizabeth Miller, dau. of Howard Potter, of New York,

[For the Potter family, which has distinguished itself in several vocations, but chiefly in the Church, see *Appletons' Cyclo. Am. Biog.,* v., 86.]

and by her had:

   I   Guy Fairfax, 1879–, Harvard, 1902, of the New York bar, etc.,

  II Howard, 1881–1906, *o.s.p.*

SOURCES:

(1) His MS. naval diary, now on file in the Navy Department, Washington, which had the distinction of being quoted by Chief Justice Cockburn in his opinion in the Geneva arbitration, and contributed a gleam of humour to that solemn proceeding. (2) His sister's *Recollections Grave and Gay.*

THE OAKHILL BRANCH

VI.   Colonel MILES CARY (*Wilson⁵, Wilson-Miles⁴, Wilson³, Miles², Miles¹*), 1789–1827, of Oakhill, Fluvanna County.

Educated at William and Mary College, 1803. A portion of the Carysbrook estate, lying on the north side of Rivanna, was set apart for him and called "Oakhill." He was J. P. for Fluvanna, and sat in the House of Delegates 1816–17. Colonel of militia. He died in Alabama while exploring the Southwest for an intended migration.

He m. 1810, Elizabeth Scarsbrooke Wilson, 1792–1830, dau. of Colonel Wilson Curle, of Elizabeth City,

[For the Curles of Elizabeth City, who were (apparently) descended, like the Carys, from Col. William Wilson, of Hampton, see *W. & M. Quar.*, ix, 125, and Brock in *Spotswood Papers*, i, 32.]

and by her had:

I   Virginia Randolph, 1812–1841, m. 1836, Lieutenant Grey Skipwith, U. S. N.,

II   Miles, 1814, of Carysbrook, De Soto County, Mississippi, see p. 123,

III   Lucius Falkland, 1815, of Williamsburg, see p. 124,

IV   William Wallace, 1818–1839, *o.s.p.*, in Arkansas,

V   Elizabeth Curle, 1819–1841, m. 1840, Rev. P. W. Alston, of Memphis, Tenn.,

VI   Sally Newsum, 1821, m. 1841, Dr. Stephen Cooke, of Arkansas,

VII   Mary Jane, 1823–1898, m. 1846, Henry D. Small of Memphis,

VIII   Octavia Wilson, 1825, d. *infans*,

VI. *Miles Cary*

VII *Lucius Falkland Cary*

VIII. *Hunsdon Cary*

Wilson Miles Cary

IX. *Rheafflery*

Hunsdon Cary

Lucius F. Cary

AUTOGRAPHS OF THE OAKHILL CARYS
The numerals indicate generations

IX   Octavius, 1827–1849, of De Soto County, Miss., *o.s.p.*, of wound received in Mexican war,

X   Wilson-Jefferson, 1828, d. *infans*.

SOURCES:
(1) Archibald Cary's *Cary Book*, 1844; (2) The *Carysbrook Memoir MS.;* (3) L. F. Cary's family Bible.

VII. MILES CARY (*Miles[6], of Oakhill, Wilson[5], Wilson-Miles[4], Wilson[3], Miles[2], Miles[1]*), 1814–1843, of Carysbrook, DeSoto County, Mississippi.

Migrated to the Southwest, 1835. One of the early planters in the Choctaw Purchase.

He m. 1839, Susan, dau. of William W. Wheateley, of Memphis, and by her had:

I   Lucius Fairfax, 1840, d. *infans,*

II   Hunsdon, 1842, of Memphis, see p. 123,

III   Susan Miles, 1844–1917, m. 1867, John Baynton Abercrombie, of Memphis.

SOURCES:
Statement of Hunsdon Cary[8], of Memphis, 1914, in *W. M. Cary Notes.*

VIII. HUNSDON CARY (*Miles[7], Miles[6], of Oakhill, Wilson[5], Wilson-Miles[4], Wilson[3], Miles[2], Miles[1]*), 1842–, of Memphis, Tennessee.

Adjutant 3rd Mississippi Infantry, C. S. A. Severely wounded at battle of Shiloh, 1862. Subsequently of the Tennessee bar.

He m. 1866, Ellen Preston, dau. of Matthew

[123]

Rhea, of Fayette County, Tennessee, and by her had:

I   Miles Fairfax, 1867–, unmarried, of Memphis,

II   Rhea Preston, son, 1871–, of the Memphis bar, m. 1893, Charlie Ewing, of Memphis, *s.p.,*

III Elinor Marion, 1884–, m. 1905, Samuel Ernest Ragland, of Memphis,

IV Hunsdon Fairfax, 1889–, dau., m. 1913, Fayette Clay Ewing, Jr., of St. Louis.

SOURCES:

Statement of Hunsdon Cary⁸, of Memphis, 1914, in *W. M. Cary Notes.*

THE WILLIAMSBURG BRANCH

VII. LUCIUS FALKLAND CARY (*Miles⁶, of Oakhill, Wilson⁵, Wilson-Miles⁴, Wilson³, Miles², Miles¹*), 1815–1845, of Williamsburg.

He was a merchant in Williamsburg and one of the leading men of his time in eastern Virginia. He was on a visit to his elder brother when the latter died, and, staying on to settle the estate, died also in Mississippi.

He m. 1835, Lucy, 1819–1900, dau. of Leonard Henley, of Williamsburg,

[For the Henley family, see *W. & M. Quar.,* i, 151, v, 38.]

and by her had:

I   Harriet, 1838–, m. 1868, William Christian, of Henrico,

[For the Christian family, see *W. & M. Quar.,* v, viii and ix, *passim.,* and Wise, *Seven Decades of the Union,* 59.]

CONSTANCE CARY
MRS. BURTON HARRISON
PARIS, 1867

II Wilson Miles, 1843, of Richmond, see
p. 125,
III Lucy Falkland, 1845–1848.

SOURCES:
Statement of Colonel W. Miles Cary[8], of Richmond, 1914, in *W. M. Cary Notes.*

VIII. Colonel WILSON MILES CARY (*Lucius-Falkland[7], Miles[6], of Oakhill, Wilson[3], Miles[2], Miles[1]*), 1843–1919, of Richmond.

Born in Mississippi but early brought to Virginia, he was at William and Mary College at the outbreak of the war between the States and at once joined the Williamsburg Company, Thirty-second Virginia Infantry, C. S. A., with which he saw service from Bethel to Appomattox. Merchant in Richmond (Sublett & Cary) until 1895, when he acquired John Randolph's plantation "Roanoke" in Charlotte County: there he resided until 1905, and then once more established himself in Richmond. He served on the staffs of Governors Fitzhugh Lee and McKinney, and always took part in Confederate reunions. He was an ardent sportsman, expert and active with rod and gun to the very end of his life. He is buried in Hollywood Cemetery, Richmond.

He m.,

1st: 1869, Ann Eliza, 1846–1875, dau. of John T. Sublett, of Powhatan and Richmond, and by her had:

I John Falkland, 1870, d. *infans,*
II Hunsdon, 1872, of Richmond, see p. 126,
III Emily Sampson, 1873–, m. 1901, Thomas Marshall, Jr., of Richmond.

2nd: 1878, Lilias Blair, dau. of J. B. Mc-Phail, of Charlotte,

[In a letter of 1868 among the *W. M. Cary Notes,* her uncle Hugh Blair Grigsby, the historian, wrote: "I derive the name of Blair

and by her had:

IV   Lucius Falkland, 1879, of Richmond, see p. 127,

see p. 127,

V   Lilias Blair, 1881–, m. 1917, the Rev. Thomas King Currie, of Augusta, Ga.

SOURCES:

(1) Statement of Colonel W. M. Cary[8], of Richmond, 1919; (2) His obituary in the Richmond *News-Leader*, April 28, 1919.

IX. HUNSDON CARY (*Wilson-Miles[8], Lucius Falkland[7], Miles[6], of Oakhill, Wilson[5], Wilson-Miles[4], Wilson[3], Miles[2], Miles[1]*), 1872–, of Richmond.

Educated V. M. I., 1892; Massachusetts Institute of Technology, 1892–93; University of Virginia, 1894–96; admitted to the Richmond bar, 1896; Richmond City Council, 1906–1908; saw military service in the mobilization for the war with Spain, 1898, and, remaining in the militia, was Major, First Virginia Infantry, 1910. Practising lawyer.

He m., 1908, Mary, dau. of George Douglas Miller, of Albany, N. Y., and by her has:

I   Hunsdon, 1909,

II   Wilson Miles, 1910,

III   George Douglas, 1912,

IV   Anne de Peyster, ⎫ 1914,

V   Mary,   ⎭

VI   Helen Franchot Douw, 1916.

SOURCES:

Statement of Hunsdon Cary[9], of Richmond, 1918.

MIDSHIPMAN CLARENCE CARY, C.S.N.
1845–1911

IX.   LUCIUS FALKLAND CARY (*Wilson-Miles^8, Lucius-Falkland^7, Miles^6, of Oakhill, Wilson^5, Wilson-Miles^4, Wilson^3, Miles^2, Miles^1*), 1879–, of Richmond.

Educated at Hampden Sidney and the University of Virginia. Of the Richmond bar.

He m., 1910, Alma Miller, dau. of the Rev. Russell H. Cecil, of Richmond, and by her has:

I   Lucius Falkland, Jr., 1911,
II   Cecil, 1913, d. *infans,*
III   Elizabeth Cecil, 1917.

SOURCES:
Statement of Lucius F. Cary^9, of Richmond, 1918.

CHAPTER SEVEN

SKIFFS CREEK AND PRINCE EDWARD

The immigrant's youngest son, "the miller," was established on a plantation[1] his father had acquired on the north end of Mulberry Island at the mouth of Skiffs Creek. His grandson, responding to the lure of a broader boundary, migrated to new lands in Prince Edward, where his descendants have since been seated. A younger branch of this family lived for one

[1] *The Skiffs Creek Plantation.* The northwestern boundary of Warwick County, dividing it from James City, was in 1643 defined as "Kethe's Creek" (*Hening,* i, 249), but has long been called "Skiffs" Creek. It is believed to have derived its name from the Rev. George Keth (or Keith) who was a minister in Virginia as early as 1617. (*Va. Mag.,* iii, 279.) In 1628 Lieutenant Thomas Flint, an ancient planter, patented 1000 acres "on the southern shore of Warwick River . . . adjoining next upon the ground granted by patent unto John Rolf, Esqre"; and thereafter, until 1647, represented the community in the Assembly. (*Va. Mag.,* i, 445.) In his will the immigrant Miles Cary devised to his youngest son the "land which lyeth up Warwick River formerly belonging unto Capt. Thomas Flint and since purchased by mee." The surviving records indicate that William Cary[2] was involved in litigation with the Flint heirs about this land, and died seized of 360 acres "at the mouth of Skiffs Creek." (*Hening,* viii, 34.) We can only conjecture that this was acquired in compromise with the Flints as it does not seem to fit the description of the Flint patent of 1628 or of Miles Cary's will. The property passed to Allen Jones in 1764, when William Cary's grandson moved to Prince Edward.

MARTHA CARY
MRS. EDWARD JAQUELIN OF JAMESTOWN
FLORUIT, 1706

generation in Prince George and another in York before it became extinct in 1805.

II. Lieutenant-Colonel WILLIAM CARY (*Miles*[1]), 1657?–1713, of Skiffs Creek, Mulberry Island, Warwick.

Inherited under his father's will the Skiffs Creek plantation on Mulberry Island. From his will it appears that he was one of the proprietors of "Warwick River Mill." J. P., Captain, Major and Lieutenant-Colonel for Warwick. Sheriff 1709. Burgess 1692, 1693, 1698, 1700–1713. He made an interesting holographic will in 1711 at a time when he expected to risk his life in active military service against the French and Indian invasions of the colony, which were then anticipated. See *Spotswood Papers*, i, 119, ii, 9, and Campbell, *History of Virginia*, ch. xlix.

He m., 1683, Martha, dau. of Lieutenant-Colonel John Scarisbrook, of York,

[For the marriage see York *O.B.* vi, 539. For the Scarisbrook or Scarsbrooke family see *ante*, p. 87, and *W. & M. Quar.*, xxiv, 200.]

and by her had:

I Harwood, 1685?, of Skiffs Creek, see p. 130,

II Martha, m. 1706, Edward Jaquelin, of Jamestown,

[For the Jaquelin family, see Bishop Meade, *Old Churches*, i, 103, and *W. & M. Quar.*, v, 50. For the wide distribution of the Cary blood and name, through this marriage, among the Amblers, Moncures and their kin, see Pecquet du Bellet, *Some Prominent Virginia Families.*]

III Miles, 1698?–*post* 1711, *o.s.p.*,

[There is no record which can be interpreted as applying to him other than the mention in his father's will as not of age in 1711, with provision that the lands in York provided for Miles should descend to his brother William in case of Miles' death without heirs. It seems probable that this happened. In his *Cary Tradi-*

[129]

tion (Richmond *Whig*, July, 1852) Anderson Demandville Abraham stated that this Miles Cary married a Jennings and was the father of John Cary, Sr., of Kingston parish, Gloucester (see *post*, p. 150). This statement has since been circulated in several traditional pedigrees, but no evidence has appeared to support it.]

IV   William, 1700?, of Prince George, see p. 138,

V   John, 1701?–*post* 1711, *o.s.p.*

[Named in his father's will as under age in 1711. His brother William refers in his will, 1742, to his inheritance of John's estate, in terms effectually to dispose of the conjectural identification of this John with the Johns of the Gloucester and York families.]

SOURCES:

(1) The will of William Cary[2], dated August 26, 1711, in *Appendix*, naming the children in the order given, and that of William Cary[3], dated 1742 (Prince George *Will Book*, G, p. 3); (2) Gleanings from public records.

III.   HARWOOD CARY (*William², Miles¹*), 1685?–1721, of Skiffs Creek, Mulberry Island.

He took the name Harwood, which has persisted among his descendants to this day, not in right of blood, but as a compliment to his father's friend Thomas Harwood, of Pocoson parish, in York. The evidence of this is an affidavit of Thomas Harwood in January, 1686, O.S. (York *Order Book*, vii, 250), in which he says: "That I, the said Harwood, amongst other discourse told the said Mr. Finney that if it pleased God I dyed without issue, after my wife's decease William Cary should have my whole estate"; followed by his will in 1700 (York *Will Book*, xi, 345), in which he carried out his promise, naming also William Cary's son Harwood. Harwood Cary[3] was one of the early students at William and Mary College. He may well have been one of the band of youngsters who, in 1704, with the connivance of Governor Nicholson and armed with the gubernatorial pistols, "barred out" the portentous figure of Commissary Blair. See *W. & M. Historical Catalogue*, 1874.

He m., *ante* 1707, Martha, widow of John Thruston, of Martins Hundred,

[The surviving proof of this marriage is an entry in the York records March 14, 1706/7, of an action of debt by "Harwood Cary and Martha, his wife, Exec'x of John Thruston," to collect assets

[130]

of John Thruston, deceased: to which may be added an entry in the account of settlement of Harwood Cary's estate in 1721, of the collection of a debt from "ye estate of Dr. Thruston, dec'd." This John Thruston was the son of Edward Thruston, "Chyrurgeon," as he styles himself, who was in turn one of the numerous family of John Thruston (1596–1675), Chamberlain of Bristol. Dr. Edward Thruston was a wanderer: while in Virginia in 1666 he married a daughter of Thomas Loveing of Martins Hundred. His son John by this marriage married first (1690), in England, Elinor, widow of John Cary, of Somerset, but later returned to Virginia and there evidently married Martha, who was his widow before 1707, when she married Harwood Cary. John Thruston's daughter by his first marriage, born in England, came to Virginia in 1718 to receive her inheritance of her father's Virginia property. See the interesting family book of the Thrustons. (*W. & M. Quar.*, iv, 23, 116, 180.) Started by the Bristol Chamberlain in 1622, it has followed his descendants through their westward migration via Virginia to Kentucky.]

and by her had:

   I William, 1708?, "eldest son and heir," named in *Hening,* viii, 34, see p. 131.

[There is no record of other issue, if any.]

SOURCES:

   (1) Reference to Harwood Cary and Martha, his wife, in *Hening,* viii, 34; (2) The settlement of the estate of Harwood Cary[3] by his brother-in-law, Edward Jaquelin, October 18, 1721, in York *Will Book,* 1720–1729, p. 92; (3) Gleanings from other public records in *W. M. Cary Notes.*

IV. WILLIAM CARY, JR. (*Harwood³, William², Miles¹*), 1708?–1784, of Skiffs Creek, Mulberry Island, and later of Prince Edward.

In 1764 he docked the entail and sold the Skiffs Creek plantation to Allen Jones (*Hening,* viii, 34 and 61, printed twice), with provision that the proceeds should be reinvested under the entail by Archibald Cary and others. From a deed dated May 18, 1786 (Prince Edward *Deed Book,* vii, p. 227), which recites the act of 1764, it appears that the trustees purchased from James Wimbish 540 acres in Prince Edward County, where William Cary reseated himself. The tradition in his family is that William Cary[4] moved first to Buckingham (where his kinsman and trustee Archibald Cary was a large landholder) in 1765 and finally established his family in Prince Edward in 1767.

He m., *ante* 1738, Elizabeth, dau. of Thomas Haynes, of Warwick,

[In his patent of 1657 the immigrant Miles Cary names Thomas Haynes as one of the head rights, in company with his own wife, and his proven kinsman Roger Daniel, so that it is possible that he was also of kin to the Haynes in Bristol. Thomas Haynes appears in the *Virginia Quit Rent Rolls* 1704 as one of the largest land-holders in Warwick, and as J. P. in 1714 (*Va. Mag.*, ii, 13). An-other Thomas Haynes, probably a nephew of this Elizabeth Cary, was a member of the Warwick Committee of Safety in 1774. See *W. & M. Quar.*, v, 250.]

and by her had :

    I   Thomas, 1738, *o.s.p.*,

    II   Martha, 1740, m. Colonel Gee, of North Carolina,

    III   Harwood, 1742, of Prince Edward, see p. 133,

    IV   Mary, 1747, m. Wilds,

    V   William, 1749, d. *infans,*

    VI   Elizabeth, 1752, m. John Bigger. See *W. & M. Quar.*, xxv, 144,

    VII   Andrew Haynes, 1755, *o.s.p.*, a soldier in the Revolutionary army,

[He was allowed a military bounty of 1000 acres in Humphreys County, Tennessee, which is referred to in Prince Edward *Deed Book*, xix, 245.]

    VIII   Edward Jaquelin, 1757, d. *infans,*

    IX   Sarah, 1758, unmarried,

x William Haynes, 1765, of Prince Edward, see p. 133.

SOURCES:

(1) York County records: (a) deed dated August 14, 1740, by William Cary, Jr., and Elizabeth, his wife, to Thomas Haynes, Gent. of Warwick, and (b) the will of Thomas Haynes, proved September 26, 1742, naming among his children his daughter Elizabeth, wife of William Cary, Jr.; (2) The will of William Cary[4], dated and proved March, 1784 (Prince Edward *Will Book*, E, 378); (3) Statement of William Haynes Cary[6], 1904.

V. HARWOOD CARY, SR. (*William[4], Harwood[3], William[2], Miles[1]*), 1742–1825, of Prince Edward.

Planter.

He m. Mary Cardwell (d. 1845), and by her had:

I Elizabeth, d. 1850, m. *ante* 1825, Thomas Harvey,

II William, *o.s.p.*, *ante* 1825, "at the foot of the Cumberland Mountains, in Tennessee."

SOURCES:

(1) Statement of William Haynes Cary[6], 1904; (2) Will of Harwood Cary, Sr., 1825 (Prince Edward *Will Book*, vi, 231); (3) Deeds by children of Elizabeth Cary Harvey[6] to children of William Haynes Cary[5], conveying the entailed lands, 1849 and 1850 (Prince Edward *Deed Book*, xxv, 412, 479).

V. WILLIAM HAYNES CARY (*William[4], Harwood[3], William[2], Miles[1]*), 1765–1852, of Prince Edward.

Planter.

He m.,

1st: Lucy Cardwell, and by her had:

I   Patsey, 1794–*ante* 1848, m. Wyatt Cardwell.

2nd: Esther Jackson, d. 1872, and by her had:

II   Harwood, Jr., 1803, of Prince Edward, see p. 134,
III   Thomas Felix, 1804–1817, *o.s.p.,*
IV   Nancy, 1806, m. Thomas Cardwell,
V   John Randolph, 1808–1827, *o.s.p.,*
VI   William Haynes, Jr., 1818, of Prince Edward, see p. 137.

SOURCES:

(1) Statement of William Haynes Cary[6], 1904; (2) Will of William Haynes Cary[5], dated 1848, in *Appendix;* (3) Will of Esther Jackson Cary, dated 1868, proved 1872 (Prince Edward *Will Book,* xiii, 93).

VI.   HARWOOD CARY, JR. (*William Haynes[5], William[4], Harwood[3], William[2], Miles[1]*), 1803–1853, of Prince Edward.

Planter.

He m.,

1st: Mary McGhee, and by her had:

I   William James, m. Sarah Ann Womack, *o.s.p., ante* 1863,
II   John Thomas, of Kentucky, m. Bathsheba Hall, and left three daughters. He d. *ante* 1904,

III   Martha Ann, 1833–1906, m. Joseph Edward Walton,

IV   Andrew Jackson, d. 1866, of Tennessee, m. Martha Ann Snead, and left a daughter,

V   Mary Elizabeth, *o.s.p.*, 1884,

[She is mentioned in the will of her grandmother Esther Cary, and herself left a will dated October 10, 1883, naming Walton and Calhoun, nieces (proved 1892, Prince Edward *Will Book*, xiv, 595).]

VI   Harwood, 1838?, of Prince Edward, see p. 136,

VII   Sarah Jane, d. 1868, m. James F. Calhoun,

VIII   Miles Haynes, *o.s.p.*, reported missing in C.S.A.,

[He left a will, dated 1863, naming all his brothers and sisters as then living, except William James, which was proved 1866 (Prince Edward *Will Book*, xii, 44).]

IX   Louisa Mildred, d. 1903, m. Horace Noble, of Hamburg, Iowa.

2nd: Mary Cardwell, and by her had:

X   Lucy Wyatt, d. 1918, m. W. T. Johnson,

XI   Emily Susan, unmarried,

XII   Wiltshire Randolph, 1851, of Montgomery County, see p. 136.

SOURCES:

(1) Statements of William Haynes Cary[6], 1904; Wiltshire Randolph Cary[7], 1918, and Mrs. Mattie E. Carter[8], of Darlington Heights, Va., 1919; (2) Settlement by William Haynes Cary[6] and Wiltshire Cardwell of the estate of Harwood Cary[6], 1853–1859 (Prince Edward *Will Book*, x, 417, xi, 27).

VII. HARWOOD CARY (*Harwood⁶, William Haynes⁵, William⁴, Harwood³, William², Miles¹*), 1838?–1890, of Prince Edward.

Farmer.

He m. 1873, Anna M. Thornton, and by her had:

VIII. BERNARD THORNTON CARY, 1878–, of Prince Edward, who m. 1909, Fannie Lillian Gilliam, and by her has:

I   Anna Daniel, 1910,
II Mildred Thornton, 1912,
III William Harwood, 1915.

SOURCES:

(1) Statement of William Haynes Cary⁶, 1904, supplemented by his daughter, Mrs. J. W. Gilliam, of Pamplin, Va., 1918; (2) Prince Edward tax and property transfer books.

VII. WILTSHIRE RANDOLPH CARY (*Harwood⁶, William Haynes⁵, William⁴, Harwood³, William², Miles¹*), 1851–, of Montgomery.

He is J. P. and a farmer living near Blacksburg in Montgomery County, Virginia.

He m. 1882, Emma McCauley, and by her has:

I   Florence Harwood, 1883, m. 1909, Nathan Francis Wells, of Washington, D. C.,
II Jone Patton, 1884–1917,
III Mae Robinson, 1887–, of Washington, D. C.,

IV   Ruth Cardwell, 1888, m. 1915, Henry Bowen Long, of Red Ash, Va.,

V   Thornton Randolph, 1890–, of Wilmore, Kansas,

He m. 1913, Alta Veleria Spencer, and by her has:

    I   David Randolph, 1915–,

   II   Harland, 1916–.

VI   David McCauley, 1892–, of Montgomery,

VII   Eugene McDonald, 1895–, U. S. A. in France, 1918.

SOURCES:
Statement of Wiltshire Randolph Cary[7], 1919.

VI. WILLIAM HAYNES CARY, JR. (*William Haynes[5], William[4], Harwood[3], William[2], Miles[1]*), 1818–1904, of Prince Edward.

Farmer. He was an interesting link with the past. His grandfather was born a subject of Queen Anne, his father of George III; he himself saw the light in the Presidency of Monroe, and lived into that of Roosevelt. The three lives spanned nearly two centuries.

He m. 1845, Betsy Logan Womack, and by her had:

    I   William Lillious, 1846–1918, m. Alice Moore,

[He was a farmer in Kansas and there left sons LILLIOUS, HOLLIS, HOMER and PERCY.]

   II   John Archer, 1847–, m. Anna Sherrille,

[He is a farmer living near Brownsville, Haywood County, Tennessee, and has a son WILLIAM SYDNEY.]

III Sarah Jane, 1849, m. John Frank Rice, of Greensboro, N.C.,

IV Thomas Randolph, 1851, d. *infans,*

V Harwood, 1853–, m. Jennie Holcraft,

[He is a farmer living near Covington, Tipton County, Tennessee, and has sons WILLIAM STEELE, DEWITT FOREST and TWYMAN and several daughters.]

VI Ann Esther, 1855, m. Lillious D. Womack,

VII Betty Logan, 1858, unmarried,

VIII Thomas Cunningham, 1860–1916, of Prince Edward, m. Mary Josephine Walton, *o.s.p.,*

IX Fannie Daniel, 1863, m. John William Gilliam, of Pamplin, Va.,

X Violet Calhoun, 1865, m. R. A. Roane, of Texas,

XI Margaret Lee, 1869, m. Francis J. Scott.

SOURCES:

Statement of William Haynes Cary[6], 1904, supplemented by his daughter, Mrs. J. W. Gilliam, of Pamplin, Va., 1918.

THE PRINCE GEORGE BRANCH

III. WILLIAM CARY (*William²*, *Miles¹*), 1700?–1742, of Bristol parish, Prince George County.

He entered 1800 acres in Prince George in 1738. (*Va. Mag.,* xiv, 29.)

He m. 1724?, Judith Jones,

[The evidence for this marriage is the tradition of it in both the Eggleston and Jones families. This family of Jones is described as originally of Gloucester, but appears in the surviving Warwick records before 1750, perhaps in consequence of the marriage of one of them with Elizabeth Cary[2] (see *supra*, p. 41), who is reputed to be the mother of this Judith Jones, and of Tingnal, Harwood, and Frances. Harwood Jones was J. P. for Warwick in 1768. Tingnal Jones moved from Warwick to Mecklenburg, where he was steward of Colonel William Byrd's Roanoke plantation. See statement of his descendant James Alfred Jones, 1872, in *W. M. Cary Notes*.

The family is still extant in Warwick and Elizabeth City. It has included those locally famous characters the Rev. "Sarvint" Jones and "Hellcat Billy" Jones, who was Clerk of Warwick before and after Reconstruction. The Allen Jones who in 1764 acquired the Skiffs Creek plantation from William Cary[4] (Hening, viii, 34) was doubtless also of this family.]

and by her had:

I Matthew Jaquelin, 1725?–*ante* 1758, *o.s.p.*,

II Martha, 1727?, m. William Goosley, of Yorktown,

[For the Goosley family and descendants of this marriage see *W. & M. Quar.*, vii, 39.]

III Judith, 1729–1773, m. William Eggleston, of Locust Grove, in Amelia,

IV Elizabeth, 1731, m. Joseph Eggleston, of Egglestetten, in Amelia,

[For the Eggleston family and their distribution of Cary blood in Indiana and New York, see Bishop Meade, *Old Churches*, etc., ii, 20; Goode, *Virginia Cousins*, 279; *Appletons' Cyclo. Am. Biog.*, ii, 315. Cf. also *Va. Mag.*, vi, 192.]

V William, 1732, of Yorktown, see p. 140,

VI Miles, 1735–*ante* 1758, *o.s.p.*,

VII Mary, 1741–1767, unmarried.

SOURCES:

(1) Will of William Cary[3], dated April 3, 1742, proved September 14, 1742 (Prince George *Will Book*, G, p. 3); (2) Statement of Mrs. Judith Cary Eggleston[5] (1760–*circa* 1860), dau. of Judith,

supra, made September 18, 1851, at Egglestetten, in *Eggleston Notes;* (3) Settlement, April 13, 1758, of the estate of the widow of William Cary³, from York records, showing that the sons Matthew Jaquelin and Miles, mentioned in their father's will, were then dead; (4) Chamberlayne, *Bristol Parish Register* (1898), p. 300, showing birth and baptism of Mary Cary in December, 1741; (5) Will of said Mary Cary, proved 1767, in Amelia; (6) Will of William Cary⁴, of Yorktown, proved July 15, 1805 (York *Will Book,* 1783–1811, p. 678).

IV. WILLIAM CARY (*William³, William², Miles¹*), 1732–1805, of Yorktown.

He was a merchant in Yorktown and sometime Mayor of the corporation. J. P. for York. Governor L. W. Tazewell remembered him as a character, familiarly known as "Uncle Billy."

He m.,

1st: 1765? . . . Moody, and by her had:

I Miles, 1766?– *ante* 1802, *o.s.p.*

[He was appointed a Notary Public, 1787, and was *second* Sheriff of York, 1801. There is no evidence that he ever married; at all events the fact that his father left all his property to his sisters indicates that this Miles⁵ was dead when his father made his will, and himself left no issue.]

2nd: 1773, Sarah, dau. of John Sheild, of York, and widow of William Dudley, of York,

[See her marriage bond in York, March 15, 1773 (*W. & M. Quar.,* i, 49), and her obituary, *Virginia Enquirer,* November 16, 1811. The son of her first marriage, Major William Dudley, married Hannah, daughter of Judge Richard Cary, of Peartree Hall.]

and by her had:

II Sally, d. unmarried, *ante* 1802.

SOURCES:

(1) Statements of Mrs. Judith Cary Eggleston⁵, and of Governor L. W. Tazewell, 1851, in *Eggleston Notes;* (2) Will of William Cary⁴, dated January 2, 1802, codicil May 1, 1805, proved July 15, 1805, leaving his property to his sisters (York *Will Book,* 1783–1811, p. 678); (3) Gleanings from York records in *W. M. Cary Notes.*

CHAPTER EIGHT

OTHER CARYS IN VIRGINIA

There were in Virginia, in the seventeenth and eighteenth centuries, other Carys than the immigrant Miles and his descendants. Some notes on them are appended.

Francis Cary   In 1649 two cavaliers, Colonel Henry Norwood, afterwards Treasurer of Virginia, and Major Francis Moryson, afterwards deputy Governor and for more than twenty-three years a large figure in the history of the colony, set sail for Virginia in the ship *Virginia Merchant.* After a prolonged and stormy voyage some of the company, including Colonel Norwood, were cast away on an island in Chincoteague Bay on the eastern shore of Maryland. Recording their adventures, Colonel Norwood says (*A Voyage to Virginia,* Force's Historical Tracts, vol. iii) : "Amongst the rest a young gentleman, Mr. Francis Cary by name, was very helpful to me in the fatigue and active part of this undertaking.

He was strong and healthy and was very ready for any employment I could put upon him. He came recommended to me by Sir Edward Thurlan, his genius leading him rather to a planter's life abroad than to any course his friends could propose to him in England: and this rough entrance was like to let him know the worst at first." Later in his discourse Colonel Norwood calls this Francis Cary his "cousin." With the aid of friendly Indians the survivors of Colonel Norwood's party at last made their way to the English settlements in Accomac (Hening, ii, 11; *W. & M. Quar.,* xxii, 53, xxvi, 133) ; but there is no further mention of Francis Cary in Colonel Norwood's narrative after the rescue, nor has other record of him in Virginia appeared. He is tentatively identified as the Francis Cary born 1628, and therefore twenty-one in 1649, the youngest brother of the ruined cavalier Sir Henry Cary, of Cockington. His ultimate fate must have been that assigned generally by Prince (*Worthies of Devon,* 184) to the youngsters of that numerous family. After the forced sale of Cockington in 1654 they are reputed by Devon tradition to have become soldiers of fortune and to have died "without issue beyond sea." This is certainly true of at least one of them, Colonel Theodore Cary, of Jamaica, but of Francis Cary no final record has appeared.

Oswald Cary, of Middlesex The parish register of Christ's Church, Middlesex (which was deposited by Bishop Meade at the Theological Seminary near Alexandria[1]), shows that Oswald Cary and Anne Jackson were there married December 19, 1681, and that he died February 17, 1690/1. Meanwhile, on April 20, 1687, "Mr. Oswald Cary" had patented 460 acres in Middlesex on Pianketank River, adjoining lands he already owned (*Va. Land Register,* vii, 582), and in 1690 bought 50 acres additional, being then described as "Captain Oswald Cary of Co. Middx., Gent." The Middlesex records also show that he was Sheriff of the County in 1690. He had a daughter who married and left Smith descendants in Virginia, but his name has not persisted. (See *W. & M. Quar.,* ix, 45.) A draft, preserved in the Middlesex records, which he drew on James Cary, of London, signed "yor dutiful son," identifies him as "my late sonne Oswell [*sic*] Cary, deceased," named in the will, dated 1694 (P. C. C. *Box,* 343), of James Cary, the founder of the house of Virginia merchants subsequently known as "Robert Cary & Co.," when they were Colonel George Washington's correspondents. This James Cary has been tentatively identified as

---

[1] This important document for Virginia colonial history is now accessible in print, having been copied and edited, in 1907, at the expense of the Colonial Dames of Virginia.

[143]

another brother of Sir Henry Cary, of Cockington, and so of Francis Cary, *supra*.

William Cary, One of the Carys, of Bristol,
of Middlesex who migrated to London during the Commonwealth was
William Cary, who died in 1664, describing himself, in his will (P. C. C. *Hyde*, 12), as "citizen and haberdasher" of Coleman Street. He had several sons, one of whom died a merchant in the Barbadoes in 1685, leaving a will (P. C. C. *Cann,* 96). The eldest is described in his father's and brother's wills as William Cary, "silkman." Before 1689 he disappears from the records in England. (See *ante,* p. 17.)

The records of Middlesex County, Virginia, show a *William Cary*, evidently a substantial planter and merchant, there resident from 1696 to 1702, when his estate was administered by his widow. (*Middlesex O. B., 1699–1705,* p. 509.)

The York records show that in 1647 "Mr. William Cary, of London, merchant," had consigned a cargo of dry-goods to Virginia on commission. Upon this evidence of family interest in the colony and the facts that they had already evinced the emigrant habit, that the "silkman" disappears from the English records, and that the dates fit, we may, pending proof of identity, conjecture tentatively that the

William Cary, of Middlesex in Virginia, was
the eldest son of William Cary, of Coleman
Street, London.

To this William Cary may perhaps be related also the *Thomas Cary,* of the succeeding
generation, who died in Middlesex, December
21, 1720, leaving a comfortable estate. (See
Middlesex parish register under that date, and
Middlesex O. B., 1710–1721, p. 208.)

Other Carys in   We find still other Carys in the
the Rappahan-   records of the Rappahannock
nock Valley   valley counties, who have not
been identified. They were all
apparently of humbler circumstances than those
heretofore named, and may have been related
one to another. They are:

Thomas Cary, imported as a servant by Major
Ralph Langley, of York, who in 1673 was ad-
judged to be 15 years of age and bound to serve
until he was 24. (*York O. B.,* v, 47.)

John Cary, imported as a servant by Captain
Richard Willis, of Middlesex, and by him de-
clared as a headright in 1699. (*Middlesex
O. B.,* 1694–1705, p. 280.)

John Cary, who, in 1732, was overseer for
"King" Carter on his Totuskey Quarter planta-
tion in Richmond County. (Inventory of the
Estate of Robert Carter, *Va. Mag.,* vii, 67.)

John Cary, who, in 1783, is recorded to have

[145]

owned one slave in Spotsylvania County. (*Va. Mag.*, iv, 105.)

John Cary, who on August 23, 1785, married Elizabeth Williams in Lancaster County. (*W. & M. Quar.*, xii, 181.)

Richard Cary, of Gloucester On July 27, 1635, a number of young men bound for Virginia on the ship *Primrose,* Captain Douglass, took the oaths of allegiance and supremacy at Gravesend. Among them was "Richard Cary, aet. 17" (*N. E. Hist & Gen. Register* (1850) iv, 189). He may well have been the same Richard Cary who, on October 13, 1653, patented 1350 acres of land in Gloucester County, Virginia. In 1662 this last named Richard joined one George Seaton in taking out a patent to 6000 acres on the Potomac in Westmoreland (afterwards Stafford) County, not far from the 3000 acres which Miles Cary of Warwick had patented in the same county in 1654. He left a will dated November 29, 1682, in which he named two sons, Richard and John. (The will is lost with the Gloucester records, but there is a recital of so much of it in a Fitzhugh deed of 1759 relating to the 6000-acre patent, which deed is calendared in *Va. Mag.,* ii, 280.)

The elder of these sons, Richard, sold in November, 1698, his interest in the Stafford land to William Fitzhugh, and in 1702 died in Kingston parish, Gloucester, where his widow, Margaret Bronaugh, administered upon his estate, as appears from a power of attorney from Margaret Cary to her brother David Bronaugh, which was recorded in Richmond County in 1704 (*W. M. Cary Notes*).

The younger son, John, left a son, John Cary, Jr., "of the County of Gloucester, gentleman," who (as appears from the aforesaid Fitzhugh deed of 1759) entered upon 1000 acres of the Stafford land in tail, and in 1752, having first docked the entail, sold the said 1000 acres to William Fitzhugh, grandson of the grantee of his uncle Richard. The act to dock the entail is not preserved in Hening and we have no further proof for this family.

It is possible (see *ante*, p. 17) that this immigrant Richard Cary was son of Christopher Cary, Bristol merchant, whose will, dated 1672 (P. C. C. *Eure*, 118), mentions sons Richard and John in such terms as to suggest that they had emigrated. If so, he was a close kinsman of Miles Cary, of Warwick.

The Green-brier Carys To the family of Richard Cary of Gloucester may perhaps be related (the proof is still to seek) a family of Carys who at the time of the Revolution were of Frederick County, Maryland, and afterwards

of Greenbrier County, (now West) Virginia:
they maintained and have transmitted a tradition
that they were derived from Bristol, through
Virginia. Their record, so far as now established, begins with a John Cary who, between
1752 and 1764 (the dates suggest that he might
have been the John Cary, Jr., of the Fitzhugh
deed of 1752), patented lands in Frederick
County, Maryland, and in 1757 married Mary
Beatty, then widow of Isaac Eltinge. (See Mrs.
R. S. Turk, *Beatty-Asfordby Genealogy,* 1909.)
Among the children of this marriage was Dr.
John Dhu Cary, who published at Frederick-
town from 1798 to 1800 *The Key,* which the
catalogue of the Congressional Library describes
as "the earliest periodical in Maryland." Of his
sons, one was George Cary, a lawyer, who moved
to Georgia and was a figure in the eighteenth
Congress; another son of John Cary and Mary
Beatty, William Cary, Sr., married, 1793, Maria
Barbara Fritchie, of Hagerstown, Maryland,
whose sons Cyrus Cary (father of the Dr.
Charles William Cary who was at the Virginia Military Institute, and 1848-49 at the University of Virginia) and William Cary, Jr., established themselves at Lewisburg, Greenbrier
County, Virginia; there they practised law and
successively sat in the Virginia Assembly, 1829–
30 and 1833–34. (Swem and Williams, *Register,*
127, 135.)

James Cary, In the surviving register of
of Gloucester Abingdon parish, Gloucester, it
appears that one James Cary was
a resident of that parish from 1689 to 1706, the
dates of baptism of his children: the last entry
of his name being "Sarah, the wife of James
Cary, departed this life September 18, 1735."
No evidence for a positive identification of this
James Cary has yet appeared. There is no entry
of his death in the Abingdon register, and, by
reason of the loss of the Gloucester County
records it cannot be proved whether he left a
will in Virginia. It has been conjectured
(Meade, Richmond *Times-Dispatch,* April 16,
1911) that he might have been James, son of
Thomas Cary[2], of Warwick; but it appears
(see *ante,* p. 41) that this is an improbable identification because the James of Warwick could
not have been born before 1673 and so would
hardly have a son baptized in 1689.

Neither has it been possible to connect James
Cary, of Abingdon, with the Richard Cary
(*supra*) who was a patentee in Gloucester in
1653.

It is now conjectured that this James of
Abingdon might have been the James Cary,
eldest son of his second marriage, named in the
will of James Cary, the London merchant, and
so a half-brother of Oswald Cary. This last-
named James died in London in 1726, leaving an

informal holographic will (P.C.C. *Plymouth,* 176) bequeathing his immediate personal effects to a niece and nephew with whom he was stopping. No mention is made of any family in Virginia, but it is not impossible that he had left one there. It may be recorded, however, that the late Captain W. M. Cary, of Baltimore, believed (on the precedent of a similar phenomenon in Massachusetts, because their name is sometimes spelled *Carey* in the earlier records) that James Cary, of Abingdon, was of origin a *Carew,* and that the spelling of his name was changed in Virginia to accord with the pronunciation.

Apparently (it has not yet been proved genealogically) the numerous Carys named Edward and John in Gloucester and Mathews were all descended from James Cary, of Abingdon. We identify among them two families, each of which begins on the surviving record with a John, viz.:

(1) John Cary, Sr., who appears in the Kingston (Gloucester, afterwards Mathews County) parish register as registering the birth of slaves from 1753 to 1769, was presumably the father of John Cary, Jr.,[1] who appears in the

---

[1] It would be convenient to identify this John Cary, Jr., of Kingston parish, with his contemporary, the John Cary, Jr., of the Fitzhugh deed of 1752, *supra,* but there is as yet no proof for such an identification. On the other hand, the recitals of the Fitzhugh deed are apparently inconsistent with the existence of John Cary, Sr., after 1752, if he was the son of Richard; yet John Cary, Sr., appears in the Kingston parish register until 1769.

same book in the same capacity during those years. This John Cary, Jr., seems to be the John Cary who married, in 1755, Dorothy, daughter of George E. Dudley, of Mathews County (see in the Kingston register the birth of Elizabeth, 1758, and John, 1761, children of "John and Dorothy Cary"), and had two sons, Dudley, who married Lucy Tabb (see the Kingston parish register and *W. & M. Quar.*, xiii, 169), and Captain John Cary (1761–1823), who served with Light Horse Harry Lee in the Revolution (obituary in the Richmond *Enquirer,* February 11, 1823), was Clerk of Mathews County in 1795, and subsequently removed, with his brother Dudley, to Georgia, where they have left many descendants, who have spread into Texas.

(2) John Cary, of York County, who married, first, Mary, daughter of Samuel Reade, and afterwards Susanna, and died leaving a will dated May 21, 1763. (See York County *Will Book,* 1760–1771.) His son, Major Samuel Cary, of Locust Grove, Gloucester Point, married Elizabeth Seawell, widow of Colonel Thomas Whiting, of Gloucester. He was an officer in the Revolution, and died in 1804, leaving four sons: (1) John Reade Cary, who was Clerk of Gloucester County many years, as was his son of the same name after him: another of his sons was Dr. Samuel Beverley Cary, who died in Petersburg in 1893, leaving descendants

in Petersburg and Richmond: two other sons moved to Zanesville, Ohio, where they left descendants; (2) Samuel Cary, who moved to Nottoway County, and has left many descendants; (3) Thomas Cary, who lived and died in Gloucester; and (4) Edward Boswell Seawell Cary, a lawyer, who represented Gloucester in the House of Delegates 1818–1820.

The Gloucester Carys and the Warwick Carys intermarried with several of the same Gloucester and York families, and so at the end of the eighteenth century were of kin on the distaff side; but no relation of their paternal blood has been proved, though persistent effort to that end has been made on both sides. This effort was stimulated by the unqualified, but utterly unsupported and unproved, assertions in Abraham's *Cary Tradition* (the advertisement published in the Richmond *Whig* newspaper in July, 1852), which still crop out in various traditional MS. pedigrees. Thus Abraham made out to his own satisfaction: (1) that John Cary, of Mathews (*supra*), was a son of that Robert Cary[5], of Buckingham, who is shown (*ante,* p. 53) to have died without issue: there was in this some vague confusion also with Robert Cary[5], of Chesterfield (*ante,* p. 62); and (2) that John Cary, of York (*supra*), was a son or grandson of that Miles Cary[3] who was son of the youngest son of the Warwick immigrant: there is, however, no evidence that this particular Miles ever grew to man's estate: the only record of him is the mention in his father's will as then a child (*ante,* p. 129).

There is current also another erroneous and in this instance a mischievous identification which has unfortunately been spread by uncritical repetition among the numerous descendants of the Gloucester Carys in Georgia and Texas, and is finally recorded in Pecquet du Bellet, ii, 67 and 116, viz.: that John Cary, of Mathews (*supra*), was the son of that name of Major Miles Cary[4], of Peartree Hall, thus substituting him for Col. John Cary, of Back River, from whom the Elmwood and Campbell families are descended. This is pure larceny by printed assertion, even though innocently perpetrated.

For a pleasant description of the households of these Gloucester Carys at "Kenwood," "Secluseval" and "Lansdowne," see the Richmond *Times-Dispatch*, April 16, 1911.

Richard and Warren Cary, of Yorktown One of the applicants to the Heralds' College in 1699 for the right to use the arms of Cary of Devon was John Cary, the Bristol merchant and publicist, a close kinsman of our immigrant Miles Cary. His life and writings are rehearsed in *Dict. Nat. Biog.* (reissue ed.), iii, 1153. He had several sons who carried on the family tradition as merchants in Bristol at the beginning of the eighteenth century. (See *ante,* p. 19.) One was Warren Cary (1683–1729), who in 1710 and 1711 was resident at Yorktown, Virginia, undoubtedly as a merchant. Thus the York records show that on October 5, 1710, he preferred a claim for "Powder & Shott and Fflints, delivered by Maj. Wm. Buckner's directions at a time when the French were supposed to come up York River"; that on May 21, 1711, he bought a lot in Yorktown from Thomas Chisman and was described in the deed as "of the parish of York-Hampton and County of York"; and that on July 25, 1711, he had a certificate for a pass for London. (See also, for a reference to him in the Richmond County records, Stanard, *Some Emigrants to Virginia,* 21.) Warren Cary returned to Bristol and there died without issue. (P. C. C. *Abbott,* 161, and *Admon. Act Book,* 1732.) His older brother, Richard Cary (1679–1730), was subsequently in Virginia. In the York records there is an entry under date of May 16, 1720, referring to "Rich^d. Ambler, Col. Diggs and Richard Cary, of the County of York," and by deed dated October 9, 1724, Richard Cary sold to Philip Lightfoot, on

[154]

behalf of his brother Warren, the latter's lot in Yorktown. In 1730, probably during another business sojourn, Richard Cary died in Virginia, without issue. (P. C. C. *Admon. Act Book,* 1730.)

John Cary, of Surry Another of the Carys of Bristol to whom the arms of the Devon family were specifically confirmed in 1699 was John Cary, of London, "one of the directors of the English Company trading to the East Indies." The pedigree he filed in the Heralds' College in support of this proceeding showed him to have been grandson of John Cary, of Bristol, and we identify him as the son of a half-brother of the immigrant Miles. (See *ante,* p. 21.) His pedigree further shows that on June 15, 1665, this John Cary married Jane, daughter of "John Floud of Virginia, Gent.," and that on February 22, 1667, his eldest son, Thomas, was "born in Virginia." He had patented lands in Accomac as early as February 23, 1663 (*Va. Land Register,* v, 218), but subsequently removed to Surry County, where the records show him living as late as December, 1669. Thus he patents lands in Surry, December 27, 1669 (*Va. Land Register,* vi, 269), and in an instrument dated that same month, describing himself as "now of Surry County in Virga.

being by God's grace intended to ship myselfe for England," constitutes his "trusty and loveinge friend Mr. Benjamin Harrison" his attorney to settle his affairs in Virginia.[1] Becoming a prosperous merchant in a large way of business in London, he never returned to Virginia; but he maintained business relations with the American Colonies (see the list of Virginia merchants in London in Bruce, *Economic History,* ii, 333). In 1690 he acquired lands, probably in satisfaction of a debt, on Bush River, Maryland. In 1691 he was one of the Committee in London for William and Mary College (*W. & M. Quar.,* vii, 164), and subsequently he sent a piece of plate to the parish church of Surry County in Virginia, which is still preserved at Brandon on the James. He had taken with him to England his ward and nephew, Walter Flood, to be educated; and also his son, Thomas Cary, who in time himself became a London merchant and the owner of a notable house at Putney.

---

[1] The tradition in the Harrison family of Brandon is that the Mary Young who married Nathaniel Harrison, of Wakefield (1677–1727), was a widow, having been born a daughter of John Cary and Jane Flood (Pecquet du Bellet, ii, 494). It may be noted, however, that neither the Heralds' College pedigree of 1699 nor John Cary's will makes any mention of children of this marriage other than the son, Thomas Cary, who went to England with his father. It is clear, however, that John Cary kept up his relations with the Surry Harrisons. There is preserved at Brandon a silver snuff-box which is inscribed: "In Memoriam Johannis Cary & Jacobi Dryden, January Primi, 1676. Beniamin Harrison."

Other Carys During the eighteenth century
on the South- there were, and doubtless still are,
side in Southside Virginia, Carys who
cannot be related to the Warwick family, although living in the same communities as some
of them. They are distinguishable also from
those of the James Cary group already noticed
(*ante,* p. 149), who may or may not belong to the
Warwick family. They may nevertheless have
been of the Bristol family, because many Virginia immigrants from Bristol settled in the
Southside counties.

William Cary, died in Newport parish, Isle
of Wight County, in 1756, leaving sons William
and Joseph. (*Isle of Wight O.B.,* vi, 243, and
xi, 140.)

Martha Cary, dau. of Mary Wrenn (for
whose will, 1747, naming dau. Martha Cary and
grandchildren William, Joseph and Charity
Cary, see *Isle of Wight W. B.,* v, 62), was doubtless the widow of the William Cary last above
named and the Martha Cary listed in the Virginia (U. S.) census of 1783 as then residing in
Surry County, having a household of six whites
and two blacks.

Joseph Cary, doubtless son of the foregoing,
who died in Surry, 1775. (For appraisal of his
estate, see *Surry W. B.,* x, 473.)

Joseph Cary, perhaps of this family, who appears in the Surry court as a litigant from 1795

to 1797, and is, again perhaps, the same who in 1796 patented a large area on Cheat River in Randolph County. (*Va. Land Register*, xxxv, 332.)

To this family we must also relate, for want of another identification, the *Mary Cary,* of Surry, who left an interesting will dated 1801, mentioning Kearnes nephews and nieces and property in North and South Carolina. (See *W. & M. Quar.*, xx, 289.)

In the Virginia (U. S.) census of 1785 are enrolled a William and Isaac Cary living in Princess Anne who may have sprung from a family of Irish Carys of which there is some evidence on the Eastern Shore.

The Fen-cing-Master We conclude the record with *Claudius Peter Cary,* an Irish fencing-master, who was a well-known character in Williamsburg at the time of the Revolution. See the notice of his death in *Virginia Gazette,* May 22, 1779.

APPENDIX I

CALENDAR OF WILLS PROVING PEDIGREE

Bristol

1570. RICHARD CARY, of Bristol,
1571. WILLIAM CARY, of Bristol,
1632. WILLIAM CARY, of Bristol,
1634. HENRY HOBSON, of Bristol,
1660. ALICE CARY, of Stepney.

Virginia

1667. MILES CARY, of Warwick,
1711. WILLIAM CARY, of Mulberry Island,
1716. HENRY CARY, of The Forest, Warwick,
1721. JAMES SCLATER, of York,
1733. HENRY CARY, JR., of Henrico,
1748. HENRY CARY, of Ampthill,
1752. MILES CARY, of Ceelys,
1763. MILES CARY, of Peartree Hall,
1772. WILSON CARY, of Richneck and Ceelys,
1785. JUDGE RICHARD CARY, of Peartree Hall,

1787. ARCHIBALD CARY, of Ampthill,

1794. JOHN CARY, of Back River,

1810. SARAH FAIRFAX, of Bath (England),

1810–1817. WILSON-MILES CARY, of Ceelys and Carysbrook,

1823. WILSON JEFFERSON CARY, of Carysbrook,

1827. MILES CARY, of Oakhill (Fluvanna),

1848. WILLIAM HAYNES CARY, of Prince Edward,

1854. ARCHIBALD CARY, of Cumberland, Md.,

1914. WILSON MILES CARY, of Baltimore.

1570. RICHARD CARYE, "the elder, of the Citty of Bristoll, marchaunt."

Will dated June 11 "anno 12° Eliz., Reginae" (1570) and proved November 3, 1570. (P.C.C. *Lyon,* 31.)

I commit my soul to God and my Body to be buried in St. Nicholas Crowde.

To my eldest son, Richard Carye, 10 *li.* To my son William Carye, 20 *li.* To my daughter Annes Carye, 10 *li.* To my daughters Frances, Elizabeth and Mary Carye, 10 *li.* each. To my father William Carye, 400 *li.*, which I ow'd him. To my daughter Lettice Mellen, 5 *li.*

I will that Joan, my wife and Executrix, shall Redeem all my lands and tenements in Mortgage; the Profits and Issues of all my lands, Tenements, etc., as well in my possession as in mortgage, to be and remain to the use of my said wife and the six last children of her Body begotten, in the manner and form following, vizt: said rents and profits to be divided into three equal parts, one to the use of my said wife for life, and the other two parts she and her assigns to enjoy for 19 years towards finding and educating my said six last children, and then all said lands and tenements to go to Christopher Carye, my son, and the heirs of his body lawfully begotten, forever: and for lack of such issue to Richard Cary, my eldest son, and his heirs and assigns forever.

[160]

All the residue of my goods, my debts being first paid, to Joan, my wife, and my aforesaid six last children upon her body begotten, in the proportions aforesaid.

The said Joan, my wife, to be Executrix; my brother William Carye and my brother Robert Halton to be Overseers.

1571. WILLIAM CARYE, "the elder, Dwelling upon the Backe in St. Nicholas Parish, in ye Citty of Bristoll."

Will dated April 2, "anno 13° Eliz. Reginae" (1571) and proved June 10, 1572. (P.C.C. *Daper*, 19.)

I commit my soul to God and my Body to be buried in the Crowde of St. Nicholas aforesaid; a Sermon to be preached at my funeral, the preacher to have 6s. 8d.

To the Poor and especially to poor Householders of Bristol, 10 li.

To my son William Carye, 13 li. 13s. 4d. To my said son's daughter, Anne, 6 li. 13s. 4d. to be paid at 21 years of age, or at her marriage.

To my son-in-law John Lacie, 10 li.

To Richard Carye, William Carye, Lettice, Frances and Elizabeth, the children of my eldest son, Richard Carye, by his first wife, 6 li. 13s. 4d. each. To Mary Carye, one of the daughters of the said Richard, 13 li. 6s. 8d.: to be paid to them respectively at 21 years or at marriage.

To my son Richard Carye's six children by his last wife, 40s. apiece, to be paid as the other children's aforesaid.

To Anne Chiles, my kinswoman and servant, 5 li.

Residue "to my son-in-law Thomas Dykinson, who I appoint sole Executor, Mr. Robert Saxie and Mr. Robert Halton, Chamberlain of Bristoll, to be Overseers."

1632. WILLIAM CARY, "the elder of the City of Bristol, draper."

Will dated March 1, 1632 (O.S.), and proved in Bristol diocesan court, June 15, 1633. The record is in *Great Orphan Books* (Council House, Bristol), iii, 311.

To my seven children by my first wife, vizt: William, Richard, John, Walter, Thomas, James and Margery, I give 10 shillings each. My youngest son Henry I leave to the discretion of his mother.

I ordain Mary, my wife, to be my sole executrix, and I appoint Mr. Henry Gibbes, Alderman, and Mr. James Diar Overseers.

1634. HENRY HOBSON, "of the City of Bristol, Innholder."

Will dated March 16, 1634, and proved May 27, 1636. (P.C.C. *Pile, 52.*)

To be buried in the parish church of All Saints, in Bristol, where I now live, near my late wife Alice.

I confirm a certain deed of trust dated 10 March 5 *Charles* (1630) between myself, of one part, and Myles Jackson, of the said City of Bristol, merchant, and Godfrey Creswicke, of the same City, Hardwareman, of the other part.

"I give and bequeath unto my grandchildren, Henry Cary, Mathew Cary, Richard Cary and Myles Cary, children of my daughter Alice Cary, wife of John Cary, draper, to each and every of them the some of five poundes apeece, of lawful money of England." To grandchildren Thomas Jackson and Henry Jackson, children of daughter Anne Jackson, widow, each five pounds.

The said legacies to be paid each of said grandsons when 21 years of age, and if any die before their portions to be divided among the survivors.

"I give and bequeath unto my grandchildren Alice Cary, Honor Cary and Mary Cary, daughters of my said daughter Alice Cary, to each and every of them the some of One hundred pounds apeece, lawful money of England." To grandchildren Margaret Jackson and Anne Jackson, daughters of said daughter Anne Jackson, to each of them the some of one hundred pounds.

The said legacies to be paid each of said granddaughters when 17 years of age or married, and if any die before, the survivors to be the heirs.

All said legacies to bear 5% interest from my death.

To my kinsman and servant Richard Burrowes £20.

To my kinsman Christopher Raynoldes, son of George Raynoldes, dec'd., £5, and to his sister Anne Raynoldes £10., when 21 years old or married.

To the Company of Innholders of said City of Bristoll, for attending at my burial, 40 shillings.

To my son William Hobson my scarlet gown.

To my kinsmen Francis Creswicke, merchant, and Thomas Hobson, Pewterer, their executors and assigns, my messuage or tenement in St. Nicholas Street in Bristol, where Arthur Stert now dwells, during the remainder of the lease, in trust to the only use of my said daughter Alice Cary and her assigns.

To my said daughter Anne Jackson "my wine license, which I bought of Hugh Hart, to draw wine by in Bristoll"; also the lease of the messuage or tenement in St. Nicholas Street, where Philip Love, merchant, dwelleth.

[162]

The residue of my personal estate to be divided between my three children, William Hobson, Alice Cary and Anne Jackson.

I appoint my said son William sole Executor, and my said kinsmen Francis Creswicke and Thomas Hobson Overseers.

Funeral Certificate.

(*Heralds' College. Book of Funeral Certificates*, I, 24, fol. 87ᵇ.)

HENRY HOBSON, late Maior and Alderman of the Citty of Bristoll, departed this mortall life at his house in ye said Citty the 21st day of March 1635 [O.S.] and was interred in ye parish church of All Saints there the 29th day following.

He married Alice, da. of William Davis of the said Cittie, by whom he had yssue, one sonne and two daughters:

WILLIAM HOBSON, his only sonne and heire, who hath borne ye office of Shreiff of Bristoll, maried Margarett Colston, da. of William Colston of the said Cittie, marchant:

ALICE, ye eldest Da. of the said Henry Hobson, maried to John Cary, sonne of William Cary, Alderman of the said Cittie: and

ANNE, his youngest Da., maried to Thomas Jackson, Marchaunt, late one of the Shreiffs of the said Cittie.

This certificate was taken the 19th day of Aprill 1637 by George Owen, Yorke herauld, and is testified to be true by the relation and subscription of the aforesaid Wm. Hobson, sonne and heire to the defunct.   (Signed)   WILLIAM HOBSON.

NOTE. *Over against the signature is a tricking of the arms of Hobson, of Bristol, viz.: Argent on a chevron azure, between three pellets, as many cinquefoils: a chief chequy or and azure.*

1660.   ALICE CARY, "of Shadwell in the parish of Stebvnheath, otherwise Stepney, Middlesex, spinster."

Will dated April 24, 1660, and proved November 14, 1660 (P.C.C. *Nabbs*, 206).

To my grandfather John Cary of Bristol, woolen draper, the full and just sum of one shilling, of lawful money of England: and to my uncle Myles Cary of Virginia the like sum of one shilling: and to my cousin William Hobson the like sum of one shilling. To the poor fatherless children of Stepney 20s. to be distributed among them by my executors within one quarter of a year next after my decease.

To every one of my nearest kindred 12 pence apiece.

All the rest I do give and bequeath unto my loving uncle Richard Cary and his loving wife, my aunt Dorothy Cary, and I make them joint executors.

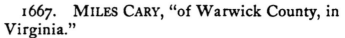

1667. MILES CARY, "of Warwick County, in Virginia."

Will dated June 9, 1667, and proved June 21, 1667, in Warwick County (*Will Book*, A, 448).

[Copy from transcript of Warwick records, made 1851 for *Eggleston Notes.*]

In the name of God, Amen:

I, MYLLES CARY of Warwick County, in Virginia, being of sound and perfect memory (praysed bee God), doe make and ordain this my last will and testament, hereby renouncing all other will or testaments formerly by me made whatsoever.

Imp*: I give and bequeath my soul into the hands of Almighty God, hoping through the meritte of Jesus Christ to have free remission of all my sinns; and my body to the earth with Xtian buriall to be decently interred by my Loving Wife; and for that temporall estate which it hath pleased God to endow mee withall, I give and bequeath in manner and form following:—

I doe give and bequeath unto my sonn THOMAS CARY all that tract or parcell of land which I now reside upon, containing by the old pattent, taken by my father-in-law, Thomas Taylor, deceased, three hundred and fifty acres of land, but since surveighed and received by me 688 acres more or less, with all that tract or parcell of land, commonly knowne and called by the name of the "Magpy Swampe," according to a destrict pattent thereof taken by my father-in-law, Thomas Taylor, deceased, containing by said pattent two hundred and fifty acres of land, which quantity of two hundred and fifty acres of land is since joyned by mee unto another parcell of land bought by mee of Zacheriah Cripps, the son of Zacheriah Cripps, deceased; yet notwithstanding my will is that the said two hundred and fifty acres, more commonly knowne by the name of the "Magpy Swampe," according to the bounds of the first pattent taken up as aforesaid, be set apart and divided from the parcel of land which I bought of Zacheriah Cripps, and be and remain with the tract or parcell of land I now live upon with all the houses, aedifices, buildings, gardens, orchards, pastures, woods and underwoods, and trees growing and to bee growing, with all the rents and profits of all leases and conveighances made out of the several tracts of land with all the hereditaments and appurtenances to any or either of the aforesaid parcells of land belonging or any way thereto appertaining, unto him the said THOMAS CARY and the heyres of his body to [be] lawfully begotten.

I doe also give and bequeath unto my sonn HENRY CARY and unto my sonn MYLLES CARY all that tract or parcell of land which I bought of Zacheriah Cripps, being according to the Ancient Pattent taken out by Zacheriah Cripps, one thousand and fifty acres, with all that tract or parcell of land taken up by mee, adjoining to that taken out of Zacheriah Cripps, but all taken into one pattent (always excepting and reserving that two hundred and fifty acres commonly knowne and called by the name of the "Magpy Swampe" to the use and purpose before expressed) which said tract of land according to the last surveigh and pattent (the said "Magpy Swampe" excepted) I give unto my sonn HENRY CARY and unto my sonn MYLLES, to be divided between them, by the runne of water which is by the great poplar in Andrew Farmers field, being the first course marked tree of the said dividend which runne of water upwards as the main runne goeth up to the dams or ponds, and so to my outward line, which runne and dams or ponds my will is shall be the dividing line between them. That is to say, I give and bequeath unto my sonn HENRY CARY all that tract or parcell of land, bee it more or less of this side of the ponds or dams, adjoining upon the lands of Capt. Thomas Bernard, deceased, with the plantation commonly knowne and called by the name of the "Forest," with all the houses, aedifices, buildings, gardens, orchards, pastures, woods, underwoods and trees growing and to be growing, with all the rents and profits of all leases and conveighances made out of the said tract or dividend of land, with all the hereditaments and appurtenances to the said parcell of land any way appertaining, unto him the said HENRY CARY and to the heyers of. his body lawfully to bee begotten.

And I give and bequeath unto my sonne MYLLES CARY all that tract or parcell of land, bee it more or less, of the other side of the runnes or dams soe farr as my outward line extendeth, and along the said line, adjoyning upon the lands of one Calvert, and adjoyning upon the lands of John Lewis, and soe along the outward line to the heade of Potash Creek, and adjoining upon the lands of Capt: Samuell Stephens (excepting and reserving the two hundred and fifty acres of land, commonly knowne by the name of the "Magpy Swampe," for the use and purpose afore expressed) with all the woods, underwoods, trees growing and to bee growing, with all the hereditaments and appurtenances to the said tract or parcell of land (bee it more or less) belonging or in any way thereto appertaining, unto him the said MYLLES CARY, and to the heyers of his body lawfully to bee begotten.

I doe give and bequeath unto my sonne WILLIAM CARY all that tract or parcell of land which lyeth up Warwick River formerly belonging unto Capt: Thomas Flint, and since purchased by mee, with all the houses, aedifices, buildings, gardens, orchards, pastures, woods and underwoods, trees growing and to bee growing, with all the rents and profits of all leases or conveighances, made out of the said tract of lands, with all the hereditaments and appurtenances to the said tract or parcell thereunto belonging or in any way appertaining, unto him the said WILLIAM CARY, and the heyers of his body to bee lawfully begotten.

I give unto ROGER DANIELL that parcell or tract of land that Goodman Heskins now lives on, and the land called "Gaole," with all the rents and profits, hereditaments and appurtenances whatsoever, whether by lease or otherwise, to all intents and purposes whatsoever in full and ample manner as I myself now enjoy it, may, might, or ever may enjoy it.

My desire is that Mr. William Beaty may have the education and bringing up of my sonne WILLIAM, and Mr. Hurle of my son MYLLES in England.

My will is that my two houses in England, the one in Baldwin Street, the other in St. Nicholas Street, bee sold by Mr. Hurle and Mr. Richard Deans, and the money in Mr. Hurle hands already and the money of the said two houses soe sold to be equally divided between my three daughters, ANNE, BRIDGETT and ELIZABETH, and to continue in Mr. Hurle his hands untill their dayes of marriage; and my will is that my tobacco that goes for England this year, and the bills of Exchange, I now send home, bee also in Mr. Hurle hands towards my sonne MYLLES his education. My Plate and Rings to be equally divided between my children.

The goods in the store to be sold by my Executors, and also the houseing at Towne[1] (which I bought of Mr. Randolph and have paid him for, as by his receipt it may appear) to be sold by my Executors, and the remainder thereof, after my debts are paid, to bee equally divided amongst my children.

I give unto ANNE CARY a negro girl called Nan, and one boy called Harry.

I give unto BRIDGETT CARY one negro girl called Bridgett.

To ELIZABETH CARY one negro girl called Sarah.

The rest of my negroes to be equally divided between my four sonns THOMAS, HENRY, MYLLES and WILLIAM; and what English servants I have I give unto my four sonns THOMAS, HENRY, MYLLES and WILLIAM.

My will is further that my stock of sheep be equally divided between my children; as also my stock of cattle be equally divided

---

[1] *This was Colonel Miles Cary's compliance with the insistence of the English government that the Virginians should live in towns. Soon after he was advanced to the Council, Miles Cary joined with Colonel Thomas Swann and Secretary Ludwell in acquiring the "old state house" at Jamestown and its adjoining buildings, then in ruins. There is a picture of the block restored in Tyler, Cradle of the Republic, 167: Colonel Cary's "houseing" was the middle one. The anxiety to dispose of it immediately after his death shows in what esteem a house at Jamestown was then held either as a convenience or an investment.*

between my said children: my horses and mares—my will is that they be equally divided between my children. My grey mare [*name illegible*] I give and bequeath unto Roger Daniell.

As for my Tobacco [debts] my will is they bee equally divided between my children; as also household Stuffs.

And my will further is that (whereas I have given and bequeathed unto my four sonnes, THOMAS, HENRY, MYLLES and WILLIAM, several tracts and parcells of land, as, by foregoing clause in this Will, may and doth appear) if any of the said Thomas, Henry, Mylles and William Cary shall happen to depart this natural life without heyers of his body lawfully begotten, that then his land goe and pass unto the next heire or brother, viz: if Thomas Cary shall happen to dy without issue of his body lawfully begotten, then his land to descend to the next brother Henry; and if Henry dy without issue of his body lawfully begotten, his land to descend to Mylles Cary; and if Mylles Cary dy without issue of his body lawfully begotten, his land to descend to William Cary; and if William Cary dy without issue of his body lawfully begotten, then his lands, and the other tracts soe falling to him, pass and descend to my three daughters, Anne, Bridgett & Elizabeth.

My will is that my debts be equally paid by my Executors, hereafter to be named, before any division or diminution of my Estate, and that no division be made but by the joynt consent of my Executors hereafter to be named, provided that my Executors be all alive at the time of division, and [in] the Colony of Virginia—that is to say, so many of Executors as are to be had [but] that no division be made untill my eldest sonne come of age.

My will further is that when division is made, that my Loving friend Mr. William Beaty have and keep in his possession my sonne William's Estate, and keep it for my said sonne William's use, untill he shall accomplish the age of one and twenty. My said sonne's maintenance for his education only to be deducted. And that the said Mr. William Beaty have my sonne Mylles Cary's part also of my Estate to possess and keep for the said Mylles Cary his use and behoof untill the said Mylles Cary shall accomplish the age of one and twenty. My will is that Henry Cary, when the Estate is divided, have his part and share of my Estate in his own possession, as also his land, formerly bequeathed to him in his own possession notwithstanding he bee not of full age.

As for my three daughters' parts or shares of my Estate (when divided) my will is, that those guardians (whom my said daughters shall then choose) with the consent of Executors, shall take it into their care and custody for the proper and sole use of my said daughters until they or any of them shall accomplish the age of one and twenty, or dayes of marriage (their maintenance only excepted); that is each or any one of the said daughters to have her part or share as she accomplish the age of one and twenty or marryeth.

I do hereby nominate and appoint my four sonnes THOMAS, HENRY, MYLLES and WILLIAM CARY, and my three daughters, ANNE, BRIDGETT and ELIZABETH CARY my joynt Executors and Executrices of this my last Will and Testament, with strict charge that they agree and act with mutual love and amity.

I doe also hereby nominate and appoint my well-beloved friends Mr. Thomas Ludwell, Colo: Nath: Bacon, Major Edward Grifith and Mr. William Beaty my Executors of this my last Will and Testament, earnestly requesting them to take the said charge and care upon them. And in token of my love to my said Executors I doe hereby give and bequeath to each of them five pounds sterling.

IN WITNESS whereof I have set my hand and seal to each syde and part of this my last Will and Testament, this ninth day of June, 1667.

MYLLES CARY   [His seal]

Signed and Sealed in the p^rsce of us:
    FRANCIS HADDEN,
    THOMAS J. KEN,
    WILLIAM   X   TANDY.[1]
        his marke

Probat. in Curia XXI die Junij 1667.
Pr. Testament: THOMAS J. KEN & GULIELMUS TANDY.
Test: WM. WOYDEN, <i>Sub. Cler.</i>
Recordat: XXIX die Junij 1667.
WM. WOYDEN, <i>Sub. Cler.</i></div>

1711. WILLIAM CARY, "of the parish of Mulberry Island in the County of Warwick, in the Dominion of Virginia."

Will dated August 26, 1711, and proved June 4, 1713, in Warwick County (*Will Book*, E, 570).[2]

[From a contemporary transcript of the original probate, now in the *W. M. Cary Notes*, which was carried away from Warwick Court House by a soldier during the war between the States, and

---

[1] *William Tandy was one of the head rights named in Captain Thomas Taylor's patent of 1643.*

[2] *Apparently some doubt arose as to the validity of this holographic will without witnesses, as on October 30, 1713, Governor Spotswood issued letters of administration upon the estate of William Cary to his widow Martha Cary.*

subsequently recovered, in New York, by the late Burton N. Harrison.]

In the name of God, Amen: I, William Cary, of the Parish of Mulberry Island, in the County of Warwick, in the Dominion of Virginia, being of perfect health and memory, Praised be Almighty God, but knowing the uncertainty of this life in this time of danger of the common enemie, do constitute and ordaine this my last Will and Testament in manner as followeth:

Imprimis: I beques my Sole into the hands of the Eternall God, hoping through the merrits of my Bless'd Saviour Jesus Christ, to have fforgiveness of all my sins.

Item: I beque my body to the Earth to be buried by my Executrix hereafter named (if she can gitt it) to burey after the Seremony of the Church of England, without any great adoe.

Item: I give unto my son Harwood Cary, after his Deare Mother Deceac'd, the tract of land I now live on, leying at the mouth of Skiff Creek in Warwick County, to Him the said Harwood Cary and the Hires of his body lawfully begotten; and in case of ffaliour of such hires Lawfully begotten, I give the said tract of land unto my Son Miles Cary and to the hires of his body lawfully begotten; and in case of the Death of said Miles or such lawful hires begotten of his body, Then I give to my son William Cary and his hires of his body lawfully begotten; and in case of ffailuer of the said William and his hires as aforesaid, then to Devolve and goe to my Son John Cary and his hires.

Item: I Give and beque unto my son Miles Cary that parcell or tract of land (after his Mother's Decee'd) which lieth in the Oaken Swamp and in Charles Parish in Yorke County, to him the said Miles and his hires forever; but in case he Deyeth before he comes to age, I give the said land unto my son John and his hires forever.

Item: I Give and Bequeth, after the Death of my Loveing wife, unto my son William Cary, the third part of Warwick River Mill, or my whole part of the said Mill, being the same I bought of Mr. John Scasbrooke, to him the said William Cary and his hires forever; And in case of his Death before he attaines to age, I Give the same as before Devised unto my son John Cary and his hires forever.

And as to what other Estate I have, after my just Debts are paid, wheather negros, horses; cattel, or any other thing, I Give and bequeth to my loveing wife Martha, Dureing her naturall life or so Long as she shall live a Widdow, and in case She should marry againe, then my will and Desire is that, that what of my Estate (not before devised) be equally Devided between my said wife Martha and all my children that shall be then alive wheather Sons or Daughters, excepting my Daughter Jaquelin, who I have allready gave her Potion, desering that what shall be so devided be done in love and Ammity without any sute of law; And if they cannot agree between themselves, that there be Indiferent persons Chosen by themselves to Devide each Child thire Share.

And further my will and desier is, that my Executrix be not compeled give any Security to any Court for the Probate of this will or any part of the Estate, Desiering my wife to take what care she can that those children, she hath to bring up, be brought up in the Christian Religion, and in what Learning she can bestow on them, not Doubting her motherly care to provide for them.

And I Doe heareby Nominate and appoint my said Loveing wife Martha my whole and sole Executrix of this my last will and testament, utterly Revoking all fformer wills by me made, as witness my hand and seale this 26th of August 1711.

WILLIAM CARY   [Seal (a scroll)]

At a Court held for Warwick County on Thursday, ye 4th of June 1713, this Will was presented in Court by Martha Cary, the Executrix, who made oath thereto, and the Court being satisfyed that the same is all of the dec'ed own handwriteing, It is therefore admitted to Record.

Test: MILES CARY,
Cl. Cur.

1716. HENRY CARY, "of the County of Warwick."

Will dated January 27, 1716 (O.S.), and proved September 5, 1720, in Warwick County (*Will Book*, i, 199).
[Copy from the original among the Ampthill muniments.]

In the name of God, Amen: I, Henry Cary, of the County of Warwick, being sick in body but of sound and perfect mind and memory, Praise be given to Almighty God for the same, do make and ordain this my last Will and Testament, in manner and form following:

And first: I recommend my soul into the hands of Almighty God, beseeching him to grant me full remission and pardon for all my sins, by the merits and for the sake of my most blessed Saviour and Redeemer, Christ Jesus, and by whom I hope to inherit a joyfull resurrection.

And as for that worldly estate which it hath pleased God to bestow upon me, I give and bequeath the same in manner and form foll'g, hereby revoking and making void all former wills by me heretofore made, and declaring this to be my last Will and Testament.

[170]

2dly: I will and ordain that all my just debts and funeral charges be paid and discharged by my executor hereafter named, and after my debts and funeralls are so paid and discharged, as aforesaid, my will and desire is that all the remainder of my personal estate of what kind soever, as negroes, stock, household goods, money, tobacco, or anything else, be equally divided between my son Henry Cary, Miles Cary, my daughter Anne Stuckey, my daughter Elizabeth Scasbrooke, and my late daughter Judith Barbar's two sons Thomas Barbar and William Barbar, except my negro girl named Rachel, whom I give and bequeath to my son Henry Cary and his heirs forever.

3dly and lastly: I do hereby nominate and appoint my said son Henry Cary whole and sole executor of this my last will and testament.

In Witness Whereof I have hereunto put my hand and seal this 27th day of January, *Anno Dom.* 1716.

HENRY CARY

[Seal bearing arms and crest of Cary of Devon.]

Signed, sealed, published and declared in the presence of:

> ROB^T. PHILIPSON,
> MILES CARY,
> RICHARD CARY.

At a Court held for Warwick County on Thursday, the first of September 1720, this Will was presented in Court by Henry Cary, jun^r., the Executor, who made oath thereto, and being proved by the oaths of Miles Cary and Richard Cary, two of the witnesses thereto, is admitted to record and is recorded in the county records.

Test: RICHARD CARY,
Cl. Cur.

1721. JAMES SCLATER, "Clerk, and Minister of Charles Parish, in York County."

Will dated November 29, 1721, and codicil dated January 16, 1722/3, proved August 17, 1724, in York County (*Will Book,* xvi, 298).

After provision for sons John and James and daughters Martha Brodie and Mary Tabb and a legacy to William Tabb [son of his deceased daughter Elizabeth]:

Item: I give to my grandson Doyley Cary a negro boy named Daniel.

Item: I give unto my grandson Henry Cary a negro boy named Jacob.

Item: My will likewise is that [as to] the negroes above given to Doyley and Henry Cary, that if either of them die before 21, the survivor to have both the negroes above alloted.

Wife Mary and sons John and James to be Executors.

1733. HENRY CARY, "son of Henry Cary, of the County of Henrico."

Will dated December 8, 1733, and proved March Court, 1734, in Henrico County.

[Copy from original in Ampthill muniments.]

In the Name of God, Amen: I, Henry Cary, son of Henry Cary, of the County of Henrico, being in a declining state of health, but in perfect sense and memory, do make this my last will in manner and form following:

I give to my Honoured Father my two negro men, named Dan¹. and Jacob. And I do constitute my said Father Executor of this my last Will and Testament, and have to this my last Will and Testament put my hand and seal this 8th day of December, 1733.

HENRY CARY, JUNR. Seal.

In presence of us:
 FOLIOT POWER,
 PAT. KER.

1748. HENRY CARY, "of the Parish of Dale, in the County of Henrico."

Will dated May 27, 1748, and proved March 2, 1749 (O.S.), in Chesterfield County (*Will Book*, i, 36).

[From a certified transcript of the record.]

Recites contract of marriage with his [third] wife Elizabeth, and in pursuance thereof leaves her £1,000. in lieu of dower. Also £120, the consideration received from the sale of her house in Williamsburg. Also household goods and plate received with her, and servants James and Flora.

Recites marriage of his daughter Judith to David Bell and that he had put David Bell in possession of 3,000 acres of land on Hatchers Creek in Albemarle, with the use of slaves Quash and his wife Dinah, George and his wife Belinda, Hector and his wife Ruthman, Moll, "a young wench," Joe and Frank, "two lads," Criss, "a girl," "a negro wench named Sarah and the said Ruthman's two children and her increase," and the plantation stock of horses, cattle, hogs, implements, etc., and devises 1,000 acres of said plantation and certain of said slaves to his grandson Henry Bell, the remainder to go to David Bell upon payment of £300.

Bequeaths to his grandson Henry Bell "a negro girl named Moll . . . for the purpose of waiting on my said Grandson, together with her increase."

Devises to his son-in-law Alexander Spiers 3,000 acres of land on Willis Creek, of which he was already in possession, with the slaves, etc., on that plantation, upon condition that Alexander Spiers shall pay to the estate £600. Mentions his daughter Sarah's "fortune" of £500.

"I do give and bequeath unto my son Archibald Cary all the residue of my estate, both real and personal, of what nature or quality soever and wheresoever lying found and dispersed, he paying all my legacys and just debts, to hold to him and to his heirs forever."

Appoints Archibald Cary sole executor.

1752. MILES CARY, "of Ceelys in Elizabeth City County, in Virginia."

Will dated October 11, 1752, and proved September 8, 1756, in Elizabeth City County.

[From transcript made 1868 of original will then on file in Elizabeth City Court.]

To sister Mary Selden £50., my easy chair, and "half the new goods in my house."

To nephew Cary Selden, chair and horses and certain household furniture.

To nephew Sam: Selden, "my troopers arms."

To nephew Miles Selden, "my fowling gun and my gold sleeve buttons."

To niece Sarah Fairfax £30 and "my mourning ring."

To niece Mary Cary, £30 and "a plain gold ring."

To niece Anne Nicholas, £30 and "a plain gold ring."

To niece Elizabeth Cary, £30 and negro girl Nanny.

To my nephew Wilson Miles Cary, "my negro man Jack, and all my plate and a ring with Diamond sparks."

To brother Wilson Cary lands in King and Queen County.

To James Roscow, son of "my brother" William Roscow, £90. 18s. 5½d., balance of £300 promised to be laid out in buying lands for him, on condition that said James Roscow "proves a good Boy and keeps close to his Book or any other Business he is putt to . . . but if he proves an Obstinate foolish boy and will not keep to his Book or other business," then to said James Roscow's brother Wilson Roscow.

To Mrs. Catherine Burkelow, his housekeeper, "for the great care and trouble she has had in my family," bed and bedstead, etc., and certain "new Goods," "a quarter cask of wine, all the tea, coffee, chocolate, spice, double refined sugar in my house," a negro wench Judy, and interest on £100.

To nephews Cary, Samuel and Miles Selden, all moneys and debts due him at his death, and crop of tobacco "then made tho' not finished," subject to current costs for "my Overseers and the negroes taxes, and charges of getting down to ye warehouse the whole crop."

Constitutes his brother Wilson residuary legatee and executor, but reciting that Wilson Cary "is very sickly," if he shall die, then Robert Carter Nicholas and nephew Wilson Miles Cary "when he shall arrive at ye age of 21 years" to be executors.

1763. MILES CARY, "the elder, of the Parish and County of Warwick."

Will dated October 11, 1763, and proved December 11, 1766, in Warwick County (*Will Book*, O, p. 549).

[From transcript of record made in 1844.]

"To my loving wife Anne" the estate she brought him, with "my chaise and Horses," in lieu of dower.

Recites conveyance to his son Richard of "my lands on PotAsh Creek, whereon my father lived," and a conveyance to his son Miles of "the lands called Perimon Ponds whereon I now live," upon condition that Miles should convey his interest in the Potash Creek lands as directed by will, now directs conveyance of those lands to Richard.

Devises also to Richard "the Tract of land I purchased of Mr. Thomas Cary, being 250 acres more or less lying in the Magpy Swamp."

Appoints son Miles guardian of person and estate of son Robert.

To "my daughter Elizabeth Watkins, my negro Girl Jane, now in her possession," and £70.

To son Richard "negro boy Dick and my negro girl Betty, and desire he may have the negro wench Tea in the devision of the Back River negros."

To son John, "negros Daniel, Franky and Tom Towlow, the younger."

To son Robert, negroes Young Ned, Matthew and Mott.

To daughter Anne Tompkins, "negro woman Bridget."

To son Miles, "my negro woman Nanny and her increase now in his possession."

[174]

To "my loving wife and each of my children," 30s. "to buy them rings."

To son John £200.

To son Robert £100.

"I desire my negro Tom Motulow have liberty to choose which of my children he will for his master within nine months after my decease."

Residue, including the rest of my slaves, to be divided equally between sons Richard, John and Robert, who, with son Miles, are appointed executors.

1772. WILSON · CARY, "of Celeys, in the county and parish of Elizabeth City."

Will dated October 10, 1772, and proved February 25, 1773, in Elizabeth City County.

[From a certified transcript of the record made in 1866.]

To "my dear wife Sarah Cary," £500., "her cabinet gold watch and rings, my Coach, Post charriot and Horses, Chair, carts and harness, and all my household Goods and Kitchen Furniture, Liquors of every sort, provisions, all the new goods in my house at the time of my death, and what new goods are sent for to Britain or elsewhere the year I shall die tho not arrived, except the Negroes Cloaths, Tools, etc., sent for my slaves in Gloucester and King and Queen, which I desire may be applied for their use. I also lend my said dear wife during her life the use of all my plate and what books of mine she shall chuse." Also use for life of all lands and slaves in Elizabeth City, with annuity of £100. per annum charged on lands in Albemarle, Henrico, Warwick, Gloucester, and King and Queen.

Annexes to Ceelys "my pew in church of Elizabeth City parish."

"Whereas, I am told that the widow of George Dudley, formerly my overseer, hath by her will left me a legacy, I give the said legacy to her son living in King and Queen, near Porapotank."

"I desire my Executors will send to England for the following books all lettered and bound in calf, viz: the *Spectators, Pamela, Clarissa* and *Sr Charles Grandison,* which said books I give to my Granddaughter Sarah Cary."

To son Wilson Miles all his lands with appurtenant slaves, viz: in fee lands in Albemarle and Henrico, and subject to his mother's life estate, in Elizabeth City, in tail in Warwick, King and Queen and Gloucester, with provision that, in event of failure of heirs, Warwick lands shall go to Warwick parish for a glebe.

To granddaughter Sarah Cary £500. on marriage with consent of her father.

To granddaughter Mary Munro Cary, a certain bond for £354.

Residue to "my four daughters, Sarah, Mary, Anne, Elizabeth, and my son Wilson Miles Cary," to be equally divided, but charged with advancements. The share of daughter Elizabeth Fairfax to be held in trust with remainder to her daughters and her son William.

To "my dear nephew Cary Selden £50. and a debt due from Colo. Lemuel Riddick."

To Mrs. Elizabeth Eyre, his housekeeper, £20. and "a suit of mourning out of Colo. Prentis' store."

Executors to lay out £100. in mourning rings. Sister Selden to have "a handsome one."

To Robert Carter Nicholas, £100.

To grandson Miles Cary, "my silver watch and my sword and Pistols, mounted with silver, and my other arms."

Recites that he was left executor of "my sister Anne Whiting" with "the Hon'ble John Blair and Col. John Bolling deceased," and stands charged with a legacy of £900.—"six hundred Pounds, part thereof, due by bond from Colo Henry Whiting"—due the legatees but paid into the hands of one James Shields, and directs the executors to secure his release, as the funds of the estate have not been under his control.

Appoints Executors "my dear and dutiful son Wilson Miles Cary, my son-in-law Robert Carter Nicholas, and my kinsman Richard Cary of Warwick."

1785. RICHARD CARY, "of the County of Warwick in the Commonwealth of Virginia."

Will dated 1785 and proved December, 1789, in Warwick County (*Will Book*, F, p. 680).

To son Richard lands known as "Peartree Hall" and "the Court House Tract."[1]

To son Miles lands known as "Balthrope" and "Marshfield."

Mentions "my daughters" without naming them.

[1]During the greater part of the eighteenth century the County Court of Warwick was held at Richneck, where the Clerk's office was maintained until about 1800. During the life of Judge Richard Cary a court-house (now used as the Clerk's office) was built on his lands, "the Court House tract," at the place now known as Denbigh, where it has ever since been maintained. This tract was presented to the county by Judge Richard Cary's eldest son, to whom he had devised it. See statement of family tradition made 1889 for *W. M. Cary Notes* by Wynne descendants of Judge Richard Cary's daughter Anne.

1787. ARCHIBALD CARY, "of Ampthill, in the County of Chesterfield and Commonwealth of Virginia."

Will dated February 12, with codicils dated February 19 and February 21, 1787, proved March 3, 1787, in Chesterfield (*Will Book*, iv, 20).

[From a certified transcript of the record.]

After specific distribution of certain house servants by name, he divides his estate equally between his three surviving daughters, Anne Randolph, Mary Page and Betty Cary, and the eldest sons of his deceased daughters Jane Randolph and Sarah Bolling, namely: Archibald Cary Randolph and Archibald Cary Bolling, including the following specific devises of lands to be charged against the respective shares, viz:

To son-in-law Archibald Bolling and his [second] wife Jane [Randolph, dau. of Richard Randolph], the plantation known as Red Oak, whereon they reside, containing 1,000 acres on Mountain Creek of Willis River, in Buckingham County, with remainder to grandson Archibald Cary Bolling [son of his daughter Sarah Bolling, deceased], who is also to have 1,000 acres additional, adjoining Red Oak.

To son-in-law Carter Page and Mary [Cary] his wife, the plantation containing 2,700 acres on Hatchers Creek and Horn Quarter road, in Buckingham County, with remainder to their children.

To his daughter Betty, 2,000 acres at fork of Willis in Buckingham, to be held in trust for her and her children by the executors "free from all disposition and control by Robert Kinkaid in case he shall become her husband."

Executors, "my sons-in-law Thomas Mann Randolph, Thomas [Isham] Randolph, and Carter Page," with "my worthy and esteemed friend David Ross," added by the first codicil.

By the codicils the specific devises of land were modified so as to provide, in certain contingencies, for sale and reinvestment, the share of the youngest daughter, Betty, being reduced.

1794. JOHN CARY, "of the Parish and County of Elizabeth City."

Will dated October 28, 1794, proved in Elizabeth City (the record now lost) and recorded also in Chesterfield, August 23, 1795, from which record this calendar is derived.

[177]

To wife Susannah, land in Charles Parish in the lower end of York County, and five house servants, in lieu of dower, but with use during widowhood of "the plantation whereon I now live."

Other slaves and residue of estate to be divided equally between "my children Miles, Hannah Armistead, Betsy Allen, Gill Armistead, John, Judith Robinson, Susannah, Nathaniel Robert, and such other child or children she may have."

Executors, wife Susannah, brother Robert Cary, and friend William Armistead.

1810. SARAH FAIRFAX, "of Walcot, co. Somerset, in England, widow of Hon. George William Fairfax, late of Writhlington in said county, deceased."

Will dated April 9, 1810, proved February 12, 1812 (P.C.C. *Oxford*, 71).

To my brother Wilson Miles Cary, £100.

To [Wilson Jefferson] Cary, first son of my late nephew Wilson Cary, Esq., dec'd. and grandson of said Wilson Miles Cary £100. and "my old family watch and gold chain."

To said Wilson Miles Cary and said [Wilson Jefferson] Cary, his grandson, all money due by mortgage on estate of my nephew George Nicholas, late of Kentucky, North America, dec'd., equally.

To my nephew Hon. Ferdinando Fairfax, whom my late dear husband made his heir after my decease, my said husband's portrait.

To my god daughter Hannah Whiting, daughter of Warner and Hannah Washington, of said State of Virginia, any one of my female negroes she may choose.

To the woman whose now name is Mary Brazier, who lived with me at Belvoir House in Virginia, a servant and an annuity.

To my nephews John Cary Nicholas and Wilson Cary Nicholas, brothers of said George Nicholas, £1000. part of my stock in American Funds, in trust for the children of George Nicholas.

To my niece Mary Munro Peachy, of Virginia, widow, seven shares in American Stock on which I have paid her the interest for many years.

Residue to my nephew Hon. Thomas Fairfax (1st son of the Rt. Hon. and Rev. Bryan, Lord Viscount (*sic*) Fairfax, brother of my said husband).

Executors: Thomas Fairfax "as to Virginia or North America," John Purnell and George Gavin Browne "as to England."

[178]

1810–1817. WILSON-MILES CARY, "of the City of Williamsburgh" (by codicil of 1817 declaring himself then a resident of Fluvanna County).

Will dated March 16, 1810 (with 26 codicils dated at intervals between March 24, 1810, and November 13, 1817), proved June 17, 1818, in the General Court of Virginia.

[From a certified transcript of the record made 1827.]

To daughter Mary Munro Peachy, £130.

To "my amiable wife Rebecca," in addition to what is secured to her by her marriage settlement, house and lots in Williamsburg with certain slaves, and £100 to furnish the house. "And I further direct that my said wife may be supplied annually" from his plantations either "above" or "below," "so long as she continues my widow, with six good muttons, two good beeves, fifteen hundred weight of fatted pork, six barrels of flour, and forty gallons of whisky": and in addition "a hogshead of best Lisbon wine."

"The pew I hold in the Church at Williamsburg to be annexed to the Williamsburg house which I bought of Doctor McClurg."

To Miss Charlotte Balfour and Miss Sarah Anderson, friends of "my late wife Sarah Cary, £25. each."

Directs prompt discharge of debt due "my friend Admiral Thomson . . . neither war nor any other circumstance" to hinder or delay the payment.

To daughter-in-law Jane B. Cary, the houses and lots in Williamsburg she occupies, with an annuity of £130., and the use of certain servants.

To godson Robert Cary Mitchell, of London, £100.

To John Ambler, only surviving child of my late sister Mary Ambler, £98. 6s. 8d.; and to the heirs of my late sister Anne Nicholas, £21. 2s. 8d. being the balance due on certain oral legacies "by desire of my late mother."

To daughter Elizabeth Fairfax, an annuity of £100. charged on the estate.

To grandson Wilson Jefferson Cary, lands and mill on south side of Rivanna in Fluvanna (*i.e.*, Carysbrook); also his books, and "Billy, a son of Islborough."

To grandson Miles, all lands on north side of Rivanna in Fluvanna (*i.e.*, Oakhill); also "my gold watch," and certain servants by name.

Also other servants and "my blooded mares and colts" to be equally divided between my said grandsons, families to go together.

"It is my earnest wish and desire that all my slaves may be well fed and clothed, and in every respect well treated, entreating my

[179]

executors and grandsons to restrain the managers and overseers from improper whipping, but if any of my slaves, as well those on the plantations as those belonging to my house and appropriated to the use of my wife, prove vicious or refractory, I authorize my executors to dispose of them, supplying their places with others."

Grandsons Wilson Jefferson Cary and Miles Cary residuary legatees and executors.

The codicils are all holographs, without witnesses. They make, change and revoke legacies in an attempt to provide with dignity and honor at once for his creditors and his family, out of a steadily diminishing estate. Thus he leaves servants to his great-granddaughters Jane Blair, Mary Randolph and Anne, daughters of Wilson Jefferson Cary, and an interest in a contingent claim to certain lots in the city of Richmond to "my dear grandson Thomas Cary Nelson." Sometimes the codicils are mere expressions of personal and political sentiments, dictated by current events. Thus:

1811—"I wish my executors and other relatives to refrain from giving in to the expense of mournings, which are often put on without real concern for deceased, and are anti-republican."

1812—"As a man of honour and a friend of my country, I declare I have lived and hope to die of the Washington school, lamenting that the good people of this State should be seduced from following and supporting the religion of their ancestors and the glorious and virtuous principles of a Washington."

1812—"Not to neglect my good nephew, the Reverend James Henderson, I give him, to put him in stock of what is essential to a clerical Christian and gentleman, 100th part of a grain of gratitude and charity, being more than I am persuaded he at present possesses, and I entreat him to render all the profits of the "Mountain Plains" to Mary Andrews, from whose family [the Blairs] he derived all his consequence."

1814—"I give to John Randolph, Esq., of Roanoke, five guineas, as a mark of my approbation of his manly and patriotic exertions in Congress in checking the persecuting and partial proceedings of some former administrations."

1814—"Finding that my affairs, through a variety of circumstances, are involved in debt, and not knowing the extent of the present nefarious measures of Administration and our Congress, who are and have been annually concerned only to register the edicts of the Administration, I direct," etc.

1823. WILSON JEFFERSON CARY, "of Fluvanna County."

Will dated May, 1823, and proved in Fluvanna County Court, January 26, 1824.

Leaves certain house servants, by name "Bailey, Lavinia, Billy the cook, Judy, etc.," to children Jane, Mary, Wilson Miles and Archibald.

Residue, including other slaves, to widow for life, with remainder in equal divisions to "my six children."

Executors, "my wife Virginia Cary, my brother Miles Cary, and my worthy friend General J. H. Cocke."

1827. MILES CARY, "of Fluvanna County."

Will dated March 23, 1827, and proved June 23, 1828, in Fluvanna Court (*Will Book*, iii, 222).

Mentions wife Elizabeth S. W. Cary and children Virginia, Miles, Lucius, William Wallace, Elizabeth Curle, Sally Newsum, Mary Jane, and Octavius.

Executors, friends Colonel Maurice Langhorne, of Cumberland, General John H. Cocke and John Timberlake, Jr., of Fluvanna.

1848. WILLIAM HAYNES CARY, "of the County of Prince Edward."

Will dated August 7, 1848, and proved May 17, 1852, in Prince Edward Court (*Will Book,* ix, 545).

Mentions wife Esther, children Harwood Cary, Nancy Cardwell, William Haynes Cary, and children of deceased daughter Patsey Cardwell.

1854. ARCHIBALD CARY, "of Cumberland, in the State of Maryland."

Will dated August 15, 1854.

Mentions "my beloved wife Monimia," children Constance and Clarence, brother Wilson Miles Cary of Baltimore, and sister Patsey Jefferson, wife of Gouverneur Morris of Harlaem, New York.

1914. WILSON MILES CARY, "of Baltimore City."

Will dated August 23, 1914.

Mentions brother John Brune Cary and sister Jennie; nephew Wilson Miles Cary, of Baltimore; cousins Constance Cary Harrison, Mary Fairfax Morris Davenport, Anne Cary Morris Maudslay, and Fairfax Harrison (to whom he bequeathed his Cary papers); and "my other nephews and nieces."

APPENDIX II

Confirmation of Arms of Cary of Devon to Cary of Bristol, 1699.
(College of Arms. Book of Grants, iv)

[PETITION]

To His Grace, Henry, Duke of Norfolk
Earl Marshal of England, etcᵃ:

> *The humble Petition* of John Cary, of the City of Bristol,
> Richard, his Brother, and their Kinsman John Cary, of the
> City of London, Merchants,

SHEWETH, That the Carys of Bristol having time out of mind
borne the Armes and Crest of the Carys of Devonshire (vizt,
Argent on a Bend Sable three Roses of the First, with a Swan
Argent for their Crest) from whom by the constant tradition in
their family they are lineally descended; And having the Honour
to be known unto the present Noble Lord Robert Cary Lord
Hunsdon, and to be own'd and acknowledged by his Lo/p. as his
Kinsmen, they Humbly Pray,

> That your Grace will please to Issue your warrant to the
> King of Armes of the Province, for assigning such Distinc-
> tions to the said Armes as may be Proper for your Petᵣˢ.
> and their Descendents to bear and use according to the Law
> and Practice of Armes.
> And they shall ever pray, etcᵃ.

(Signed)   JOHN CARY,
           Rᴰ. CARY,
           JNO. CARY.

[CONSENT OF EDWARD CARY, OF TOR ABBEY]

UPON request made to me by Mr. John Cary, of the City of Bristol,
and his kinsman Mr. John Cary, of the City of London, Merchants, That I would certify what Relation they have to my
Family;

These are to certify to all whom it may concern,

[182]

That I, EDWARD CARY,[1] of Torr Abbey, in the County of Devon, Esqr. (Heir male and Principal Branch of the Family of the Carys of Devonshire) do hereby Declare, that I have heard and do believe That the Carys of Bristol sprung some Generations past from a younger Branch of the Carys of Devonshire, And I do, therefore, hereby acknowledge them to be my Kinsmen, and consent and desire that they may be permitted to use and bear the Paternal Coat-Armour of my Family, with such due and proper Differences and Distinctions as to his Grace the Earl Marshall and the Kings of Armes concern'd shall think fit.

In Witness Whereof I have hereunto put my hand and Seal of Armes, this Eighteenth day of June, 1699.

(Signed)   ED. CARY   [L.S.]

JOHN HESKETT, of the City of Exon, Gent., maketh oath that the Certificate hereunto annexed, was by this Deponent (this 19 day of August instant) produced unto Edward Cary of Tor Abbey, in the County of Devon, Esqr., who then acknowledged the said Certificate (and the name Edward Cary thereunto subscribed) to be his proper handwriting; And that the said Edward Cary did in this Deponent's presence affix his Seal of Armes thereunto.

(Signed)   Jo: HESKETT.

Jurat apud Aishburton in Com.
Devon, decimo nono die Augusti
Anno Regni R^s Willi.
Tertii, nunc Augt. etc. undecimo,
coram,

ROGER CAUNTER, *in Canc. M^ro. Extr.*

[WARRANT OF THE EARL MARSHAL]

WHEREAS John Cary, of the City of Bristol in the County of Somerset, Richard his Brother, and John Cary, of London, Merchants, have by Petition Represented unto me, That that Branch of the Carys, seated at Bristol aforesaid, having time out of mind borne and used the Armes of the Ancient Family of the Carys of Devonshire, scil^t., Argent on a Bend Sable three Roses of ye First with a Silver Swan for their Crest, as descended from a Collateral Branch of the said Family, they therefore humbly Pray That they

---

[1] *This was Edward Cary (1650–1718), of Tor Abbey, the head of the Devon family, a stout Jacobite, who was to be involved in the adventure of the Old Pretender in 1715. See Herald and Genealogist, viii, 114. It will be noted that he does not date his certificate in the year of William III. As he was the repositary of a consecutive family tradition, his certificate is of substantial genealogical value.*

[183]

may be permitted still to continue to bear the same with such due and proper Differences as are usual in like cases:

And forasmuch as the Right Honble Robert Cary,[1] Lord Hunsdon, has Personally own'd That he does Believe the Pet^rs are descended of a Collateral Branch of the said Family, and has requested me to allow and confirm the same:

And that the Pet^rs have Produced unto me an attested Certificate, under the hand and Seal of Armes of Edward Cary of Torre-Abbey in the County of Devon, Esqr., the principal male Branch of the Carys, setting forth that he does Believe the Carys of Bristol to be a Collateral Branch of his Family, sprung forth some Generations past, and does therefore consent and desire they may be permitted to bear and use the Paternal Armes of the Carys, with due and proper Differences,

I, HENRY DUKE OF NORFOLKE, Hereditary Earl Marshal of England, having duely considered the Premises, do hereby order and appoint Garter and Clarenceux Kings of Armes to Exemplify and Confirm the foresaid Armes and Crest with such fitting Differences and Distinctions as are proper for Collateral Branches, unto the said Pet^rs and their descendents, according to the Law and Practice of Arms, Requiring that the said Allowance, and their Petition, together with these Presents, and also the Certificate of the said Edward Cary of Torr-Abbey, be entered by the Register in the College of Arms.

And for so doing this shall be a sufficient Warrant.

Given under my hand, and Seal of my Office of Earl Marshal, this 30th day of August, 1699, in the Eleventh year of the Reign of our Soveraign Lord William the Third, by the Grace of God

---

[1] *This consent was doubtless of value to the applicants at the time but it has no weight as evidence to-day. Robert Carey (1650–1702), seventh Lord Hunsdon, was next to the last representative of a family which had been utterly ruined by their adherence to the Stuarts in the civil wars, temp. Charles I. He had himself been a journeyman weaver in Holland when he unexpectedly succeeded to the Hunsdon peerage in 1692, and thenceforth subsisted in England on a pension allowed him by William III. If his family was Cary at all, except in name, his Dutch education and Dutch maternal origin for several generations undoubtedly disqualified him as a competent witness as to the traditions of the Devon family with which none of the Hunsdons had had any intimate relations for more than two centuries.*

It was doubtless upon some tradition of this "recognition" of kinship by Lord Hunsdon that the Virginia antiquary Richard Randolph founded his statement to Hugh Blair Grigsby that Colonel Archibald Cary of Ampthill was the heir to the Hunsdon peerage.

King of Engl^d, Scotland, France, and Ireland, Defender of the Faith, etc^a.

(Signed) NORFOLKE; E. M.

To Sr Thomas St. George, Knight
Garter Principal King of Arms,
and Sr Henry St. George, Knight
Clarenceux King of Armes.

[GRANT BY GARTER AND CLARENCEUX KINGS OF ARMS]

To All and Singular to whom these Presents shall come,

Sr Thomas St. George, Knight, Garter Principal King of Armes, and Sr Henry St. George, Knight, Clarenceux King of Armes, send Greeting:

Whereas, John Cary, of the City of Bristol in the County of Somerset; Richard his Brother, and their Kinsman John Cary, of London, Merchants, have by their Petition Represented to the most Noble Prince Henry Duke of Norfolke, Hereditary Earl Marshal of England, etc^a., That that Branch of the Carys seated at Bristol aforesaid, having time out of mind borne and used ye Armes of the Ancient Family of the Carys of Devonshire, scilicet, Argent on a Bend Sable three Roses of ye First with a Silver Swan for their Crest, as descended from a Collateral Branch of the said Family, they therefore humbly Pray that they may be permitted still to continue to bear the same, with such due and proper differences as are usual in like cases;

And forasmuch as the Right Honble Robert Cary Lord Hunsdon has Personally Own'd That he does believe the Pet^{rs} are descended of a Collateral Branch of the said family, and has requested that the said Armes may be allow^d and confirm'd to them:

And it appearing also by an attested Certificate under the hand and Seal of Armes of Edward Cary of Torre Abbey in Com. Devon, Esq., the principal male Branch of ye Carys, setting forth that he does believe the Carys of Bristol to be a collateral branch of his Family, sprung forth some generations past, and does therefore consent and desire they may be permitted to bear and use the Paternal Armes of the Carys, with due and proper Differences;

His Grace having duely considered ye Premises did by Warrant or order under his hand and Seal of his Office of Earl Marshal, bearing date the 30th day of August last past, Order and Appoint us to Confirm, Allow and Exemplify the foresaid Armes and Crest, with such fitting Differences and Distinctions as are proper for Collateral Branches, unto the said Pet^{rs} and their Descendents, according to the Law of Armes:

[185]

KNOW YE THEREFORE that wee, the said Garter and Clarenceux, in pursuance of the said Earl Marshal's Order, and by virtue of the Letters Patents of our Offices to each of us respectively granted under the Great Seal of England, have Allowed, and do by these presents Allow and Confirm:

unto the said JOHN CARY, OF BRISTOL, and to RICHARD his Brother, the Armes and Crest hereafter mention'd, vizt:

Argent on a Bend Sable three Roses silver, in a Canton or an Anchor of the Second; And for their Crest, on a Wreath Argent and Sable, a Swan proper, charged on the Breast with an Anchor Sable, as in the margin hereof is more plainly depicted:

And to the foresaid JOHN CARY, OF LONDON, their kinsman, the said Armes with the variation

of the Bend to Engrail'd, and the Anchor in the Sinister Chief, and the Swan charged on the Breast with a Red Rose;

To be severally borne and used forever hereafter, by them the said John, Richard and John Cary, and the Heirs and other Descendents of their Bodies lawfully begotten, in Shield, Coat Armor, Penon, Seal, or otherwise, according to the Law and due Practice of Armes, without the lett or interruption of any Person or Persons whatsoever.

In Witness Whereof, Wee, the said Garter and Clarenceux Kings of Armes, have to these presents subscribed our names, and affixed the Seals of our respective offices, this 25th day of September in the 11th year of the Reign of our Soveraign Lord, William the Third by the Grace of God, King of England, Scotld, France, and Ireland, Defender of the Faith, etca, *Annoq. Dni.* 1699.

(Signed) THO. ST. GEORGE,
Garter Principall King of Armes.

HEN: ST. GEORGE,
Clarenceux King of Armes.

[CERTIFICATE FROM THE TOLZEY BOOK OF BRISTOL]

(*College of Arms.* 3 D, XIV, fol. 53b)

I, *James Hollidge,* Esq., Chamberlain of the City of Bristol, do hereby certify that, upon inspecting the ancient Book for regist'ring and recording the names of Persons who had been Mayors of the said City, I do find that one William Carye was Mayor of the same City in the year of our Lord 1547, in the 38th year of King Henry the 8th.

Witness my hand this seventh day of Octor *Anno Domini* 1710.

JA: HOLLIDGE, *Chamb'lain.*

[186]

And also that one William Cary was Mayor of the said City
in the year 1611, 9º Jacobi 1ᵐⁱ.

JA: HOLLIDGE, *Chamb'lain.*

1313.	LAWRENCE DE CARY	Senister,
1350.	JOHN DE CARY	Bayliffe,
1353.	JOHN DE CARY	Bayliffe,
1532.	WILLIAM CARYE	Sheriffe,
1546.	WILLIAM CARYE	Mayor,
1599.	WILLIAM CARY	Sheriffe,
1611.	WILLIAM CARY	Mayor,
1612.	CHRISTOPHER CARY	Sheriffe.

This is a true copy extracted out of the Tolzey Book of Bristol,
this 27th day of November, 1710.

Witness my hand,

JA: HOLLIDGE, *Chamb'lain.*

INDEX

CPSIA information can be obtained at www.ICGtesting.com
Printed in the USA
245052LV00013B/151/A